LADY
IVY
and the
IRISHMAN

LADY
IVY
and the
IRISHMAN

CLAIRVOIR CASTLE *Romances*
BOOK FIVE

SALLY BRITTON

Published by Pink Citrus Books
Edited by Karie Crawford of Cookie Lynn Publishing Services
Cover design by Blue Water Books

Sally Britton
www.authorsallybritton.com

First Printing: May 2024

To each woman who's felt pressured to silence her inner voice,
may you find the courage to be authentically yourself.

CHAPTER 1

JULY 2, 1821

"My friends say being an Irish baron isn't as good as being an English baron."

Teague Frost blinked down the breakfast table at Fiona, his eleven-year-old sister. She stared at him, her dark brown eyes inquisitive. "Did your friends say why?"

"They say your heir cannot sit in the House of Lords when you die."

Given that Teague was not anywhere near expiring, nor did he have an heir or any way to obtain one as a bachelor, he stared incredulously at his younger sister. At ten o'clock in the morning, already exhausted and not looking forward to the day ahead of him, he was not in the best frame of mind to discuss the drawbacks of being an Irish member of Parliament.

"Your friends are right enough. All Irish lords in the House of Lords must be elected by the Irish peerage."

"Why? All an English lord has to do is wait for his father to die, and then he gets to sit in Parliament."

Teague wrapped his hand around his cup of coffee. "It is complicated, Fi."

The child sighed and went back to her breakfast, humming

softly to herself between bites of egg and sausage. Her humming during meals wasn't the best of habits, but since it made her happy, Teague said nothing. Neither did her governess, when she was about.

His mother would have asked her to stop, had she been at table. Unfortunately, the baroness was in bed with a headache. His other sister was a married woman, completely gone from Teague's household.

Which meant the only person to converse with was Fiona. And Fiona seemed of a mind to discuss politics.

"When will women get the vote, do you think?" she asked with a tilt to her head. "Before I am grown?"

"That is unlikely."

"Why? Máthair says that even though women may not have a vote, we influence politics more than you men will ever know."

His lips twitched. "Does she now?"

"She does." Fiona adjusted her posture and pointed her fork at him. "I think I'm as smart as any boy my age. Why couldn't I run for the House of Commons?"

He leaned back in his chair and regarded her with amusement. "It's complicated."

She huffed. "You already used that answer once."

"I'm certain this is something your governess ought to school you in."

"Do you know why or not?"

"I know why, but sitting at my breakfast table, when I'm hardly awake enough to enjoy a bite, isn't the best time to be after explanations. Especially when I know none of them will satisfy someone as stubborn as you."

Fiona considered his words a moment before she nodded. "Fair enough. But you will explain sometime, will you not?"

"I will. Sometime." He looked at the clock hung over the door. He needed to leave to make his committee meetings on time, but his mind remained in a fog of exhaustion from staying out late the evening before.

Keeping awake to attend the evening events of London Society was necessary for a man in politics. Too many nights in a row made mornings difficult, on occasion, but he'd managed well enough.

He worried for his mother, though. The parties that kept on until the wee hours of the morning rarely agreed with her. Mixing in large crowds often made her anxious. Yet she kept at it, arguing politicians relied on the women in their lives to work behind the scenes.

He wished she wasn't right on that account.

After a brief glance at his sister, ensuring she had turned her attention to the book she had brought to the table, Teague opened the paper beside his plate. He skimmed the lengthy report on the Queen's legal justification, and its rejection, for attending the King's coronation. He glowered at the long list of laws dredged up, at the numerous lists of consorts and wives of kings' past and how they had or hadn't been present when their mate and monarch received the crown.

"Ridiculous," he muttered to himself, moving along to the next page. The government had gone mad, refusing to acknowledge the wife of their king as his consort. Politics aside, it gave all of Europe reason enough to laugh at the English.

He read through the announcements of plays in this or that royal theatre, his eyes lingering over a review for a particular performance. He had accepted an invitation to see a newer play, called *A School for Scandal*. It was purported to be a comedy, which he supposed he needed.

He'd attended a new tragedy written by a fellow Irishman, yet watching the melancholy story unfurl half a dozen times in the previous weeks had affected him. Perhaps he ought to have seen it once only, but Irish pride in a fellow Irishman succeeding, and in such a way as to gain the praise of so many English critics, had kept him going.

He had even had dinner with the playwright, John Banim, to discuss the themes of friendship and loyalty in *Damon and Pythias*. Two things Teague hadn't much personal experience with if he was truthful with himself. A fictional farce had the potential to improve his mood.

A few inches over from the theatrical announcements were the lists of nobles departing London until Parliament gathered again in the new year.

His eyes caught on a familiar name. *The Duke and Duchess of Montfort, along with all (principal) members of their family, quit London for their familial home in Leicestershire on Wednesday.*

Teague's mind filled with his memory of Clairvoir Castle, the country residence and family seat of the duke. The castle—with its gold-bricked edifice and elegant turrets, the ramparts made for promenading rather than defense, and the beauty of its gardens—had left an impression upon his mind he hoped to keep all his life. He'd spent a Christmas there, more than a year ago, when his sister and the duke's heir had fallen in love with one another. He'd visited last spring for their wedding in the castle's chapel.

He hadn't returned since then, as his own affairs, estate, and politics kept him far too busy.

Still, he wondered if Lord and Lady Farleigh, his brother-in-law and sister, were part of the *principal members* of the family soon to make their way to the rolling hills and peaceful woods of Clairvoir Vale.

When was the last time he'd spoken with Isleen? Weeks ago, when the two of them had found each other invited to the same party. He saw his sister's father-in-law more often than anything. At clubs, in political circles, in places where Teague felt weary rather than comfortable.

He closed the paper and tossed it onto an empty chair to his left, across the table from his sister's seat.

"What has made you grumpy this time?" Fiona asked from her place.

"Nothing we haven't already discussed," he admitted, forcing himself to smile even though he felt exhaustion weighing on his mind and heart. He had been at work in the House of Lords from January to July, seeing and hearing more meaningless motions and bills than he could remember. Some motions had passed that were helpful, but others exacerbated problems for his people in Ireland and the common laborers across the Kingdom. Everywhere he turned, he found more bluster and nonsense than he had patience for. "It is always the same."

"Then you should stop fretting about all of it, if there is nothing new," Fiona said, buttering a slice of toast with a knowing grin. "We quit London next week."

"That we do." Teague passed his hand across his eyes. "On to our next adventure, I suppose."

"Máthair said we're visiting Isleen."

"Did she now?" Teague raised his eyebrows. "I hadn't heard this news. Do we have an official invitation?"

Fiona shrugged. "I know only what Máthair tells me." She took a large bite out of her toast. "But if we are invited, we will visit, won't we?"

"We will." Teague couldn't deny his mother time spent with her married daughter, nor the luxury and enjoyment of staying as a guest of the duke and duchess at their home. Even if he had his own estate and obligations to see to.

He rose from the table and ruffled his sister's hair as he passed her chair. "I must be off. I won't be back for dinner, and I am out late at the theater this evening."

Wrinkling her nose, Fiona's query verged on a whine.

"When do I get to come with you? Must I really wait until I'm presented at court?"

"And not a day before."

She grumbled something about the "unfair treatment of youth" before taking another large bite of her meal, and Teague left the room with an amused grin. Fiona couldn't wait to grow older. Poor mite was in for a shock when she saw all that came with age and Society's expectations.

At least he had the theater to look forward to that evening.

CHAPTER 2

The hypocrisy of buying the best seats in a theater with the best view of the stage, then ignoring everyone upon that stage, frustrated Lady Ivy Amberton to no end. She wanted to enjoy the play, not listen to her sister-in-law's complaints about her acquaintances in Society. But Ivy's brother, the Earl of Haverford, never seemed to mind missing a performance as he absorbed his wife's gossip.

Here, in the second act, one of the characters on stage spoke with vigor, while Fanny's words interspersed with the dialogue of the actor.

"Oh, the devil! no man knows what to say at the time when one most wants to say it. I'll go over it again—"

"—if I have to hear Lady Bilton's story of her pug one more time—"

"—I beg pardon, but you know one can't help these things."

"—and the excess of stupidity ought not be brought up—"

"—I find that talking clears the mind wonderfully."

Ivy sat on the edge of her chair, leaning toward the box's rail, and nearly went so far as to cup a hand around her ear, the better to hear what went on between the actors. But her hands

7

were already full. One held the theater glasses her late father had gifted her when she had come out into Society, five years previous. He'd been delighted with the contraption, which he'd bought while they were together in Paris the summer before he died.

A "delightful way to see the world," he had called them, amused with the simplicity of the idea. "Everyone will own one of these before long. Changeable Claude Glasses."

They were simple, made only of wood, thin metal frames, and colored glass, but they had accompanied her to every theatrical performance she had attended since she'd made her curtsy.

With a flick of her wrist, Ivy could change the lenses through from the normal spectacles of a theater-goer to rose-hued glass, then blue-tinted, then yellow-tinted, thus changing the way the world looked to better admire it anew. Each pair of lenses, framed in delicate wires, joined at the stick with an ingenious pivot mechanism. It was a simple matter to fold one set down along the handle to allow another to act as the primary pair.

Her other hand grasped the rail. She needed it there to keep balanced on the edge of her seat as she leaned forward, her gaze fixed intently on the stage below, completely absorbed in the performance before her.

Ivy's hair fluttered slightly in the warm air, her neck arched as she stretched her head out over the edge of the theater box, and she felt as though she reached for something out of her grasp. The rest of the world had fallen away, leaving the performance to captivate her attention. Fanny's complaints were not so loud now.

She wished one of her sisters had come. Juniper had a cold, though, and Betony didn't care for the theater. That left Ivy with only the company of her half-brother and sister-in-law.

So rarely did she experience people and places to her taste, dependent as she was on her sister-in-law's approval, that she was determined to savor every second of the play.

Caught up in the magic of the performance below, Ivy sensed rather than saw a movement from beneath their box. Glancing down, she saw a man in the box beneath hers, a handsome one at that, leaning on his rail. Looking up. His eyes fixed on her and an amused smile played at the corners of his mouth.

How long had he been staring? A flicker of embarrassment warmed her cheeks, the same as when Ivy's sister-in-law or brother caught her doing something they deemed improper. But this man wasn't her brother; he held no power over her actions.

Let him stare, even laugh if he chose.

A rebellious wave of defiance washed over her. She was here to enjoy the performance, to lose herself in the story, and she wasn't about to let anyone else's opinions stop her from doing that. With a toss of her head and a small smile, she returned her focus to the stage, more committed than before to enjoy every second of the performance, no matter who was watching.

Her grip on the rail slipped in her distraction and she tilted forward, far enough that her stomach dropped in fear of a fall.

A strong grip on her forearm steadied her, giving her a moment to grip the rail with both hands, steadying herself. When the hand holding her theater glasses hit the rail, the stem snapped in half. She watched, hopelessly, as the multi-hued spectacles fell down—

Her brother pulled her back before she saw the fate of her father's gift.

"Will you not sit in your chair as you should?" Lord Haverford whispered harshly in her ear. "You nearly pitched out of the box. People were *staring*."

Her brother had hauled her backward, firmly placing her into her seat, but Ivy's eyes remained on the broken stick in her hand.

That was all that remained of her theater glasses. Half a stick of polished wood, the end of it splintered and jagged. The gift from her father, gone.

"Honestly, Ivy," he said, tone impatient in the semi-darkness of the box. "We cannot take you anywhere without you acting like an addlepated child. What are you trying to do? Leap to the stage from our box?"

"Everyone was looking at you," his wife added, her fan fluttering in front of her face, resembling an agitated moth's wing. "Gawking at the actors as though you've no manners. It is shameful."

Ivy gripped her little stick tighter and turned her glare to her sister-in-law. For one glorious instant, she considered saying what she wished to say. *"Better to look as though the play bores me, I suppose? Putting on a sour face, like yours? Gossiping about all my friends?"*

She bit her tongue.

Though Ivy had achieved her majority at the age of one and twenty, she was as much at the mercy of her half-brother and his wife as she had been at seventeen, when her father had died. Now, at five and twenty years, she itched to leave their overly critical care and set up a household of her own.

Hopefully taking her two younger sisters with her. Juniper would reach her majority in a matter of weeks, but Betony was only nineteen. Still. Both were old enough to know their own minds, weren't they?

The sisters' late father had left their half-brother as executor of his will and as their guardian. This made him the man who held the purse strings, and he had ensured that the entire inheritance from their father was kept in trust until each of his half-sisters was either wed or he deemed them capable of setting up house for themselves.

Dependent on her brother and sister-in-law's whims, Ivy

swallowed her words and bowed her head, making herself the very picture of ladylike contrition.

"Please forgive me, Fanny. I didn't realize I had drawn inappropriate attention."

Fanny sniffed. "See that it doesn't happen again. Be still, Ivy."

Nodding her agreement, Ivy wrapped her hands around her fan and the stem of her lost theater glasses. She held her gloved, cream-colored hands grasped in her lap, staring at nothing.

She wouldn't cry. She hadn't cried in front of her two judgmental guardians in years. They only used her emotions against her. Once, her father had praised her for her passionate expressions, her exuberance and excitement for taking in the world around her.

"Watching you reminds me so much of your mother. She had a love for the world and everything in it that was honest and open." He had said those very words to her the night of her first ball, which he had spared no expense to hold in her honor. She had laughed and danced all the night long, unashamed of enjoying the sparkle of the chandeliers and beauty of the music.

She had never been happier. Her father had been proud of her. He'd been certain she would take London by storm, be declared a diamond, the favorite of all.

And then he had died less than a fortnight later. An attack of the heart, his physician had said. Nothing could have prevented it. Except, perhaps, less excitement.

Ivy kept still and quiet, hardly hearing the actors until the orchestra played, the audience rose to applaud, and the curtains closed.

Act two had finished, and it was Fanny's favorite part of attending the play. The part where her devoted friends, whom Ivy privately thought of as Fanny's minions, would visit her box one by one to impart some salacious bit of gossip. The earl had already muttered an excuse to leave, slipping out before the first feather-bedecked lady stepped in, leaving Ivy to sit in her chair and act the part of a doll, saying nothing and posing prettily.

Precisely as they had trained her to do.

Teague hadn't meant to look up. He couldn't even give a reason why his gaze drifted from the stage. He had been enjoying the play, laughing as the disguised uncle spied on his nephews, when he'd glanced up. Then he'd seen her, thanks to the angle at which he sat in his box and she in hers.

A woman with delicate features, leaning forward and illuminated by the soft glow of the stage lights below. Her neck arched gracefully as she stretched her head out over the edge of the theater box, craning to catch a better view of the performance. A gust of cool air brushed by Teague as he leaned forward, surprised by the beauty hovering above him.

She didn't see him at first. Her whole attention was focused on the stage as her lips parted in anticipation of a laugh, her eyes alight with excitement. The loose curls of her hair, shining amber in the lights, quivered slightly as she leaned further out, oblivious to everything but the play.

With a smile playing at the corners of her mouth, she was the picture of a woman caught up in the magic of the theater, lost in the spell of the performance before her.

Teague's heart responded with an excited thump, recognizing in the unknown woman a kinship of sorts. Few people of his status came to the theater to watch what happened on the boards. Most were more interested in the other audience members and the dramas of scandal and gossip. This woman, enthralled as she was with the unfolding comedy, caught his attention. Few English ladies ever seemed to show their true feelings, preferring to feign boredom. This one...she was different.

She looked down. Her gaze met his and she froze, startled to find him watching her, as he realized he was wearing a ridiculous smile.

She smiled back. Then she lifted her chin, dismissing him, in favor of returning her attention to the actors and their speeches. Teague didn't want to look away. What sort of gentleman stared at a woman he didn't even know?

Then his heart lurched upward as his stomach dropped in fear. The woman's whole body jolted, as though she'd lost her balance or been struck from behind. He rose at the very same instant she caught herself and something fell from her grasp.

He dove forward to catch it without thought, his hands closing over the object and his ribs protesting as they crashed against his box's rail.

Sir Andrew, a baronet and friend to Teague, grasped Teague by the shoulders with a muttered oath and pulled him backward.

"What madness is this, Dunmore?" he demanded, calling Teague by his title. "If you wish to join the actors on stage, there are better routes!"

"Sit down, both of you," Lady Josephine, wife to the baronet, said quietly. She also happened to be the Duke of Montfort's eldest daughter, sister-in-law to Teague's sister. An admirer of all forms of fiction and storytelling, from what he could gather. "Lord Dunmore, are you all right?"

He sat back in his chair and Sir Andrew did the same with a huff.

"I am well. The box above—" How did he explain the woman whose beauty had completely enchanted him? "—someone dropped this." He held the object out in one hand and finally realized he had caught what appeared to be several pairs of spectacles affixed to one another, a broken handle explaining how their owner had lost her hold of them.

"Dear me." Lady Josephine laid a hand over her heart. She kept her tone soft, mindful of the boxes around them. "That would have hurt, had it landed on someone's head."

Sir Andrew raised his eyebrows, impressed. "A heroic act, then. Well done, Dunmore. You see, Josie, our friend proves yet again that Irishmen are a welcome addition to Society." He winced when his wife smacked his shoulder with her fan.

"Do stop teasing, Andrew. Someone will hear you and take you seriously. Lord Dunmore isn't nearly well enough acquainted with your sense of humor to make it acceptable to jest in that way."

"Apologies, Dunmore," Andrew said quietly, rubbing where his wife's fan struck. "I hadn't realized my wife found it her duty to defend your honor. I meant nothing by it."

"I am well aware, Sir Andrew." Teague waved away the apology, not even hiding his smile at their antics. He'd spent enough time at the club with Sir Andrew to know the man's jests were a sign of friendship. "Though Lady Josephine is welcome to continue wielding her fan on my behalf if it pleases her."

The woman's smile brightened and she saluted him with her fan, then turned her attention back to the stage. Sir Andrew settled more comfortably in his chair before he took his wife's hand in his, watching her more often than he glanced at the stage.

The two were besotted with each other. Teague didn't minded. They were good company and didn't usually try to make conversation in the middle of an actor's monologue.

He fiddled with the spectacles, folding and unfolding them, wondering if their loss would make it difficult for the lady above his box to enjoy the rest of the play. He'd seen people with tele-scopes before, watching plays through the long stems of jewel-crusted spyglasses. There were many women at that moment making use of lorgnettes, delicately made spectacles with dainty handles of ivory and silver.

This strange thing in his hands, though, was unlike any device he'd seen before, yet it was a simple construct. Hesitantly, he raised the rose-colored pair of glasses to his eyes. They worked exactly as he expected, bringing the objects and people upon the stage closer through their lenses and turning everything to the shade of a gentle blush.

A shame the handle had broken. The lady would likely be able to replace it, if she found someone willing to tinker with the unusual contraption.

Teague grinned to himself. He would have to return it to her, of course, and perhaps gain an introduction. Perhaps he could ask her if she was enjoying the play. The play he hadn't paid any attention to since the moment he'd seen the woman.

Best to rectify that. The end of the second act drew near, and he'd have to hurry up the stairs immediately after, before the crowds of people filled the halls and made them impassible. He settled in, still only half aware of the story unfolding on stage. His thoughts were entirely upon the woman and what he would say as he returned her property.

As the curtain fell, Teague slipped from the box with a quick promise to return to Sir Andrew and Lady Josephine. He was upon the carpet in the corridor in seconds, darting into the main staircase to take it up another level. He had stepped onto the top landing when the doors opened and gentlemen and ladies poured out, the swell of their chatter breaking upon the quiet like surf upon a sandbar.

Teague had to slide between ladies fanning themselves and gentlemen complaining about the stuffiness of the evening. At last, he made it to the curtained doorway of the box above his own. The curtain had already been pushed aside, allowing him to enter.

He found two ladies inside, one a decade or more older than himself, and the other the woman who had dropped the dual telescopic device in his hand. They both looked up as he entered, but Teague's gaze stayed upon the younger of the two.

He bowed. "I must beg your pardon, ladies, for this breach in etiquette. Baron Dunmore, at your service." Why did his native Irish sound so thick on his tongue? There would be no doubt from whence he'd come, even after so few words. He made a greater effort to hide it with the next. "I have the privilege of enjoying the evening's performance from the box beneath your own."

The woman with a sour expression and tall purple feather in her hair narrowed her eyes at him. "My husband is not present, Lord Dunmore, to make appropriate introductions. If you have need of him, he may be found in the gentlemen's parlor."

The countess was exactly what he'd come to expect from English matrons when confronted with his Irish brogue.

"Ah." He winced. "Thank you, madam. I had hoped we might forgo the usual method, given that I am here to return the property of the young lady." He nodded to the woman who had remained silent. He realized the pink in her cheeks had disappeared, leaving her rather pale instead.

His breach in decorum hadn't been all that terrible, surely.

"Ivy?" The woman's eyebrows rose to the top of her forehead. "What property have you given this man? Do you know him?"

The woman stood quickly. "No, Fanny. We have never met. But he has my opera glasses. I dropped them a moment ago."

Somewhat relieved, Teague managed to smile at her again and held the contraption out to her. "Indeed, miss."

"Lady Ivy Amberton," she corrected softly, dropping her gaze and bending in an abbreviated curtsy. "This is Lady Haverford, my brother's wife." Her tone was not what he had expected after seeing the open display of her emotions before. She sounded far more subdued than he'd imagined.

The countess stood, her lips puckered and eyes pinched. "How do you do." She wasn't truly asking, her tone flat, her eyes narrowed. Nothing about her stiffly held posture indicated an ounce of interest in him.

"Lady Haverford. It is a pleasure." It wasn't. Lord Haverford belonged to the party in opposition to Teague's own, and he'd had several choice things to say about having the Irish in Parliament. Haverford proclaimed himself a traditionalist, a man who believed the past had achieved perfection. Any progress or reforms were challenging the natural order of things. "I have met Lord Haverford in Lords many times. He is highly respected by many."

The many that Teague often caught himself wishing would all retire to their countryside homes and decide not to come back again.

"I cannot recall him making any mention of you," the countess said, remaining in her chair. "Return Lady Ivy's property, if that is why you came."

He looked at the woman who had so captivated him with her enjoyment of the play and then her defiance at his watching her. How could she, lovely and enthusiastic as she was, be related to one of the most unpleasant and unmovable men in Society?

She leaned closer to him. "I apologize for my sister-in-law," she said, her voice almost too low for him to hear amid the buzz of conversation in the theater below. "She isn't fond of meeting strangers."

"I can understand the discomfort." He held the joined spectacles toward her. "Your property, Lady Ivy."

"Thank you, Lord Dunmore." Again, her softly spoken words confused him. She sounded as though she had been chastened, or that she feared raising her voice to even a normal speaking level. She took the device with both hands and held it against her stomach and when she raised her eyes to his, they were filled with gratitude. "Not many would have taken the trouble to return such a silly item. I wasn't certain I would see them again."

As he opened his mouth to respond, someone nudged Teague from behind. He stumbled a step forward and moved out of the doorway, making way for a woman in dark blue silks and smelling strongly of roses.

The woman barely glanced at him as she stormed across the floor and collapsed into the vacant chair beside the countess. "Here now, Lady Haverford, what think you of Mrs. Garrett's eldest wedding a foreigner?"

The two of them immediately forgot everything else around them and fell into a passionate conversation about the private affairs of others. Teague stared at them in confusion.

Had he been dismissed without realizing it? Then he looked again at Lady Ivy, who still clasped her multi-colored spectacles to her midsection and stared at her sister-in-law with confusion.

Teague took a single step closer to the wall and the movement drew Lady Ivy's attention. She glanced once more at her sister-in-law, then came closer to Teague, closer than she had a moment before to accept her property from his hand.

"I am sorry, Lord Dunmore." She winced and Teague offered her a reassuring smile.

"Perhaps I ought to have waited to return your property, but I didn't want to chance missing you."

Lady Ivy's brows drew together in apparent confusion.

"A lady who attends a play to actually watch the story unfold is as rare as a fairy in these parts."

Her lips twitched. She had a sense of humor, then. That made her less like her brother already. "I suppose there are more fairies in Ireland, your lordship?"

"I am told there are." He gestured subtly to her hands. "I

have never seen anything like your spectacles, Lady Ivy. It would be a shame to lose something so unique."

She nodded and looked down at the item in her hands, turning it over. "My father gifted them to me. They are a combination of a *lorgnette* and Claude glasses. To let a viewer enjoy many shades and notes of color."

"A fascinating idea. I noted a slight magnification for each pair of lenses, too."

"For those who are not as gifted with far-sightedness. Such as myself." She glanced over her shoulder at the two gossiping women, then peered up again at him. She was half a head shorter than he, with the dark hair and dark eyes that made him think of rich earth, chocolate, coffee, and deep forests. His favorite things. "You were kind to return them to me with such haste, Lord Dunmore. Thank you. I will not forget it."

He ought to say something. He knew he ought to. But not a single clever thing came to his mind, which was an oddity for him. The Season was nearly over. He'd be leaving soon. She likely would, too. Haverford's holdings were in the southwest of England, while Teague would journey northeast to the Duke of Montfort's estate.

He had run all the way up to her box without much of a plan. He'd wanted to meet her. Now that he had, there was nothing more to say. Not to an English noblewoman, even if she surprised him with her sweet openness. So unlike the other ladies he'd tried to speak to in English ballrooms and parlors.

Even if he'd wanted to, there wasn't even time to ask which ball she would attend next, or if he might take her on a drive through the park. It was unlikely her brother would even allow such a thing, given how little Haverford and Teague had in common, politically or otherwise.

So he stepped back toward the open doorway. "It was a pleasure to meet you, Lady Ivy. I hope you enjoy the rest of the performance." He bowed again. "Good evening."

The gentle sadness in her eyes left him with an ache in his chest, as though he'd had the air forced from his lungs. Despite the flicker of interest that had sparked in his thoughts upon first sight of her, the timing was all wrong.

Perhaps she sensed it too, for the air between them hung heavy with unspoken words and unexplored possibilities. It was the sort of meeting that happened in the best of stories, he thought wistfully.

However, there wasn't time for a second act . The curtain had already fallen on the London Season, and their paths were unlikely to cross again for months, if not an entire year.

A bittersweet smile appeared on her lovely face. "Good evening, Lord Dunmore. And good bye."

He left the box and returned to his own, but he sat farther back. Away from the rail, denying himself a chance to look up on the slim chance that Lady Ivy would sit within his view. He watched the play to its end, departed with his friends, and looked over his shoulder only once as they left the theater.

His gaze immediately collided with Lady Ivy's, though she descended the stairs to the ground floor and he had nearly walked out the doors into the night. In that brief moment, Teague wished he had seen her weeks, if not months, before that evening.

The crowd swept him out the door and, once in the warm night air, he heaved a sigh of regret.

CHAPTER 3

The morning after attending *School for Scandal*, Ivy sat with Fanny in the Yellow Room, a westward-facing sitting room Fanny preferred when she had a headache from being out late the evening before. Juniper and Betony sat together on a settee, the former sketching the profile of the latter.

No one said a word.

Personally, Ivy found the room's yellow-green wallpaper and furnishings more likely to induce a feeling of nausea than cure a headache. But she and her sisters went where their sister-in-law bid. Ivy sat quietly in a chair at a distance from the fire with the newest copy of *Ackermann's Repository*. She turned the pages as quietly as she could, as even a rustle of paper would elicit a glare from Fanny.

After Fanny's lecture on holding conversations with strange men the evening before, Ivy wished to avoid her sister-in-law's censure. No matter how unfairly Fanny distributed it.

How could Fanny blame Ivy for the appearance of a baron in their theater box? If anything, her brother was at fault for pulling her about and making her drop her theater glasses. Which were, thankfully, unharmed after their sudden downward flight. Once she replaced the stem-like handle, all would be well.

Her fingers paused, holding a page she stared at without thought, her mind busy remembering the man who had rescued her treasured belonging. An Irish baron, with dark eyes and a smile that had made her stomach twist and her fingertips tingle.

If only her brother had been present to make a proper introduction. If only they had met at the beginning of the Season rather than at its end. If only she had been brave enough to suggest he call upon her, or that they might both take a walk in the park the next day.

If only.

Something had passed between them that had left her breathless, yet the knowledge of what could never be tainted the moment.

Unless they met again. Perhaps next Season.

When she came to the page with the new beadwork patterns she had sighted before, Ivy stopped and examined the details carefully. Though *Ackermann's* published the simplest of instructions, in the past she had found ways to incorporate the idea presented on the page into her more complicated work. Carefully, she traced the design of beads made to resemble ivy and flower buds with her fingertip.

A soft rap on the door preceded the entrance of a footman. He carried a silver tray bearing a single card. "My lady, a caller has arrived for Lady Ivy."

While her sisters stilled and glanced her way with raised eyebrows, Ivy's heart skipped a hopeful beat. What if it was *him*? Had the handsome baron decided to pay a call on her after all?

Fanny's nose wrinkled as she took the card from the tray. "We are not at home today. You know that, John." Fanny called all the footmen John, whether or not that was their name. She also refused to use spectacles, or even the daintiest of quizzing glasses, though she had to narrow her eyes and hold the card at a specific distance to read the print.

"Yes, my lady," the footman, whose real name was Davis, said with a tone of deep respect. "As it is Lady Josephine Wycomb, I thought it best to be certain of my lady's schedule."

"The duchess's daughter? Again?" Fanny gave up trying to read the card and dropped it on the platter. She cast Ivy an incredulous expression. "I suppose you may accept her visit. We have no wish to insult Her Grace by refusing her daughter. Even if she is negligent as to our schedule." She waved Ivy away. "You may receive her in the East Room."

"Thank you, Fanny." Ivy rose and looked at her sisters to find both of them wearing beseeching grimaces. "May my sisters come with me?" she asked Fanny. "Perhaps a few moments of respite will help your headache."

Fanny believed it her duty to keep them all under her watchful eye whenever she could, but apparently she'd had enough sherry and wine the night before to make her relax her usual strict standards.

"Fine. Do *not* do anything to disgrace us." She spoke as though she expected the grown sisters to cause chaos the moment they left her sight.

Ivy left the book on her chair and led her sisters out of the room at a staid pace. The moment the door closed behind them, they looked at each other with unrestrained relief.

"She spoke as though we'd leap upon Lady Josephine like lions or some such thing." Juniper's nose wrinkled.

Betony giggled. "Even if we did, Lady Josephine would never tattle on us."

"Hush, both of you." Despite the door between them and their half-brother's wife, the idea of Fanny overhearing them made her feel small and ill. She'd faced Fanny's idea of punishment for speaking freely and critically of her guardians—weeks of being reminded in chilly tones of all the things Fanny and

William had done for Ivy's good. Hours spent reading aloud from a book of sermons meant to teach young ladies how to behave. Telling guests, with Ivy present, how difficult it was to look after someone "entirely ungrateful."

Thoroughly humiliated, Ivy hadn't said a word against her sister-in-law's treatment of her for a long time.

She led Juniper and Betony across the corridor to the only sitting room that welcomed the late morning sunlight. Davis had already disappeared to escort Lady Josephine upstairs.

Though they were distant relations to the duchess's daughter, Ivy hadn't formed a close relationship with Lady Josephine, now wife to Sir Andrew Wycomb, until last Season. This year, Lady Josephine had visited Ivy three times during the course of the Season, which was more times than Ivy had hoped for, given their brief acquaintance. They had met at a ball hosted by the Sicilian ambassador, the Conte di Atella, after Parliament reconvened.

The duchess, born Lady Cecilia Boxbury, was a cousin to Ivy's mother, Elizabeth Russell. A fifteen-year-old Cecilia, prior to her marriage, had embroidered the white cap infant Elizabeth had worn on her christening day. With such a difference in age, and later in station, the cousins hadn't been close, but Ivy had always been cognizant of the relationship.

One could hardly forget a kinship to a duchess. So when the duchess's daughter had become an acquaintance, Ivy was thrilled with the possibility of a new friend *and* a rekindling of familial ties.

Given the rank and importance of Lady Josephine, Ivy's brother and sister-in-law had allowed the friendship.

The duchess's daughter, now a baronetess through marriage, entered the room with a wide smile, her confidence in herself and her place in the world evident with every movement and line of her bearing.

"Cousin Ivy, I am grateful you allowed my visit. I know it

isn't Lady Haverford's at-home day." She settled on the couch near Ivy, her blue eyes bright with good humor. "Cousins Juniper and Betony, it is a delight to see both of you again. Though I'd hoped to keep the purpose of my visit a surprise." She winked at them, then met Ivy's gaze. "I couldn't wait to speak to you, and sending a card ahead felt like too much bother when I could come myself."

Confused, Ivy settled on the couch between her sisters, the three of them facing the other lady in her chair. "I am always pleased to see you, Lady Josephine."

"Oh, enough of that nonsense. When we are not surrounded by those who worry about such things, please call me Josephine or Cousin. We are near enough in age, and we *are* family. Besides, we decided we were friends the last time I called upon you."

Ivy relaxed and allowed herself to return Josephine's smile. "True. Then you must call me Ivy." She glanced at her sisters, who swiftly repeated the sentiment before falling silent.

Josephine grinned and reached across the space separating them to take Ivy's hand in a friendly grasp. "I haven't stopped thinking about our last conversation, the night of the musicale at the French embassy. Do you recall? We were speaking of our plans for the summertime."

Unfortunately, Ivy remembered that evening with great clarity. Her brother had been severe in his critique of her, making certain Ivy knew how disappointed he was in her lack of talent when it came to instruments, as she had not been invited to participate in the evening's *programme*. Shortly after the earl's diatribe, which had taken place behind a column in the ambassador's home, Lady Josephine had arrived with a pained expression on her face. Though Josephine hadn't spoken of it, Ivy suspected the baroness had overheard every word Lord Haverford said.

"You are going to stay with your family," Ivy recalled,

brushing a stray curl from where it tickled her ear and mentally swiping away the unpleasant memory. "At the castle where you grew up."

"Indeed." Josephine gave Ivy another gentle pat on the hand. "It is a beautiful place, truly my favorite in all the world. My father and mother are happiest when we are all under the same roof, and my husband has practically lived there the last decade or so anyway."

If only Ivy and her sisters had close family like the duke and duchess, rather than a half-brother who never seemed satisfied by anything she did and a sister-in-law who saw Ivy as a project rather than a person.

Ivy allowed herself to be happy for her friend, though. "I am glad for you. Everything you have said about Castle Clairvoir makes it sound like a palace from a fairy tale. May I write to you?"

Perhaps she could live vicariously through her friend and pretend her own summer at her brother's estate wasn't quite so long and dreary.

"I hope there will be no need," Josephine answered, startling Ivy from her thoughts. "I want you to come with me, as my particular guest." She laughed at Ivy's open-mouthed awe, though not unkindly. "You needn't worry. I spoke to my mother first, of course, and she assured me you are most welcome." She made a point of looking at both Juniper and Betony, who had turned stiff as statues. "All of you are welcome, and we will have room to spare. My family hosts dozens of people at a time, and you three would be a welcome addition to any party. Not to mention that you are our cousins, so you have more reason to visit than most. Please say all of you will come."

Hope made Ivy's heartbeat quicken, and she felt her younger sisters staring at her, begging her with their eyes. Dare she say yes? She didn't even have the authority, surely. "I'm not certain my brother will allow it."

"Oh, my father promised to speak to him today, at his club. Lord Haverford will say yes. His Grace is quite persuasive, you see. It comes with being a duke." Josephine's smile softened as she spoke of her father, as did the gleam in her eyes. "How could your brother say no?"

Time away from her sister-in-law, far from beneath the critical eye of the earl, appealed to her. At five-and-twenty, Ivy ought to have more freedom than she did at present. And having her sisters with her? It made the prospect even better.

With her brother holding her purse-strings until she married or he deemed her competent enough to set up her own household, she was as helpless and dependent as she had been at seventeen when she'd lost her father. Treated more like a child than a woman grown, in a household she had once loved but now felt like an unwanted guest when she walked down its corridors.

"Unless you would rather not come?" Josephine asked hesitantly, her eyebrows drawn together.

Juniper nudged Ivy's shoulder and, when Ivy glanced over, her sister gave her a hopeful smile.

Ivy had remained silent too long, so she hastened to make her answer clear. "I would dearly love to visit. *We* would be honored. If our brother agrees, we can be ready in a matter of hours." She stood and paced to the window, looking out into the sunlit London morning before spinning around to face her friend, allowing herself to hope. "If you truly wish for us to come, I can think of no place I would rather be. And if you are certain the duke and duchess will not mind—"

"They are happy to have you." Josephine grinned first at Ivy, then the other two. "I promise. We will make this summer an absolute delight for everyone." Josephine stood and opened her reticule, withdrawing a folded square of paper. "Here is the invitation from my mother, directed to your sister-in-law."

With wide eyes, Ivy accepted the paper. "You had this at the ready?"

"Of course." Josephine smirked and folded her hands in front of her. "I am a duke's daughter. That makes me quite skilled at negotiation. We are approaching from several fronts. My father to your brother, me to you, and my mother to your sister-in-law." She beamed at Ivy. "I will take my leave of you now so you will have time to speak to Lady Haverford and begin your preparations." Josephine came forward and wrapped her arms gently around Ivy. No one had held her that way in a very long time. Not since her father's death. Though it had surprised her, Ivy returned the embrace without hesitation.

"Thank you for inviting us, Josephine," Juniper said, bouncing up to her feet. Betony stood, too, with pink cheeks and a wide grin. Josephine gave each of them an embrace, then turned to Ivy one last time.

"Thank you for agreeing to come."

Though she said it as though Ivy had done the baronetess a great favor, Ivy's eyes filled with grateful tears. The opposite was true.

Lady Josephine had granted Ivy's dearest wish—an escape for herself and her sisters, an opportunity for them to experience freedom for the first time in a very long time.

CHAPTER 4

A summons to her brother's study didn't necessarily mean anything of consequence. Sometimes, Ivy's brother had a question about an expense he thought Ivy had knowledge of. Other times, he asked if she had anyone she wished him to invite to dinner. Once or twice, he had even asked her opinion on a household matter when her sister-in-law was not readily available for something he considered a "domestic concern."

Ivy suspected this particular meeting, requested a quarter of an hour before dinner, had something to do with the invitation from the duchess and duke. She hadn't yet put her gloves on, carrying them with her as she went down the stairs to her brother's domain. The study, which had belonged to their father, didn't look as it had during Ivy's growing up years.

When her father had sat behind the desk in the evenings, he'd been surrounded by a halo of light. His eyesight wasn't the best, so he kept bright lamps on the desk to illuminate papers or books placed on its surface. A surface Ivy couldn't truly remember seeing, as it had always been covered in documents, notes, magnifying glasses, and cast-iron paperweights shaped like exotic animals.

William kept the desk spotless. The wood had been polished until it gleamed, and not a single thing rested on its surface unless the earl was using it at that very moment. Consequently, that evening only a single sheet of paper, cut to a small square, rested before him on the desk.

He never dithered in speech when he had a topic in mind, so when he spoke without any sort of polite conversation, Ivy wasn't surprised. "I met with His Grace, the Duke of Montfort, this afternoon. From what Fanny has said, this will not come as a surprise."

"No, it doesn't." She sat without being invited. William often forgot to let others know they could sit in his presence. She did not take it personally, but would not wait upon him to remember, either. "I had a visit from Lady Josephine and the invitation from the duchess this morning."

Her gaze drifted to look behind him, and she wondered if feeling lonely after looking at bookshelves was a common affliction.

The loneliness she felt in her own home often took her by surprise.

Her father's shelves had overflowed with books, globes, maps, and trinkets from his travels. The disarray wasn't touched by servants, except for light dusting, as the late earl had known where everything was precisely because there was no reason to it.

"Ordering it to someone else's arbitrary idea of organization would undo everything," he'd said once when Ivy offered to tidy the shelves for him, thinking he didn't trust a maid to do the job.

William's shelves were nearly empty. He had a few tall books with dark red leather binding, a small bust of a philosopher he rather liked, and a tidy collection of poetry he had never read but had been a gift from the Prince Regent. His Royal Highness apparently rather liked poetry and tried to share his fondness for it with others.

"The invitation was a surprise, I take it?" he asked.

Ivy directed her gaze to her brother. "It was, yes. I haven't spoken to Her Grace for some time, though Lady Josephine and I are frequently guests at the same parties."

"It comes at a good time," her brother said, tapping the paper in front of him with his finger. "I intended to have this conversation with you when we adjourned to the country. I have looked over the numbers, Ivy, and I have decided you must marry."

She stilled, her lungs trying to close up while her thoughts caught up with what her ears had heard. "I beg your pardon. Did you say marry?" And what had *numbers* to do with such a thing as matrimony?

"Yes. The sooner you do, the better." He tapped the paper again. "While you have ample funds to set up a comfortable household in some less fashionable place, Bath or York, perhaps, I think it a shame for the income to do nothing other than pay your bills for the remainder of your life. Though you would be a comfortable spinster, you would still be a spinster. The money would go nowhere, be passed on to no one, and you would be too much of a novelty in any neighborhood where you settled. You would be a spectacle."

The bleak prediction for her future shook Ivy's tongue free at last. "I have no intention of remaining a spinster, William. I haven't met the man I wish to marry yet, but I would like to marry someday."

She needn't be alone. She could have her sisters with her—if he'd only release her funds.

"That is a relief of sorts." He sat back in his large chair and laced his fingers together on the desk. "Though it changes nothing. A woman with her own household and funds, living independent of guardians and family, is an object of curiosity. Already, Fanny and I worry over your habits. We have checked many of your odd impulses, but without our direction, you are likely to slip into greater instances of peculiarity rather than conform to the expectations Society has for marriageable women. Thank goodness we haven't seen the same level of oddities in the younger girls."

Her mouth opened and closed without a sound. Her brother thought her odd? So odd, in fact, that he didn't think she should live on her own?

"You require the supervision of a responsible husband," he went on, tone certain and expression bland. "A man who will oversee your funds and ensure you conform to the duties and behaviors of your sex."

A laugh that had nothing to do with amusement escaped her throat. "You do not trust me to set up house or be responsible for myself? Not in the least?"

Women her age supervised households as mistress and housekeeper, taught as governesses, ran schools, arranged social calendars, and even ran businesses. Most of her friends from youth were married with children, managing estates, assisting their husbands' political careers, and even traveling the world.

"I trust you to have good intentions," her brother corrected with an air of consolation. "Your lack of experience and the evidence of your behavior to date, however, show you unlikely to do more than become—"

"An object of curiosity," she said, repeating his earlier words. "What do you think I will do? Start a scandal? Wear my nightgown in public? Take up hunting in Hyde Park?"

Just once she would like her brother, like anyone, to tell her she had done well. A kind word of praise had become so rare to her that she had come to crave even the smallest of compliments.

His expression turned from bland to unamused, which was rather different, though Ivy couldn't have explained how.

"It is rude to interrupt," he said. "It is worrying you came up with a list of such absurd behaviors without pause. No, Ivy, I do not expect you to become a fool. I do expect you will portray yourself, perhaps convert yourself entirely, into a creature no man will wish to marry, if you are left to your own habits and strange ways."

"What horrible thing is that?" she asked, her bare fingers gripping the arms of the chair so fiercely her knuckles turned white. "A witch? A progressive? Perhaps—" she put her hand over her heart for emphasis, as she knew her brother despised one sort of woman above all "—a female emancipationist?"

His eyelids fell halfway closed and his lips thinned. "You think yourself amusing, Ivy, but you are proving my point. An independently-minded woman is a danger to herself and the foundations of our society. Our father indulged you past the point of reason. I had hoped Fanny's example and my own influence upon you would improve your behavior and unorthodox mannerisms." He sighed as though he was the one whose character and entire identity had been called into question. "Thank the Lord your sisters are not nearly so stubborn as you."

The censure hurt, and it remained up to her to find a balm for the pain. No one else would.

Ivy wanted to stand and pace the room, as she had when she and her father shared friendly debates in the past. William would see such movement as agitation on her part, or perhaps even think pacing an unladylike display of emotion.

"I am capable of living independently," she said in as calm a voice as she could manage, and she felt she did well at sounding reasonable rather than furious. "Even more so, I think I could set up a proper house for myself *and* my sisters."

His eyebrows raised at that, and Ivy realized she was skating perilously close to the line William had drawn for appropriate behavior. He wasn't as strict as Fanny, but she had no wish to push him to that point.

Softening her tone, she tried for a pleading air rather than continue to give voice to her shock. "Perhaps you would explain to me, if you would be so kind, why this is a conversation we must have now. Have I committed some terrible misdeed that requires immediate expulsion from your household? Or is there another pressing reason you think marriage the solution to a problem I have no awareness of existing?"

"Fanny needs to turn her attention to our own daughters," he said, referencing his two female children. The two little boys were both away at school until the family returned to their country house. "Florence and Henrietta are at an age when they need their mother's guidance."

The girls were thirteen and eleven, and as Fanny had mostly ignored them since their birth, William's comment made little sense. They were too young to enter Society and they had an excellent governess.

"The less time Fanny spends worrying over your unmarried state and your social standing, the better." He finally picked up the paper and held it out to her over the desk, requiring Ivy stand to take the single sheet from him. "As you are not ready to manage yourself, and Fanny has done all she can for you, I decided it best we stop delaying the inevitable and find you a suitable husband. Preferably before you are considered on the shelf, though luckily your blood and your dowry extend the time frame for such a thing considerably."

The paper bore three columns. The first was a list of numbers which appeared to be an estimation of household expenses for a woman living in Bath. The second column was a list with the heading "benefits of marriage," and the last was a list of "points against spinsterhood."

She would have laughed had the matter not concerned her entire future.

"There isn't anyone I wish to marry." She tried to ignore the way the paper blurred as her eyes grew damp. She couldn't think of a gentleman who had shown more than a passing interest in speaking with her, let alone offering courtship.

A pair of warm brown eyes and the lilt of an Irish accent briefly came to mind, but she shook her head impatiently. A single encounter with a man she nearly injured by dropping an object on his head didn't mark the start of a lifelong romance. Lord Dunmore had seemed pleasant enough, and certainly handsome, but he was a stranger who hadn't even hinted at hoping to see her again.

He had already spent far too much time in her thoughts. He might not even be a good person. He could hate children and be the sort of man who always refused to eat chocolate cake because he considered it "too rich." Perhaps he drank to excess. Or kicked puppies.

Her brother's voice broke into her ridiculous suppositions with an unpleasant tone of impatience.

"Are you even listening to me, Ivy?"

Ivy shook her head and raised her gaze from the paper she'd pretended to study. "I am terribly sorry. My mind was taken away by the absurdity of this interview."

Oh, dear.

He frowned, the expression breaking his indifferent mask at last. His disapproval didn't strike her as any better than his previous attitude. "Being inattentive is not mannerly, Ivy. I will forgive you this once, as it seems my decision has shocked your delicate sensibilities."

She bit her tongue and simply stared at him, waiting until he exhaled a rather put-upon sigh through his nose, making his nostrils flare far more than anyone would find reasonable.

"Before your thoughts took leave of our conversation, I said it does not matter whether you have a current prospect or not. Finding a husband is a simple matter when one is practical rather than sentimental."

Was it with such brilliantly inane comments that her half-brother had won himself a wife? If Fanny had conversations such as these with William on a consistent schedule, it was no wonder the woman lacked sympathetic virtues.

"You cannot force me to marry," she said with a measure of calm she did not feel. Legally, her brother had to care for her, especially while holding her inheritance in trust. William also believed in upholding obligations, and he considered himself obligated to her and her sisters, due to their father's wishes and will.

"Do not act as though I am some sort of fictitious villain." He remained perfectly calm. A true villain would have laughed somewhat maniacally by now, like Iago from *Othello*. Or at least issued some terrible threat with a swirl of a black and scarlet cloak.

William didn't have enough imagination to own such a cloak, let alone know how to wield it dramatically.

"No one will force you to do anything. The idea is unpleasant." He stood, and she remained sitting, staring up at him across the desk. "Take the summer to think things over, if you wish. But you will marry if you want access to your funds and to set up your own household."

"It wouldn't be mine," she argued. "It would be my husband's."

"Even better. All the joy of putting things to order without any of the worry over grocer's bills." He patted the top of his desk. "Come now, Ivy. You had to know this day would come. We cannot continue to chaperone you everywhere, nor devote so much time to you, when we have our own worries and children to attend to, not to mention settling the futures of Juniper and Betony. It is time for you to accept your future as a lady, not act like a spoiled child."

The last two words, spoken with a whip-like crack, stung her heart. Spoiled? Never. Perhaps she had been coddled and cared for once, when her father was yet alive. She'd also been educated, debated, praised, and encouraged. But not spoiled.

How she wished to go back to the way things were.

"Come now. We are late for dinner."

Fanny abhorred tardiness, even if there were no guests present.

He came around the desk and offered her a hand. Ivy ignored it. Perhaps it was a childish thing to do, but she wasn't yet wearing her gloves. Putting them on gave her all the excuse she needed to avoid touching her brother, who withdrew his arm and gestured for her to precede him out the door.

Marriage. And she had the summer to *think things over*. Then what? Pick a gentleman from the crowded ballrooms the way she selected a hat from a stand?

The summer no longer seemed long enough, Clairvoir Castle or not, because it sounded as though it would be her last summer as a free woman.

She had better make the most of it.

CHAPTER 5

Traveling to Castle Clairvoir in July meant far better road conditions than in December, the last time Teague's coach had crept up the hill to the duke's family seat. He sat across from his mother and his sister's governess, Mrs. Gibson, with Fiona at his side. All the carriage windows were open, despite the risk of dust, to let air flow freely and keep the passengers cool despite the warmth of the summer's day.

Fiona bounced up and down on her side of the bench, her nose stuck just outside the window, her whole body straining for the first glimpse of the castle. "James will be surprised to see that I am taller than he is now," she said with an air of triumph.

"He may have grown a few inches himself," Teague said, arms folded and eyes watching the trees.

He was thinking of Lady Ivy again. Ever since their chance meeting in the dim light of the theater, her smile had haunted him. He'd tried for a week to talk himself out of his interest in her. Why should he give an English woman, as like to scorn him for his place of birth as naught, even a moment of his thoughts? Yet she had remained, and he had resolved to see her. If only to prove to himself she was like the rest, finding him an oddity at best and an irritating upstart at worst.

He'd attempted to call on her the day before departing London, far too eager to see if the connection he'd sensed was more than a wistful notion. But the footman at the Haverford's town home had informed him she'd been invited to visit cousins in the country, leaving Teague with unanswered questions and restless thoughts.

"Boys never grow as quickly as girls," Fiona said with a smug grin. "Máthair said so. Didn't you?" She turned an appealing smile to their mother.

"I said it happened that way on occasion," the baroness corrected, waving her fan somewhat languidly. "As most young men eventually outpace young ladies, I wouldn't be touting a thing that is beyond your command, daughter."

Fiona at least appeared to consider that advice when she turned back to the window. Teague smiled, amused as ever by his youngest sister. Perhaps they had indulged her over-much, as she was the baby of the family and had come into the world not long before their father left it. Fiona had come to think herself capable of many things, growing bold and sometimes brazen in speaking her mind. He found it endearing, and his mother had yet to express concern, but her English governess had hinted that something ought to be done before Fiona entered Society in a few years' time.

It didn't seem fair, though, to stifle the girl. Not when a boy making the same sort of statements would be praised for his intellect and confidence. Teague would leave her be at present. Time would take care of maturing her far better than a reprimand from him ever could.

The castle came into view as the carriage left the shadows of the wooded hill, and Teague found himself bending to take in the sight even as his sister cheered for their arrival. The yellow-hued brick glowed golden in the afternoon light, a flag raised from the tallest tower assuring everyone the duke was at home. Teague couldn't help but smile when he spied a welcoming party waiting on the lawn stretching away from the castle.

The ducal family and their guests stood in the sun, the ladies beneath parasols, and one eager boy waved from the wall. "Lord James seems pleased to see you," Teague said with a grin.

"As he ought to be. I am likely the most interesting friend he has," Fiona replied with easy confidence. She stuck the top half of her body out the window, waving back vigorously. The governess gasped and reached forward to hold Fiona by the waist, as though fearful the girl would tumble out of the carriage.

Teague guiltily took hold of his sister. "Fi, you had better sit."

She did, her grin broader than before. She snatched her bonnet up from the seat between them and put it on her head, tying it hastily, if somewhat messily, beneath her chin. "We only saw each other twice in London, you know, before he went off to school again."

"I know." Máthair gave her daughter an amused half-frown. "Remember to exercise your manners when you curtsy to their graces before you run off to play."

Fiona agreed, and none too soon. The carriage stopped before entering the portico, where guests usually departed their vehicles beneath the castle roof, entering the building through a long corridor lined with shields and banners before coming into the guardroom. Today, that formality was unnecessary because Teague's family were kin to the duke and duchess through his sister's marriage to the duke's heir.

Teague left the carriage first and handed down his mother, sister, and the governess, before extending his arm to escort his mother up the short set of stairs from the ground to the raised stone terrace, where they met with Isleen and her husband, Lord Farleigh, Simon Dinard.

"Máthair!" Isleen rushed forward to embrace her mother as though it had been months since their parting and not a fortnight when they had last been together in London. "I am so glad you agreed to come. Thank you, Teague, for making the time." She released their parent to embrace him next, and Teague's heart softened to see his sister so well and happy. He smiled over her shoulder at her husband, who had wrapped their mother in an embrace, too.

Simon greeted Teague with a clasp of his arm. "Welcome to Clairvoir once more, brother."

"Farleigh. My sister hasn't razed the castle yet, I see. Very un-Irish of her."

Isleen cast him a dark look as she wrapped her arm around her husband's. "You best take care, Teague. I'm an English countess now, and I have been instructed on how to properly use the cannons."

He laughed, even if it still pained him somewhat to feel he'd lost his sister—well, not to the enemy. But to the English.

He offered his elbow to their mother. Fiona hopped from one foot to the other, waiting for them to walk the twenty steps to where the duke and duchess stood with the rest of the household's occupants. Simon and Isleen led the way.

His mother murmured softly to him, "They have made a good match of it, haven't they? I never thought it would be an Englishman what would win Isleen's heart. And a future duke, at that."

"They are well-matched," he agreed easily. He was happy for them both, truly. The two were quite enamored with one another, having celebrated the one-year anniversary of their marriage the previous March. He almost envied them.

As though she had heard his thoughts, his mother whispered, "I need to find you a lively *cailín* willing to put up with your politics, then I can have some peace until Fiona comes of age."

"Now, Máthair. I trust your matchmaking skills, but I've yet to see a woman who could put up with me as well as you have. I've no doubt you'd be searching far and wide—" Simon swept Isleen to one side, revealing the family waiting to welcome them.

And Lady Ivy.

Standing next to the duchess, her figure bathed in sunlight, a wide-brimmed bonnet shading her eyes, was the woman from the theater. Time paused for Teague, and he quite forgot how to breathe.

Lord Dunmore and Lady Farleigh were brother and sister.

Ivy's shock fizzed through her like a lightning current as Lord Dunmore stepped into view. The Irish baron seemed as surprised as she was, given how his eyes grew to double their size. He stared at her, as though he didn't quite believe what he saw. Warmth rushed into her cheeks, and she stood frozen a moment longer than everyone else as the polite greetings were made.

"We're pleased to have you here again, Lord Dunmore," the duke intoned.

Ivy's thoughts were still unraveling the unlikely coincidence, a twist of fate that had quite tangled her thoughts. She remembered Lady Farleigh mentioning her brother, but never by title. The same Irishman she hadn't forgotten, could not forget since their chance meeting in London, was somehow *here*.

"Lord Dunmore, allow me to introduce Lady Ivy Amberton," the duchess said with a graceful gesture.

Lord Dunmore grinned unabashedly at Ivy. "We've met before. In London. At the theater."

Voice wavering slightly, she added. "Yes, it was quite the unexpected pleasure."

"How wonderful. I'm pleased you know one another." The duchess swept her hand to indicate Ivy's sisters, standing just behind her. "Have you met her younger sisters, Lady Juniper and Lady Betony? Their mother was a cousin of mine."

"I haven't had the pleasure." Lord Dunmore bowed to them both. "Ladies, it is an honor."

Ivy couldn't stop staring at him as he moved through the informal reception line, greeting everyone. In the gaslit theater, he'd been quite handsome. Here, in broad daylight, he was even more attractive to behold. Warm, dark eyes. A noble bearing. A smile that made her want to tease it from him at the next available opportunity.

Her cheeks warmed at the somewhat brazen thought.

Lady Farleigh—his sister—leaned close to Ivy and whispered, amusement twinkling in her eyes. "It seems the world is smaller than we think, Lady Ivy."

Ivy nodded, her gaze flickering towards Lord Dunmore. He caught her looking this time and sent a confident, crooked smile in her direction.

Did he remember their first encounter as vividly as she did? Had she improved in the sunlight, too?

Upon meeting Simon's bride for the first time, only the day before, Ivy had found the woman's Irish accent charming. Of course, it had immediately reminded her of Baron Dunmore. Yet she hadn't said anything to Lady Farleigh about the Irishman she'd met. To assume all Irish people knew one another wasn't at all intelligent, and some might even consider the assumption rude.

Ivy hadn't heard a thing about Lady Farleigh's brother until breakfast the morning of his arrival, her second day at the castle.

They had never once spoken of him by his title. They had referred to the coming guests as "Isleen's brother" and "Isleen's mother" and "Fiona" when they spoke. She had even heard his Christian name, "Teague," mentioned by Lady Farleigh.

It hadn't seemed at all possible that the arriving Irishman would be *the* Irishman. The only one she knew. The one she had thought of again and again since their single, brief meeting.

How had he come to be here, of all places? His sister married to one of Ivy's relatives!

The rest of the introductions were made without any further surprises.

As the duchess and Baroness Dunmore fell into conversation, Lord Dunmore found his way back to Ivy's side. "When I went to your brother's home, they told me you were away for the summer."

"Yes." She babbled while bobbing her head up and down, somehow unable to stop herself from acting ridiculous. "Her Grace invited me here. For the summer. We're cousins. On my mother's side."

"I think the duchess said that already, Ivy." Juniper had remained next to Ivy while their youngest sister had drifted to the duchess' side, everyone milling about there on the lawn and chatting like old friends.

Ivy's cheeks felt as though they were aflame. She winced and forced a weak laugh. "Yes, thank you, Juniper. The family tree feels a little convoluted at times, is all."

The Irishman's grin turned all the more charming when he spoke. "As one unexpectedly related to a future duchess, I can empathize."

Ivy had to clamp her teeth together to keep from saying something strange aloud. Like complimenting his smile. Or asking questions about his sister. Or asking why he hadn't come to visit her in London sooner.

Juniper looked from Ivy to the baron with a gleam of

mischief in her eyes, but said nothing to detract from the awkward silence. It was almost as though she enjoyed it.

Lord Dunmore studied Ivy a moment, his smile turning from amusement to confusion. "Is everything—"

"Fi," a voice said abruptly from beside her, making Ivy jump. She looked down to find her cousin James with his arms crossed impatiently. "Now that you've done the polite thing, do you want to stop standing around and come see the new colt in the stables? He was born a fortnight ago."

The little girl at Lord Dunmore's side gasped happily. "May I go, Máthair?"

Lady Dunmore assented with a nod. "You may. Off with you, then. Mind you return soon."

"Thank goodness," the duchess murmured as the children ran away. "James has been speaking of nothing but showing Fiona that colt since the creature took its first breath."

The mothers shared an amused glance, then went back to conversing as though they were the oldest of friends. Perhaps a future of shared grandchildren made it an easy thing to get along.

The duke steered Lord Dunmore into a conversation about the journey, and Lord Farleigh stepped closer to form a triangle for the three men, cutting off Ivy's sight of the Irishman. Thankfully, before she made a greater cake of herself.

Juniper nudged Ivy's shoulder with her own. "You never said anything about meeting a handsome Irishman in London," she said, the words somewhat accusatory. "And now he's here."

Ivy took her sister by the arm and took several quick steps away. "Hush. Someone will hear you." She wanted to melt into the ground. "Did I look as surprised as I felt?"

Someone did hear them. Lady Farleigh appeared on Ivy's other side. "You looked like you'd seen the fair folk." Her expression turned mischievous. "Surprised, but not unpleasantly so."

Ivy ducked her head, casting her sister a horrified glance. What would the lady think, hearing them talk of her brother? She stammered out a response. "He did a kindness for me, and I didn't expect to see him again. I hope I didn't act foolish. I promise I am not usually such a ninny when introductions are made."

"Who would think such a thing? Not I." Lady Farleigh's expression turned speculative. "What is it you think of my brother, Lady Ivy? Now that you've met him twice over."

If she hadn't already turned pink with surprise, Lady Farleigh's question would have caused the flush all on its own. Did she think Ivy had intentions toward Teague Frost? She spoke with more haste than care, "One can always benefit from new friendships."

"Mm-hm. That is true enough." Lady Farleigh tipped her head forward. "Do you find him handsome?"

Her jaw fell open and she squeaked out, "Handsome?"

Juniper stared at Ivy as though her sister had grown a second head.

Lady Farleigh smiled and loosed a quiet laugh. "I am teasing you, Lady Ivy. He's charming enough, I know, but it's rather bad of me to speak so of my brother."

Ivy glanced over her shoulder at the baron and found him watching their group. When she caught him staring, he was not sheepish or apologetic. Not at all. Instead, the polite smile he wore grew wider.

Ivy turned away and wished she had brought her fan to cool her cheeks and give herself something to hide behind. How could one feel both pleased and anxious at the same time?

"See now, he's made you blush. Troublesome fellow." Lady Farleigh cast a glare in his direction. "Pay him no mind. He's far too satisfied at the moment."

Juniper finally chimed in, bless her. "The accent helps. The moment a gentleman utters a familiar word with a more exotic twist to it, what lady can help but find him interesting?"

"True enough. One of our dear friends married a man from Sicily. It is always a pleasure to hear him speak of even the most mundane things, like food."

Happily, Ivy took a step back from the conversation. The strange twist to her stomach, experienced the moment she'd found Teague's eyes on her, hadn't faded away. Instead, it caused a sensation she hadn't experienced in several years. A friend of hers had called the feeling a "magnetic spasm of attraction." It sounded somewhat like an illness in those terms, and not nearly so pleasant as it actually felt.

Memory of the last time she'd experienced such a thing went back to her days visiting Oxford with her father, when a handsome scholar had flirted with her while her father had visited an old professor.

A more recent memory of her half-brother's parting words to her, however, came to the forefront of her mind all too readily. The spasms that recollection caused were far less pleasant than what Lord Dunmore inspired.

A cloud passed over Ivy's thoughts, dimming the day and its surprises. As the small crowd of the duke's family and guests went inside, Ivy took the first opportunity to slip away. Her sisters were consumed in conversation with the duke's unmarried daughters, Lady Isabelle and Lady Rosalind, and did not notice her absence.

She needed the gardens and sunlight. Ordering her thoughts and feelings took precedence over pleasant conversation. Her half-brother had given Ivy much to think about.

CHAPTER 6

I vy gently pushed open the door to the castle's library, seeking solace within the comforting presence of books. It didn't matter where she was in the world, being surrounded by volumes of knowledge and stories soothed her heart and mind.

The grand room, with its towering bookshelves and ornate furnishings, was lit by the soft glow of the setting sun. Streaks of amber and emerald shone through the large stained-glass windows, casting their rich patterns on the wooden floor. Atop the shelves were busts of historical and mythical figures alike, all of them pleasant featured so one needn't feel as though Athena glared down upon them while reading.

Wandering along the wall of shelves, she allowed her fingers to glide across the spines. She paused at one shelf when a title caught her attention, and she delicately tugged the book from its place.

Pamela, a novel her father had often described as old but beautiful. She opened the leaf and turned to the page where the bookseller's mark resided, along with the original year of publication, 1740. Incredible that, for nearly one hundred years, people had found pleasure in the pages of a single story.

Lost in her own thoughts, she was unaware of another presence until a familiar voice startled her. "What marvelous treasure did you find, Lady Ivy?"

She looked up to find Lord Dunmore, his tall frame leaning against one of the towering bookshelves, watching her with a teasing glint in his eye.

Her lips parted in surprise. Where had he come from? Perhaps one of the couches facing away from where she had entered. Wordlessly, she held the book out to him, the title page visible.

Eyebrows raised, he straightened and came a few steps forward to better read the print. "*Pamela*? An intriguing choice."

Ivy looked at the volume in her hands, then up to meet the baron's gaze. Her tone took on a defensive edge as she responded, "It's a lovely work of literature."

"Is it?" He tilted his head to the side. "I am only passingly aware of the contents. I didn't think it a novel young ladies were encouraged to read, given the nature of the heroine."

"But it's about so much more than Pamela," she said, somewhat aghast that he hadn't read it. That he didn't know about the story inside. "My father used to say the novel's value came from how it presented virtue and the dynamics between servant and master. We used to discuss whether Pamela herself deserved praise for steadfastness, or if her story was about her manipulation of others to rise in social ranks."

She wanted to bite her tongue midway through her explanation, but the words fell from her tongue as though she were holding a literary debate rather than speaking with a near-stranger. A handsome near-stranger, at that.

Lord Dunmore leaned in slightly, intrigued. "Which camp do you fall into, Lady Ivy?"

She pondered for a moment, closing the book and holding it against her chest, arms folded over it. "I believe there's merit in viewing Pamela as a woman of her time, navigating the expectations of others. But it's also a reminder that stories—and people —aren't always as straightforward as they might seem."

His eyes twinkled with amusement. "Much like our present company?"

Ivy swallowed. "Perhaps. One can never be too careful in discerning the intentions of others, your lordship."

The baron chuckled and crossed his arms, leaning his shoulder against the bookcase once more. "A great truth. No matter how you feel about books, we certainly ought to use such caution around people. Although it can be difficult when we cannot study a person the way we study a page."

She certainly wished she could give greater scrutiny toward him. The initial shock and flutter of excitement she had felt when he had arrived the day before had altered to irritation. Mostly with herself. There was absolutely no reason for her to be pleased to see him again. They meant nothing to one another. He'd done her a kindness at the theater. That was all.

Yet the way he stared at her now, the way he had looked at her with such pleasure the day before, made her question his motivations. A man as charming as he shouldn't be permitted to smile in such a way, as though he'd saved that smile precisely for her. Fanny would certainly take issue with such an open smile directed at an unmarried woman.

The thought of Fanny made Ivy immediately defensive. "Yet here you stand, Lord Dunmore, peering at me as closely as some would peruse a difficult passage in a book."

His grin widened and she wanted to bite her tongue. Fanny would be mortified that Ivy would speak to a peer that way, but the Irishman seemed delighted. In fact, he seemed rather flirtatious.

"Forgive me, lady. I had no wish to make you uncomfortable." He turned his gaze to the shelves. "Though I find you an interesting study, to be sure."

"I cannot think why." She bit her tongue.

His eyes brightened as he focused on her once more. "Can you not?"

Despite herself, she rather liked his attention. When was the last time a gentleman had spoken to her with interest and kindness?

But Fanny would disapprove, and the admonishments of her sister-in-law echoed in Ivy's memory. Loudly. *"A lady ought never draw attention to herself, nor make herself a spectacle. Certainly, she shouldn't invite the attention of men. Modesty, demure posture, and silence are the most appropriate attributes of an unwed lady."*

Ivy lowered her gaze to the book in her hands.

When she didn't answer, he returned his attention to the shelves. "His Grace has a splendid library. Every time I peruse the shelves, I find something of interest. I could spend the whole summer in this room, I think. Reading."

A safe topic meant asking a safe question. "Do you have a literary recommendation, Lord Dunmore?"

His grin widened. "Perhaps something a bit more...contemporary than *Pamela*. There are modern tales that mirror the age-old dance of romance quite well."

Warmth crept into her cheeks. Surely she had imagined the interest in the undertone of his voice. She hadn't said a word about the romance of the novel.

"I appreciate classics," she replied with a measured tone. "There's something timeless about them. And re-reading old favorites is rather soothing, I find."

Teague's expression turned quizzical. "You're not fond of surprises, then?"

It wasn't that Ivy disliked surprises; it was the uncertainty they brought with them. Sometimes her honest reaction to them was at odds with what was expected of her.

"They can be pleasant enough, I suppose."

Those dark eyes of his were still uncertain. "What of meeting me again, Lady Ivy? Was that a pleasant or unpleasant surprise?"

The directness of the question took her aback, and she stammered over the hasty and polite response that spilled from her lips. "P-pleasant, of course. Why wouldn't it be pleasant? You did a kindness for me."

A hint of disappointment clouded his eyes. His posture changed and he looked to the windows. "I am glad I could be of service to you, then. Especially given that those glasses of yours seemed rather important."

As one who had schooled herself in polite behavior for years, Ivy immediately recognized the withdrawal of his more open personality, of his easy conversation, and regretted the loss of both immediately. Why could she never get things quite right?

"Discovery is far more interesting to me than surprise," she said, stepping toward him again, bringing her within easy reach. If she liked, she could have touched the lapel of his coat. Caught hold of it to drag his attention and good humor back to the conversation. She resisted that overly impulsive thought. "Like this castle. There is so much to find here. Every corner tells a story. Speaking of which, have you seen the ballroom? It's lovely. The paintings there are quite rich with history."

Lord Dunmore's eyebrows rose and a startled chuckle escaped him. "Ah, so we're discussing architecture and history now, are we?"

Ivy didn't know precisely why she wanted to coax his smile back. It was pleasant. He was handsome. The combination of the two made her stomach flutter. "If you wish. I am fond of history."

That tilt of his head made her wonder if he found her curious or interesting. Perhaps both. "As am I. Though I must admit that a moment ago, I was trying to delve into a different kind of history—ours."

Ivy's mouth opened and closed without sound, as she couldn't find the words for addressing such a blunt statement. Finally, she squeaked out, "Ours? One meeting in London and an unexpected reunion here hardly constitutes a history, Lord Dunmore."

"Yet it's a start, isn't it?" He moved closer, eyes searching hers. "Every great tale begins with a single moment. Our meeting again, entirely by accident, feels like something out of a story." He nodded to the shelves, his eyebrows raised along with the corners of his lips. "Does it not?"

Caught in his gaze, Ivy felt a twinge of vulnerability, and warmth spread across her cheeks as her pulse quickened. "My past experiences have taught me to be cautious," she admitted softly. "It's not you, Lord Dunmore. One can hardly trust a moment of serendipity to lead to the happy conclusions in works of fiction."

Teague's expression softened. "I understand caution, Lady Ivy. But, sometimes, amidst the games and dances of society, a genuine connection is worth the risk."

Watching him, Ivy hadn't any idea what risks she *could* take. She'd been freer, more prone to wildness and daring, before her father's death. However, her brother and sister-in-law had labored and lectured until she'd learned how often her natural inclinations went against the bounds of propriety. She had her sisters to look out for, too. They depended on her.

She didn't have time for frivolous things. William wanted her to marry. Fanny wanted her to behave respectably. Her sisters counted on her to secure a match that would set all of them free from their half-brother's watch.

A summer's flirtation with an Irishman wasn't likely to help any of those things.

Perhaps he glimpsed something of her confusion in her gaze

and took pity on her. Teague's eyes wandered momentarily to the bookshelf where she'd found *Pamela*. He plucked a slender volume from its companions and handed it to her.

"Of course, risks ought to be weighed. Have you read *The Vicar of Wakefield*? In it, the vicar says, 'When lovely woman stoops to folly, and finds too late that men betray, what charm can soothe her melancholy, what art can wash her guilt away?' I've seen men and women both make mistakes because they acted without thinking."

Who was this Irishman who quoted random snatches of literature at her mere moments after flirting outrageously?

She tilted her chin upward. "And you? Have you acted on impulse, only to regret it later?"

He chuckled, the light in his eyes dimming a touch. "Once or twice. Each mistake has been a lesson. Sometimes, I learned about the world. Other times, about myself."

Ivy found herself drawn into his honesty, sensing a depth in him that intrigued her. "What lesson do you take from our current moment?"

Lord Dunmore returned the book to its place and looked at her. "That sometimes, serendipity isn't merely about chance. It's about recognizing the importance of the moment and the person you're with."

The man was clever. "Are you something of a philosopher, Lord Dunmore?"

He laughed, the sound soft in the library. "All Irishmen are philosophers, Lady Ivy. Especially when in the company of a lady they wish to impress. Though it seems I am failing spectacularly at it today."

Her heart gave a painfully hopeful twist. He wished to impress her? Why?

Ivy was about to respond when she caught a glimpse of movement in the doorway to the corridor. One of the duke's footmen—Sterling, she thought, given the man's height—briefly put his head into the room. His stern expression, though she doubted it was directed at her, and swift stride past the room reminded her they weren't completely alone, not even in a castle of Clairvoir's size.

"Is something wrong?" the Irishman asked, bringing her attention back to him.

"Oh. No. But—"

A chime from the clock above the hearth interrupted their exchange. She glanced towards it, then back to the baron, feeling an odd sense of reluctance mingled with relief. "I suppose we should prepare for dinner."

He offered a nod of agreement, but as she moved to slide *Pamela* into its home again, he spoke. "Perhaps we could continue our exploration of classic tales and personal histories over a walk tomorrow? The gardens here are quite enchanting. Unless you have seen them already?"

Caught off guard, she replied honestly instead of cautiously. "I haven't seen much of them yet. I'd like that." Not only did she take *Pamela* with her, she also took hold of the book he'd recommended. She held both close to her chest.

"Excellent. I look forward to it." He bowed his farewell.

As Ivy stepped away from the man and went through the door of the library, her thoughts thrummed at speed with her racing pulse.

Why did he have such an effect on her? She wasn't typically this open with people, especially not men she barely knew. His presence was magnetic, an unyielding force that seemed to draw the words from her lips. Was it his clever wit, or perhaps the gentleness she sensed in his eyes?

She felt the weight of *Pamela* in her hands, the pages heavy with a near century of readers' emotions.

Was it so wrong to desire connection, to want to feel something, even if they were the dreamed up emotions in a novel? Life wasn't a storybook, and she wasn't an imagined character free from consequences. Every word she uttered, every gesture she made was watched. Judged.

Her sister-in-law's words echoed in her mind. *"A lady must always be in control of her emotions, her reactions."*

Perhaps the trouble was that Lord Dunmore inspired something in her to behave more like she had in the years prior to her father's loss. The free-spirited, open-hearted girl who viewed the world through a lens tinted with curiosity and wonder. He stirred a part of her she thought she'd buried deep, hidden from the gaze of society.

Her fingers traced the spines of the books as she held them closer.

Lord Dunmore was right, of course. Every great tale started with a single moment. One couldn't always tell what sort of story would be told after reading the first page. One simply had to read more.

Was this another fleeting connection, doomed to be extinguished by life's cruel realities, or was it the start of something new and interesting? She felt the tug of anticipation and caution war within her.

It was merely a walk in the garden. With a man she'd met in London. A trusted guest of the Duke of Montfort. She hadn't accepted a contractual agreement or committed to an act of war.

Everyone took walks in gardens.

She reached her chamber door, taking a deep breath to steady herself. Perhaps, just perhaps, she could allow herself to enjoy a moment of serendipity, a happy accident. But with caution.

Always with caution, she thought as she stepped into her chamber, letting the weight of their conversation settle in her heart, telling herself she wouldn't examine it later.

Knowing already she'd fail at that promise.

CHAPTER 7

The morning passed pleasantly enough for Teague, though he found himself checking his pocket watch with increasing frequency as the afternoon and his appointment with Lady Ivy approached. He'd breakfasted in private with his family, so they could have his sister Isleen all to themselves for the first time since her marriage to Simon. Then he'd closeted himself with the duke and Lord Farleigh to discuss the last meeting in the House of Lords and what they'd not managed to achieve.

"We have the summer and autumn to sway others," the duke said to the younger men. "Never underestimate the power of house parties and hunting trips to discuss political matters."

Teague nodded, the weight of the duke's words not lost on him. "Indeed, Your Grace." The informality of such events gave members of Parliament a chance to be heard or express themselves without concern that their party would get wind of their private thoughts. Politicking was something of an art, both inside and outside of the Houses of Parliament.

Lord Farleigh chimed in, his usual earnestness in his tone. "There is something about being away from the noise and urgency of Town. Here, amidst the rolling hills and quiet solitude, I think men must face their own thoughts in a different way."

The duke leaned back in his chair, a knowing smile playing on his lips. "We must also remember the ladies. They hold sway in their own right. Many a vote has been influenced over tea in the drawing-room, not just brandy in the study. Her Grace is preparing a list of guests for the coming picnics, games, and balls. I hope you will both take note of who attends our entertainments."

Teague's gaze drifted towards the window, the lush green of the estate grounds beckoning. "Speaking of which, I am due to accompany Lady Ivy for a stroll in the gardens." He had no wish to make a secret of it.

"Lady Ivy?" The duke's eyebrows raised at Teague's respectful nod. "My wife is quite fond of her young cousin. She strikes me as an intelligent lady, though I think she holds back a great many of the things she wishes to say." He chuckled. "Perhaps the influence of Josephine and Isleen will encourage her to speak her mind more often. I am often intrigued by what our esteemed ladies have to say about the state of our kingdom."

Simon, Lord Farleigh, chuckled. "Isleen rarely leaves anyone wondering about her thoughts on most topics." The warmth in his tone as he spoke of his wife, Teague's sister, was unmistakably affectionate. It was good she had found someone, an entire family, that did not mind her differences. "Do you miss her debating at the breakfast table, as she now does with me?"

"Every day," Teague admitted with an honest grin. "Though I don't miss her smugness when she bested me in our discussions."

Simon's gaze turned somewhat unfocused. "I cannot say I mind too much. My wife quite enjoys being right. The improvement to her mood is beneficial in other ways, too."

Teague resisted the urge to groan. Happy as he was for his

sister's marriage, he didn't have to sit and listen to his brother-in-law turn soft and silly about their relationship. He exchanged a glance with the duke, whose amusement subtly glimmered in his eyes.

With a polite smile, Teague rose from his seat. "I had better be on my way to my appointment, then. One ought to never keep a lady waiting. Your Grace, Farleigh, your conversation has been most enlightening."

"Enjoy your time in the gardens, Dunmore," the duke said. "Oh. One more thing."

Teague paused halfway through his bow. "Your Grace?"

The duke raised his eyebrows. "Good luck drawing out Lady Ivy's conversation. I have a feeling she will have a great deal of worth to say to a man who is willing to listen."

With the duke's parting comment, Teague excused himself to prepare for his walk in the gardens with Lady Ivy. He stood before the ornate mirror in his room, fingers deftly working on the buttons of his waistcoat. The deep chocolate brown of his attire was an echo of his eyes, a shade so dark and rich that it brought warmth to any ensemble. Isleen used to tell him that he wore the color well—another thing she'd been right about.

He brushed non-existent dust from his trousers, trying to distract himself from the nerves building in the pit of his stomach. The afternoon walk with Lady Ivy wasn't merely a stroll in the gardens. It was an opportunity, a chance for him to get to know her, to understand the puzzle she presented.

He allowed his mind to drift back to the theater, to the dimness interrupted by the soft glow of the gaslight, where he had first been charmed by her open enjoyment of the play.

In the library the day before, her voice, despite the hesitancy with which she spoke, had carried tales of far-off places and hinted at a depth of thought he hadn't encountered in some time. Yet, behind her words, he had sensed a barrier. A hint of caution had crept into her eyes, making him wonder about the stories she wasn't telling. About the parts of herself she hid.

Rubbing his chin thoughtfully, he contemplated the upcoming encounter. The mere thought of Ivy evoked a multitude of feelings—curiosity, attraction, and a smidge of uncertainty. He didn't want their next meeting to feel like an interrogation. Nor did he wish to plunge headlong into the waters of intimacy, making her uncomfortable.

The English and Irish nobility had many similarities, of course. The Irish were less reserved, as a rule, when it came to expressing their thoughts and feelings on a matter. He'd no wish to scandalize her ladylike sensibilities. And she was English, even if he'd yet to see the aloof indifference he'd come up against time and again in others of her class.

A knock on the door interrupted his musings. "Come in."

The door flew open to reveal Fiona, her face bright with mischief. Over her shoulder, James peered into the room, the mischievous twinkle in his eye mirroring the girl's.

"We've escaped the nursery," Fiona declared, putting one fist on her hip. "And we're off to explore. Your room is the first we're claiming for Ireland."

"And England," James said from behind her, holding up a telescope to peer through it at Teague's furnishings. "You agreed we could both have any new territory we found."

"Fine." She narrowed her eyes at him. "Though I think England's taken more than her share of land already."

The solution to Teague's dilemma had appeared, right there in front of him. He'd not hesitate to accept such luck.

"Fiona, James. The exact two daring adventurers I needed to see." Teague adopted a conspiratorial tone. "How would you both like to join Lady Ivy and me on our garden exploration? There will be ample land to lay claim to out of doors."

The children exchanged excited glances. In their world of

make-believe, the prospect of fresh air and gardens was always welcome.

Teague leaned in closer, whispering, "There could be hidden treasures in the garden. And I might need your expertise to make my way through hostile lands."

The children nodded solemnly, fully engrossed in the narrative Teague wove.

"Excellent. Best get your hats, then take yourselves off to the guardroom. I'll wait for you, along with Lady Ivy. Be as quick as a wink."

As they scampered off to prepare for their expedition, a weight lifted off his chest. Having them along would add a touch of innocence and levity to the walk, a buffer that would ease any lingering tension. The footman trailing behind the children at a discreet distance passed Teague, barely pausing to give a slight bow.

"Ah, Sterling. You have nursery duty today?" Teague asked.

"Indeed, my lord."

The guard's stern expression gave nothing away, and Teague hadn't ever asked if the duke's personal guards liked certain duties or patrols over others. All of them struck him as serious individuals, and he couldn't quite imagine them outside of their roles of the duke's private militia.

"Then I suppose I will see you in the garden, too."

"Yes, my lord." Sterling bowed and went on his way, trailing after the children he had been assigned to watch over. Though one would hope children remained out of the realm of political disagreements, some unsavory characters who disliked the duke wouldn't hesitate to use his sons or daughters to exact revenge or as political leverage.

The year before, there'd been an attempt on Simon's—Lord Farleigh's—life. Teague still shuddered when he thought of his sister, Isleen, being the one to stumble upon the plot and thus save the duke's heir from the violence intended for him.

Looking back at his reflection in the mirror, the Irishman grinned. Deepening an acquaintance with the lovely English-woman while playing a part in the children's expedition promised an entertaining afternoon at the very least.

At most?

Serendipity, he thought to himself with a shrug. He would enjoy whatever good luck fortune sent his way. He left his room with a light step, making his way through the corridors and down the staircase to the guardroom.

The guardroom was a sprawling space, meant to mimic castle halls from ages past, with alternating black and white marble tiles leading the eye to various antiquities collected by the duke and duchess. Old shields lined the walls, along with lances, sabers, and suits of armor.

The tall, diamond-paned windows from the floor above allowed in rays of light that danced on the floor, creating transient patterns, brightening up what might otherwise feel like a heavy entryway for a castle of such size.

Amidst this grandeur, Teague's gaze was irresistibly drawn to a single figure. Lady Ivy stood near a fireplace at the far end, studying a suit of armor. She bent slightly, her fingers tracing the intricate patterns on the metal breastplate, her expression a blend of curiosity and awe.

As he approached, he noted that her movements were graceful, even though she appeared lost in her thoughts. There was something ethereal about the way she drifted across the marble with every step she took, reminding him of tales of the faerie folk.

Perhaps that's why he found himself liking her more and more. She reminded him of something out of reach, not like the indifferent ladies of English Society, but far more fanciful.

"Good afternoon, Lady Ivy." Teague bowed as she turned, putting every ounce of charm he could into his grin.

A reserved smile graced her face. "Good afternoon to you,

Lord Dunmore," she replied, inclining her head in acknowledgment.

Before he could engage in any further pleasantries, two youthful voices echoed through the room from the stairs above.

"Hurry, or they'll not think a thing of leaving us behind." Fiona's voice came from the stairs an instant before she appeared.

Fiona and James spotted Ivy and charged toward her, their excitement barely contained.

"Lady Ivy, you'll represent England with me on our journey, won't you?" the young lordling asked with wide eyes.

"Teague *must* be for Ireland," Fiona added with a tip of her chin. "It's only fair."

To Teague's amusement, Ivy's eyes widened slightly as she listened to them explain their purpose as they had to him minutes before. It was evident she hadn't expected to see them there, let alone accompanying him for the walk. Instead of showing any signs of annoyance, her eyes sparkled with a hint of mirth.

"I will happily represent my kingdom," she agreed with a note of solemnity in her words, placing one hand over her heart. Satisfied, the children scampered ahead, darting through the door the moment a footman opened it for them.

"I thought you might be in need of protection during our garden tour." Teague nodded toward the children. "They were quite willing to ensure I am on my best behavior today."

Ivy's amused laugh more than repaid him for the effort, the sound light and cheerful. She wasn't affronted or reluctant in the slightest. He rather liked that.

She stepped ahead of him out into the open air, walking through the courtyard.

"Indeed? Are there times when you are not on your best behavior?" she asked, casting a glance at Fiona and James. They had darted ahead, voices raised in light argument about which direction they ought to go first.

"I suppose there must be," he acknowledged. "Else how would I know what my best was, if I didn't also have a worst and everything else in between?"

Ivy's eyes sparkled at him as she shook her head, then she gave her attention to the children as Fiona danced back to her side to show off the map she had found in the nursery. It was a map of the gardens.

"Isleen drew it for me last time I visited. She said she had to draw up maps of the castle and gardens, again and again, or she'd never learn where everything is. She has to *know*. Someday, she will be the duchess and she will have to help Simon take care of all of it."

"That is an important responsibility," Lady Ivy noted with a serious nod of her head. "What sections ought we to explore today?"

James came back with a huff. "We won't see any of it if everyone keeps going so slow, plodding along like donkeys. I think we ought to take this route." He touched the map, his fingers tracing a path as he explained which gardens were best for their game and which were "better for the bothersome, boring conversations the adults are always having."

Teague's heart swelled with warmth at the exchange. Hearing Ivy's soft laughter, watching her easy interaction with the children, he felt an unexplainable sense of contentment. As they moved towards the gardens, he dared to hope that this afternoon might reveal *why* he found the woman so intriguing.

It wasn't like him, really. To see a pretty lady and make a point of pursuing an acquaintance. If his mother had noticed, he would have a difficult time convincing her not to plan a wedding. She would order Irish lace by the yard if she thought there was a chance of him finding a bride.

That wasn't what he was doing. At least, not yet. Certainly not with an English lady.

Why had he even thought of the word *wedding*? He cast the single most dangerous word to bachelors throughout the kingdom into the darkest recesses of his mind.

The gardens sprawled out before them, vast and meticulously manicured, sloping downward from atop the hill where Clairvoir Castle stood, like giant steps leading down into the valley.

Fiona and James darted ahead, the boy holding the telescope to his eye and pretending to scrutinize their surroundings. Sterling kept his distance from all of them, but tall as he was, he couldn't be ignored entirely.

"There!" James cried out, pointing at a common daisy. "A new variety of flora. I shall name it... James's Delight."

"We really ought to have had that Mr. Gardiner fellow with us," Fiona said, opening a notebook. "And Mrs. Gardiner. They know so much about flowers." Fiona had met the entomologist and his wife, whose interest also lay in the natural sciences, the summer before. They lived nearby and regularly visited the duke's family to study the gardens and their creatures.

"They know too much," James countered with a scowl. "Mr. Gardiner can talk about a single damselfly for hours."

Fiona ignored him, going to the nearest bed of bright pink roses.

"Oh, look," she cooed, spotting a butterfly that rested momentarily on a blooming rose before taking flight again. "A rare, winged creature. I'll make note of it."

The children's imagination and zest for exploration lightened the atmosphere. Teague and Lady Ivy shared an amused glance, she as clearly entertained as he was by their game.

"It appears we've embarked on a groundbreaking expedition," Teague said with mock gravity, watching as Fiona and

James bent to examine a shiny beetle on the path. "Captain Cook couldn't do such a fine job of the thing."

"Indeed. I doubt these gardens have ever witnessed such enthusiastic explorers before." Lady Ivy tucked a stray lock of dark brown hair behind her ear, and he immediately wondered whether her hair was as soft to the touch as it looked.

Then he mentally chastised himself for wondering such an ungentlemanly thing.

As they strolled side by side, they reached a section of the garden dedicated to a larger variety of flowering plants, creating a layered work of natural art and color. Teague, seizing the moment, bent down to pluck a bloom from a vibrant geranium.

"This one," he said, holding the delicate flower up, "reminds me of someone. Graceful, vibrant, and standing out effortlessly amidst the many." He offered it to her with a bow.

She accepted the bloom, ducking her chin slightly as she smiled. "Very charming, sir. And which flower represents you, Lord Dunmore?" She didn't seem to take him seriously in the least.

He considered for a moment before pointing at a white rosebush set back in the garden beds. "Perhaps this? A bit prickly, but not lacking in charm."

"You know yourself to be charming?" The dry amusement in her voice felt like a challenge.

"I must be." He feigned surprise. "How else would I merit the company of so fine a person as yourself?"

"Do all Irishmen offer flattery as freely as you, sir?"

"I haven't any idea. I haven't met all the men of Ireland. Though I'd wager a fair few of them have a gift for paying pretty compliments to deserving ladies."

She laughed at that, twirling the flower he'd gifted her between her fingers. "Perhaps I ought to visit Ireland, then, to test such a thing for myself. I imagine it would do wonders for building my confidence." There was the barest hint of wistfulness in her words, and he suddenly wondered what the men of England were about that they hadn't showered her with pretty words at every chance.

"Ah, you needn't make the journey for so simple a thing." He kept his hands tucked behind his back as they walked, not even daring to brush her arm with his. But he dared in that moment to offer her a wink. "I'm happy to pay you all the best of compliments while in your company. In fact, I consider it my duty."

"To build up my pride?"

He shook his head. "To tell you the truth of things. And the truth is, you've a smile as lovely as the sun on a spring morning."

Her cheeks pinked and her eyes went dark with caution. Did compliments make her uneasy when he offered them up too bare? He changed tack immediately.

"Though your taste in literature is questionable, reading dusty old things like *Pamela*."

"I read Shakespeare, too."

"Even worse." He clicked his tongue against the roof of his mouth. "You know, I've heard a rumor that the Bard stole most of his ideas from an Irishman."

"I have never heard such a thing."

"Of course not, you being English."

The playful banter kept her relaxed, and he maintained a distance of several feet between them as they walked.

As they wandered further, the curiosity he'd seen Lady Ivy exhibit before finally showed itself. "You've spoken fondly of Ireland at every turn. What do you miss most about your home when you're here, in England?"

Teague let his eyes travel across the distant trees at the bottom of the hill, looking at the immense expanse of land.

"Where do I begin? I miss the clover-covered meadows stretching to the horizon, the lively music that floats in the very air, and the tales about the ancient heroes told by the hearth at night. Most of all, the sense of belonging. There's a unique pull the land exerts on the soul itself, something all Irishmen feel whether we are poor or wealthy, noble or servant. It is a thing I've experienced nowhere else."

Ivy's tone softened as she spoke, holding the flower he'd gifted her near her lips. "I almost envy your love for your homeland. It's been a very long time since I have felt that sort of belonging anywhere. I understand why you miss it."

"When did you last feel that sense of belonging?" he asked, watching her expression change to something almost wistful.

"Before my father died. Years ago. It wasn't so much the place as it was the way I felt in his company. He traveled a great deal, and he brought my sisters and me with him sometimes." Her expression softened as she kept her eyes ahead, seemingly watching the children scamper about between the hedges. "Nothing too exotic, of course. We went as far north as Scotland, westward to Wales, southward to Weymouth, and east to Dover. He always made me feel like I could be myself. Say whatever it was I was thinking, for example, without any fear of censure or disapproval."

"An honest way to live," Teague murmured, studying her profile with interest. "You don't speak your mind as freely now?"

"No." Her gaze lowered to the flower. "As a member of the House of Lords, I'm certain you must know the importance of measuring your words, that our society is often bound by expectations and judgments. A single word or action can influence opinions and shape reputations. As a lady with younger sisters to look after, I'm constantly on my guard against saying or doing anything that might cause judgement. In the absence of my father, it's more crucial for me to safeguard my family's name and uphold its honor. There's little room for anything else."

Teague's brows knitted together in understanding. "That is true. The upper classes have their expectations and rules. They are rarely kind to those who fall short or are different in ways they do not expect."

He watched as Sterling moved along the hedges, eyes on the children. Another reminder of what it meant to occupy a central role in Society. Danger. Constant vigilance.

"If I might be so bold, Lady Ivy, I believe there's a strength in being one's true self. Often it is the very thing that sways opinions, because honesty stands out in a sea of pretense."

She looked up at him, a touch of vulnerability in her gaze. "It's not that simple. Not for me." He thought she might say more, explain her reasoning, but she turned her gaze away from him and watched the children instead.

They walked in silence for a few moments, Ivy still tracing the petals of the geranium with her fingers. The playful mood had taken a serious turn, but with an intimacy of mind Teague appreciated. She had confided in him.

Lady Ivy stirred his curiosity. He wanted to know the depths of her thoughts, the facets of her character. He'd never been one to ignore the lonely either, and there was something of loneliness in the lady's eyes.

If he could ease her discomfort with a kind word or a touch of humor, he would. It would be a shame for one as lovely as Lady Ivy to retreat behind walls of silence and formality.

The English were terribly stuffy at times. He wondered how much they lost by maintaining that sort of behavior.

"The children certainly don't hold back their thoughts," he commented lightly, nodding towards Fiona and James, who were at that moment engaged in a lively debate about the height of the surrounding hedges.

Lady Ivy watched them with a tilt to her head, her mood visibly lifting. "No, they certainly don't. It's refreshing, isn't it?"

"It is," he agreed with a grin. "Perhaps we can take a page from their book and allow ourselves a little more freedom now and then. Just in this garden, for today. What say you to that, my lady?"

She looked at him, a playful glint returning to her eyes. "I think, Lord Dunmore, you might be a bad influence on me. You're a near stranger. You cannot possibly expect me to throw aside caution and speak to you as I would a close companion."

"Not yet, it seems. But I'll tell you true, Lady Ivy. I don't intend to give up." He winked at her.

She narrowed her eyes at him in return. "Why not?"

Indeed. Why not?

"Because a lady who isn't content to look at the world the way it is, but wants to see it through the lenses of what it could be, is a lady worth knowing. In this Irishman's opinion, anyway."

The pink returned to her cheeks as she turned away, and Teague presented her with his most sincere smile before calling out to the children, "I think that's time enough arguing about the shrubbery. Let's go look at the frogs a bit before we return for tea."

CHAPTER 8

I vy stepped into the sitting room she shared with her sisters. Two bedrooms joined with this smaller chamber, giving the three of them the ability to have private family conversations away from the other inhabitants of the castle.

Juniper and Betony looked up when the heavy wooden door closed with a soft thud behind Ivy. Golden late afternoon sunlight streamed through the windows, bathing the room and her sisters in a warm glow.

"Where have you been all afternoon?" Juniper asked, tucking a ribbon into the book she had been reading.

Betony sat bent over a tray full of tiny glass beads and dark, thick thread while she wielded a thin needle, sewing the beads to a reticule. She kept her focus on her work as she spoke. "In the library again, I would wager. Given that the duke has a host of books on every subject imaginable and our dear sister is always curious."

"It is rather freeing, to read whatever we wish without Fanny commenting on the appropriateness of our choices." Juniper grinned and held up her own selection. "I'm reading about the Golden Age of Piracy."

Fanny certainly wouldn't approve of such a topic for young ladies. Ivy was cheered enough by her afternoon in Lord Dunmore's company that she didn't resist the playful desire that overtook her.

Ivy put her nose in the air and affected her sister-in-law's superior tone and accent. "See here, Juniper. Pirates are not gentlemen. Therefore, a lady ought not be aware of such persons. I insist you put that book away and take up something more appropriate. A treatise on embroidery, perhaps."

Feigning horror, Juniper put a hand to her cheek. "Dear me. Perhaps you are right. Although there is a pirate mentioned as being called 'Gentleman Jack.' Perhaps I may still read about him?"

Ivy bit back a giggle. "I suppose you may read of him. But *no others*, my dear. Imagine if the patronesses of Almack's found out that you filled your head with such horrid things."

Betony snorted. "If they are everything that Fanny has said, the patronesses of Almack's can be no better than harpies or gorgons." She caught a bright red bead on her needle before glancing up at Ivy with raised eyebrows. "You still haven't said where you were. Do not think we've forgotten the question."

Warmth spread through Ivy's cheeks. "I went for a walk in the gardens."

Juniper and Betony exchanged a glance.

"And?" Juniper prompted.

"With a blush like that, there must be an *and*." Betony put down her needle, a certain sign of her interest in her eldest sister's tale.

"*And* we ought to dress for dinner." Ivy turned to the door that led to the smaller of the two bedrooms, with just one bed, she had claimed for herself. The other room was larger, with two beds, for her sisters.

"Ivy, what have you been up to?" Juniper leaned forward in her seat. "You know we won't tell anyone."

"Not a single soul," Betony agreed with a hand placed over her heart. "If you don't tell us—"

"—we will do our best to find out," Juniper finished with a grin.

Ivy looked between her sisters and let her shoulders drop with her resignation. "It wasn't anything secretive. As I said, I went for a walk in the gardens. Lord James was there, along with Miss Frost. The two of them were playing at exploring, and that tall footman was there, too."

Betony's lips parted with a gasp. "Were you flirting with the footman?"

"You weren't," Juniper said, her eyes going large. "Were you?"

That would be worse than the truth. Ivy squeezed her eyes shut as she shook her head. "I wasn't flirting with anyone. I never even spoke to that man. I was walking with someone else."

"Who?" both sisters said at once, obviously at the end of their patience.

"Lord Dunmore." Ivy kept her eyes squeezed shut another moment, but when neither of her sisters made comment, she dared open one to take in their reactions.

They were looking at one another with highly amused expressions. Betony raised her eyebrows, and Juniper's lips were turned upward in a smirk.

Ivy folded her arms over her chest. "Neither of you seem shocked by that particular admission."

It was Juniper who stood and mirrored her stance first. "Perhaps because you have made a point of *not* mentioning him. Several times. Since he arrived."

"What do you mean?" Ivy tucked a curl behind her ear, briefly glancing away from her sisters.

Betony rose, too. "You've spoken *around* him enough times. It was rather like circling a particular word in a poem again and again. 'What do you think of the Irish family? The baroness is lovely.'"

"'The little girl seems to be a special favorite at the castle,'" Juniper added. "Then you talked of what it must be like in Ireland at this time of year."

"You wondered aloud if they would stay long, at least twice." Betony came a step closer. "Everyone noticed your reaction to seeing him *again*, and how careful you both were in speaking of your mysterious first meeting."

Juniper nodded smartly. "Which you never told us about."

Betony's brow furrowed as though a new thought had occurred to her. "And you *do* tell us everything, except things you think will worry us. Does that mean we ought to be worried about Lord Dunmore?"

Ivy turned from her sisters and went to the window, fingers brushing the delicate lace curtain back as she took in the view. The garden below was saturated in amber hues, the flowers almost luminous.

Closing her eyes for a moment, she turned her face to the sun's fading warmth on her skin, letting it summon the memory of walking along the garden pathway as vividly as the real one stretched out below the window, where the woods met the manicured landscape in a riot of colors.

"No. You needn't be worried about Lord Dunmore." When the silence stretched behind her, she released a sigh and let the curtain drop from her fingers. She turned to look at her sisters, the two of them watching her with open expressions, waiting for more explanation.

What should she tell them?

It had been a perfect afternoon, in a perfect place, and with perfect company. The baron's words echoed in her mind, his voice a gentle baritone that seemed to have the power to simultaneously soothe and unsettle her.

She remembered the careful manner in which he'd listened

to her, the intensity in his eyes, the genuine interest he'd shown in the few words she'd dared to say. The world had faded away, leaving the two of them—and the children—to quietly wend their way through flowers and shrubs. He'd shared stories about his travels, family, and hopes, making her feel as though he held her in some esteem, as though she wasn't a mere stranger requiring polite conversation. Someone he already trusted.

"You've turned all serious," Betony noted, her eyebrows drawn sharply together. "Yet you say not to worry? What is it, Ivy? Has he said something unkind?"

"No. He wouldn't." Ivy shook her head and went to the chaise near the hearth. She sat with a sigh, her fingers finding and absentmindedly twirling a loose strand of hair. "Fanny wouldn't approve of him, I think. Nor would William."

She didn't need to look up to know her sisters were exchanging another knowing glance. She felt it, just as she felt their concern.

Despite the casual nature of her interaction with the baron, she felt a connection to him—a pull that she wasn't certain she ought to acknowledge. Not to her sisters, and certainly not to herself.

As she remembered the timbre of his voice, the way he'd said her name, Ivy's heart quickened and a shiver traced her spine. She could almost feel the ghost of his fingertips brushing her arm as he pointed out a bloom, igniting a rather curious spark in her core.

He'd also flirted at nearly every turn, which had flattered what remained of her vanity and feminine pride.

"Who cares what William and Fanny think?" Betony asked at last, the question bursting from her with impatience as she came forward and sat down next to Ivy, snatching up her hand in a fierce grip. "Ivy, you *like* him."

Juniper abruptly sat on Ivy's other side. "You do! Look at her cheeks bloom like a pair of roses. Did he flirt with you?"

"Did he compliment you?" Betony asked. "Or ask to walk with you again?"

Ivy shook her head quickly and tried to laugh away their sudden interest. "He was a perfect gentleman. I certainly didn't flirt with *him*, which is all that matters. I think he must flirt with everyone, given how casual he is about it. Besides, we are both guests in the duke's household. We passed an enjoyable afternoon together in the gardens. There is nothing else to be said." She cleared her throat. "Tell me how you enjoyed your afternoon with Lady Isabelle and Lady Rosalind."

"Absolutely not," Juniper said softly. "Because there *is* more to say about Lord Frost."

"There is *much* more to say," Betony said with enthusiasm, a stubborn tilt to her chin. "Because you like him."

"I like a lot of people." Ivy could be as stubborn as her sister.

Juniper tried a gentler tone. "All right. Say that we believe you. That you like him no more than you do anyone else. What was it the two of you talked about while you walked?"

"I didn't take notes," she protested, somewhat weakly. "We talked of many things."

Lord Dunmore had surprised her. From their initial introduction and the snippets of conversations she had overheard the evening before, she had painted an image of him: a handsome nobleman with traditional beliefs, bound by his political aspirations, society's expectations, and family concerns. Yet, during their walk, he had hardly spoken of any of those things. Instead, he had shown a curiosity about *her* she hadn't expected.

She smiled at the memory of his teasing, the way he had made her laugh, and how he had listened intently to what she said. She had seen a man not of privilege, but of understanding and empathy. He had seemed to genuinely want to know her, to inspire an open conversation and exchange of ideas that no one had sought from her since the loss of her father.

"That smile—something he said made you smile like that," Juniper said. "Oh, he flirted with you more than a little, I think."

"Out with it. Or I will take up a needle and torture you until you tell." Betony's tone held some impatience, but her expression was one of worry. "What did he say to you, Ivy?"

He'd said something that had struck her to her heart. She repeated it aloud, tone soft, "'I believe there's a strength in being one's true self.'"

The cadence of his voice as he spoke, near to matching the way other well-educated Englishmen spoke, but still—there was something different in the manner of his speech. He spoke in conversation with a lilt others used as they recited poetry.

If he believed such a thing, she had to admire him for it.

"Is that all?" Juniper sat back. "It has made you smile as though he'd confessed affection for you."

"Oh, hush." Betony gave Ivy a sympathetic squeeze of the hand. Though she was the youngest, she'd often seemed the most sensitive of the three of them. Perhaps even the most intuitive. "Obviously that wasn't all he said. But it made an impression on Ivy. Didn't it?"

Slowly, Ivy nodded. "He was quite sincere. I haven't had anyone suggest that being true to myself was a good thing. Not since Papa died."

Juniper closed her eyes and leaned her head back against the chaise. "Fanny would prefer us to be copies of herself."

Betony nodded her agreement. "William would have us be at hand when he has need of us, then tucked away in cupboards the rest of the time." She patted Ivy's hand again. "I can see why you would admire someone expressing such a sentiment, Ivy."

With her budding admiration came hesitation. Ivy had been hurt before by fleeting connections. Ladies who promised kind companionship, disappearing the moment they had secured a husband. Gentlemen who spoke with her, only to wander off the moment she said something unconventional.

Could she trust this initial impression of the Irishman, or was he just another person adept at saying what one wished to hear?

The memory of their garden walk continued to repeat itself in her mind. The way the sunlight had danced on his hair, the faint scent of his soap, the warmth of his fingers when he'd momentarily touched her arm to point out a particularly beautiful flower.

It ought to embarrass her, the amount of detail that had etched itself into her memory after such a short time in his company.

"There was more to it than that," she confessed at last, softly. "I feel silly about it. We were only on a walk, in a garden. We do not know one another very well. Or at all, really. A handful of interactions does not make a true connection."

"A summer at this castle might." Juniper rose. "And getting to dinner on time will contribute to a positive impression on him. It is nearly time for the evening meal and none of us are dressed."

Betony rose, too, tugging Ivy up with her. "Dress quickly and I will help you with your hair. Then we can see if Lord Dunmore looks at you with more than friendly admiration."

With a groan, Ivy tried to retake her seat, but Betony kept firm hold of her. "If the two of you start staring at him, I will be mortified. Please, can we pretend I never even spoke his name?"

Her sisters laughed without mercy as the two of them gently tugged and pushed her to her door, admonishing her to wear her prettiest dinner gown.

Once the door closed behind her, Ivy sighed and leaned against it. Regardless of her reservations and her sisters' teasing, one thing was undeniable: Lord Dunmore had made a lasting impression on her. She hoped that, in time, she'd find out what that meant for her peace of mind.

CHAPTER 9

The ladies within the castle walls had gathered in the music room, where a grand piano held a place of honor beside the large windows. Ivy leaned her hip against the large instrument, the polished wood cool beneath her fingertips. Beside her, Lady Josephine flipped through a collection of sheet music, her brows drawn together in concentration.

"Ah, here's the one," Josephine exclaimed, pulling out a sheet adorned with intricate notes. She handed it to Ivy. "Do you remember this? Miss Bateman played it during that recital in London, though it felt more like a dirge than the beautiful piece it is."

Ivy's eyes studied the tune, her fingertips tapping the wood as though she played the melody as she read it. "Mrs. Beardmore's *Grand Sonata in F Major*. Goodness, this is the same piece?"

"It is," Josephine replied with a soft laugh. "Perhaps we ought to give this to you to play for our musical party, so we might hear how it is meant to sound."

"I cannot claim mastery of the instrument," she said with a little frown, studying the notes with greater interest.

"Ivy much prefers a clarinet," Betony said, coming to peer over Ivy's shoulder at the music. "Though I haven't heard her play one in ages."

Before Ivy could demur or do more than shoot a quick glare at her sister, another voice chimed through the room.

"We have one," the duchess called out from her seat in a plush armchair across the room, her voice musical all on its own. "If you should like to try it, Lady Ivy, that is. Fetch it for her, won't you, Sterling?"

The guard-acting-as-footman, and the only male in the room, swept from the corner where he had been successfully unobtrusive and took a case from one of the shelves along the wall. He was to Ivy's side before she could form her protest.

The man bowed as he opened the case, then proffered it to her. Ivy's eyes drank in the sight of the clarinet, and her fingertips touched the smooth instrument reverently before she caught herself and snatched her hand away. She sent a warning look to Betony, who stood smiling innocently at her side.

Heat stole into her cheeks. "I thank you, Your Grace. I will not need it. My skills will suit the piano, I think." She hadn't played the clarinet in three years. Not since her sister-in-law had caught her practicing the instrument. Her words, her disapproving tone, still echoed in Ivy's memory.

"The clarinet? Really, Ivy? Such an instrument for a lady of your standing. It's not exactly...fitting, is it? There are far more elegant choices, surely. Puffing your cheeks in and out like that, holding your arms at such graceless angles."

The joy had gone from the instrument, though Ivy missed putting it to her lips. She had likely lost the ability to play well, given the amount of time that had passed since she'd last expanded her lungs to the extent required of an elegantly held note.

"Are you certain?" Josephine asked from Ivy's other side, her voice soft. "We keep all the instruments maintained. If the family doesn't play an instrument, a servant does, so nothing is ever out of use for long. We also have specialists in from London once a year who check everything and make necessary repairs."

Sterling hadn't moved, but remained still as a statue, holding the case.

Ivy shook her head. "No. Again, thank you. You may put it away, Sterling." She gave her attention back to the papers scattered atop the piano and turned the sheet music over. "I prefer the piano."

The guard withdrew, depositing the case on the shelf, then disappearing back into his corner.

"You needn't fear censure here," Betony said so quietly that Ivy barely heard her. She shook her head once, sharply.

From the corner of her eye, she saw Josephine's eyebrows draw together, her lips parted for another probing question, but a new voice interrupted the conversation.

"Music is a joy in this place," Lady Farleigh said as she approached on Ivy's other side, the lilt of her Irish making her cheerful tone playful. "Even my husband sings on occasion while I accompany him on harp or piano."

"Does your brother sing, too? I cannot think I have heard Lord Dunmore join in song before," Betony asked, after a quick glance at Ivy.

At some point, Ivy would have to either gag her sister or lock her in a tower where she couldn't get out to betray Ivy's secrets with silly questions.

Lady Farleigh grinned, her expression turning quite gleeful. "Was there ever an Irishman who didn't enjoy bellowing like a frog?" Then she waved a hand to dismiss her own words. "Though we tease him terribly, my brother has a fine voice. He could charm the fairy folk with the right song. Invite him to sing with us and he will certainly perform. I think he likes to make a spectacle of himself when he can."

Josephine giggled. "No wonder he gets along so well with my husband. The two of them can be ridiculous together."

Ivy couldn't imagine a duke's heir performing for anyone if he would be seen as ridiculous. But then, she didn't know Lord Farleigh—Simon, as he'd asked to be called—all that well. If the musical party took place in his home, his standards might loosen enough to perform. But not to the point of silliness.

The dowager duchess, a woman who hadn't shown much levity in Ivy's company thus far, sat down at the instrument the younger women had surrounded. She put her hands on the keys and played a simple scale with a wince. "I still prefer the harpsichord."

Josephine snorted. "Grandmama, you do *not*. What a falsehood! You told me when I was ten years old that you begged your father to replace your old harpsichord with a pianoforte."

"Did I?" The dowager raised her eyebrows. Then she played a complicated piece, her eyes on her granddaughter throughout, and Ivy felt her mouth drop open in surprise. She didn't know if her own fingers could fly across the piano keys with such speed as the older woman played. When she struck a final, emphatic note, she smiled benevolently at the younger women and folded her hands in her lap. "Yes, I suppose I do prefer this sound to the other."

"That was astounding," Ivy said, leaning over the instrument slightly to better smile at the woman. "Your Grace, what was that piece?"

"Something from France." She waved the compliment away. "Have you each chosen pieces for the performance next week?"

"Not quite," Lady Farleigh said, grinning at her grandmother-in-law. "Will I scandalize everyone if I sing something from the Irish Rebellion?"

"I doubt it, especially given the outcome of that particular point of history." The dowager duchess's eyes gleamed with mischief. "What were you thinking? *The Boys of Wexford*, perhaps? Or *Irish Soldier Laddie?*"

"Neither." The Irishwoman grinned broadly. "*The Wearing of the Green.*"

"Isleen," her mother warned from the other side of the room. "What would your brother think of you stirring up an argument with your in-laws' neighbors? Sing something without politics tied to it, my girl."

"*If I Were a Blackbird?*" Lady Farleigh batted her eyelashes at her mother, the picture of innocence.

Ivy nearly snorted as she tried to choke back her laugh. Every tune named by Lady Farleigh had a fair dose of Irish pride and a whisper of rebellion to it. But the last was a near tragic song, hardly appropriate for a night of gaiety and song.

"Only if you want to make all of us weep, *mo stór*," her mother said. "You are that determined to be difficult today. How does your new husband put up with you?" Though Ivy winced at the critical words, she noted the tone didn't sound like a censure at all. Instead, Lady Dunmore seemed teasing. Tender.

Lady Farleigh didn't act the least bit as though she'd been chastised.

"I am difficult every day." Lady Farleigh smiled brightly. "But I mention that song because I know it is your favorite. Let me sing it for you, Máthair."

The baroness patted her daughter's hand. "Very well. I would like to hear it, in truth. Thank you, Isleen."

Juniper approached with sheet music in hand, standing across the instrument from Ivy and Betony. "I found a duet for us, Betony, if you'll sing the refrain in soprano." She passed Betony the sheet music, and Ivy wondered if she could join their selection to avoid doing a part on her own.

Her Grace came to the instrument, standing behind the dowager duchess, looking all of them over with a fondness that warmed Ivy's heart when she found herself included in it.

"Music has a way of stirring the soul," Her Grace said, the wrinkles deepening around her eyes as she smiled. "Whether it brings tears or smiles, I am happy for all of it. Thank you for the idea to have a musical party, Josephine. Will a week be long enough for everyone to practice?"

A murmur of ascent followed her question and the duchess gave a satisfied nod. "Excellent. I will send out invitations to our neighbors who will wish to attend and invite another performer or two."

Lady Dunmore released a heavy sigh. "Back home, in Ireland, music is a thread that binds us. Teague still hums the melodies of our land. I've often thought if the Irish and English spent more time appreciating one another's cultures, we would all get along better. Perhaps we could persuade my son to join us in song, too."

"His Grace will have a few guests here who could benefit from such an evening." The duchess shared a look first with her mother-in-law, then her daughter—the dowager duchess, the present duchess, and the future duchess. "An evening with music could be a meeting of our worlds, if we agreed on a blend of Irish and English tunes."

Lady Farleigh, pausing in her perusal of the music spread atop the piano's lid, looked up at her mother-in-law. "You wish to make a political evening of it then, Your Grace?"

Ivy's ears perked up at that. Fanny insisted a woman had no place in the world of politics. The duchess, however, seemed amused by the question.

"There are many ways we women contribute to the running of this country," the duchess murmured, a secretive smile turning her lips upward. "There are times when shouting turns to cannon fire, but there are others when a soft word of change follows a song."

"Music in a drawing room isn't where anyone would expect

to find political change," Ivy said out loud, without thinking first.

When all eyes turned to her, she immediately dropped her gaze. Betony tensed at her side. Her shoulders crept up toward her ears, waiting for a rebuke the likes of which her brother or Fanny would give any one of them for speaking upon a subject considered unladylike.

Ivy swallowed and apologized quickly. "I beg your pardon. I spoke out of turn."

Silence met her apology and she wished to sink into the floor, or roll herself up in the ornate rug beneath the piano. Yet —a rush of excitement went through her blood, too. When was the last time she had expressed her thoughts so openly to more than a single sympathetic ear? Her throat closed and she clenched her hands at her side, waiting for the reproof.

"No, you didn't, Ivy." Josephine touched her arm, gently. "You mustn't apologize. We have conversations like this all the time. I don't think we realized you were unaware of such things, as your half-brother is a well-known voice in Parliament."

William didn't ever speak to Ivy or his other half-sisters about politics. He'd told them it wasn't a woman's place to discuss such heavy matters, even if their father had often spoken freely of such things in their presence.

"It took me some time to see what can be accomplished in drawing rooms and at dinner tables," Lady Farleigh added from her place near Juniper. "When Teague joined the House of Lords, I didn't realize how much of the politicking was done away from Parliament and London."

"It is a secret not everyone learns," the dowager said, her tone resolute. "For every man who stands and blusters about taxation and tariffs, there is a woman in his household who has complained about the cost of sugar. Or a farmer among his tenants who cannot sell his wheat."

"Though our influence is subtle," the duchess added. "We

can still make it count." She regarded Ivy with a soft look in her eyes. "You needn't let the idea weigh on your heart, Ivy. I am afraid we forget ourselves at times. Two duchesses, a countess, a baroness." She nodded to each of the women in turn. "Each of us tied to a man who can sway the nation."

"I am most relieved I married a man with few political aspirations," Lady Josephine murmured, turning her attention back to the music. "Though Sir Andrew and I help Simon and my father as often as we can, through whatever small influence we have."

Ivy looked at the other women with a greater appreciation, and a rather new perspective, too. Things had changed as surely as if she had used another shade of glass to view them. Instead of seeing them tinted more blue or pink, they were tinted with a brighter shade of fortitude.

Envy crept out of one corner of her heart as she listened to them talk freely with one another. They were so easy in their speech, in their expression of thought and emotion. They acted as she had once thought family ought to act, though the only example she'd had of such a thing previously had been her own relationship with her father.

"What would you like to play, Ivy?" Josephine asked, turning her attention back to Ivy at last. "Or will you sing?"

"I...I am not certain." Ivy picked up the sonata and carried it to the window, as though to use the light to better study the notes.

The duchess joined her there, eyes sharp and understanding. "Music, my dear, has many uses. It can make us feel things we resist. It can stir our hearts. It can also reveal to us truths we deny, such as who we are or who we want to be. It frees us. Perhaps that is a thing to consider while you make your choice."

Ivy nodded thoughtfully, turning the duchess's advice over in her mind. Who was she? Who did she want to be? What music could possibly go along with either of those things?

The conversation turned to the picnic and games planned for the next afternoon. The duke and duchess would invite most of their neighbors to the event as a way to open their home and mark the beginning of summer's festivities. It sounded rather marvelous.

Hopefully, Ivy wouldn't shame her hosts by acting strangely in front of their friends and neighbors. There would be enough people present that any poor behavior on her part would likely make its way back to William and Fanny. She had to be the perfect model of a lady—no matter how much she wished to act otherwise.

CHAPTER 10

Teague strode across the sweeping lawn, the sounds of laughter and lively music floating on the summer breeze. Groups of lords and ladies dotted the hillside, parasols and glasses of punch in hand. In the distance, children scampered about in anticipation of the games.

"No lady on your arm today, Dunmore?" his brother-in-law Simon, Lord Farleigh, remarked as he fell into step beside Teague. "You must be the most eligible bachelor in three counties."

"Irish counties, perhaps. Not English." Teague chuckled. "My sister may have found love at your family's estate, but I'm not in any great rush."

"Come now. I've seen the way your eyes follow a certain lady whenever you think no one is looking," Simon said with a wink.

Heat prickled Teague's neck, but he kept his tone light. "I haven't the slightest idea whom you could mean."

Simon's eyebrows raised. Thankfully, he changed tactics. "What are your hopes for the festivities today?"

Teague gestured to the grounds. "I simply want to experience all of your family's renowned hospitality this summer."

His gaze drifted across the festive scene, searching for one face in particular. There—near a flowering trellis, in an elegant blue gown—stood Lady Ivy. Catching his eye, she offered a tentative smile before turning back to her conversation with the duchess.

"There you are again. Stealing glances at Ivy. The two of you have spent a lot of time speaking with one another. Have you enjoyed getting to know her?"

Teague tried to appear nonchalant. "We've had some pleasant conversations. She has a uniquely insightful perspective."

Simon smiled knowingly. "Insightful indeed. Take care, my friend. Reputations are fragile things." He gestured discreetly to where Lady Ivy stood speaking with other guests. "Especially for an unattached young woman."

Teague's jaw tightened, not appreciating the thinly veiled warning. "I assure you, I have nothing but respect for the lady."

Clapping Teague on the shoulder, Simon nodded. "I've no doubt. Forgive my caution—a lifelong instinct where my family is concerned. Eyes and gossip follow more closely than you know."

"I'm not about to give anyone fodder for gossip, Simon. I've my own reputation to worry over. I am being friendly enough, but I prefer to focus my time on the summer's delights."

"Speaking of summer delights..." Simon inclined his head discreetly to where Lady Ivy now stood alone. With an enigmatic smile, Simon departed.

Teague watched him go, irritated but contemplative. With a fortifying breath, he banished his troubling thoughts and turned his attention to where Lady Ivy awaited. An irrepressible grin spread across his face as he went to her.

"Lady Ivy," a familiar masculine voice said from behind her as she bent to enjoy the fragrance of some of the duchess's flowers. "How do you fare this fine day?"

She looked over her shoulder to find Teague Frost standing a few feet away, his dark eyes dancing.

"Thus far, I am well." She returned his wide grin with a slight smile of her own. "Though I admit to some trepidation about that." She gestured to the crowd of people forming nearer the castle as carriage after carriage lined the hill's drive. The faces of children appeared in carriage windows and the vehicles with open tops were full of people laughing and calling out to one another.

The baron waved when an enthusiastic child in one of the carriages caught his eye and flapped her arm about with gusto. She doubted he knew the girl, but when a child waved, one always ought to return the gesture. It was only polite. "They're all harmless enough, I think. So long as they are kept fed, no one ought to bite."

She couldn't help a laugh of surprise. "I suppose that is something to be thankful for, and the duchess has an impressive feast laid out in the shade. Every possible cold dish one could want, pies aplenty, and more pastries and puddings than I have seen in my life."

"Her Grace never does things by halves. She fed the entire village on the day my sister married Lord Farleigh, a wedding breakfast that went on until it became a wedding dinner."

Ivy tilted her head to one side, trying to imagine that feast. She'd never seen anything like it, likely because not everyone could afford to be as generous as the ducal family. Though her own family had enough and to spare, it was difficult to concep-tualize what the duke had at his disposal.

That made her voice a thought she would normally keep to herself. "I imagine that was something of a surprise, your sister marrying into a duke's family, given how few dukes there are with eligible sons. They both seem quite happy. My cousin says it was a love match."

His gaze left hers to find his sister standing near where the guests had formed a line. Lady Farleigh, who had insisted on Ivy calling her Isleen, welcomed all who came with a grace and kindness that well suited her position as future mistress of the castle. The guests parted from her with smiles as they filtered through the area set aside for the picnic and into the gardens and amusements set about for the afternoon.

"I cannot claim I expected her to find her other half in an Englishman, much less one with such a revered title and heritage. Indeed, a surprise. Lord Farleigh is a good man, and he makes my sister happy." His tone sounded almost wistful for a moment, and Ivy well enough understood such a thing. Watching others find their happiness sometimes caused difficulty with being content in one's own life. He gave his full attention to her again and leaned close. "I'm told many an English rose mourned his loss in the marriage market."

Ivy giggled, but swiftly stifled the sound by biting her lower lip. There had been a great deal of gossip—a flood of it, actually —when Simon had announced his betrothal shortly after the family had returned to London for the Season.

"I imagine it would be somewhat disheartening to learn a future duke no longer had need of wifely candidates. Who can blame them for their disappointment? A woman of our set is bred for one purpose, and that purpose is marriage."

"I am well aware." He huffed and folded his hands behind him, but there wasn't any real heat or displeasure in his words. "My sisters regularly remind me of the unfairness of the world and a woman's place in it. I assure you, I am well-versed in the frustrations they have expressed. Let us talk of something outside of the subject of matrimonial prospects."

She cast him a sideways glance as she inspected a climbing rose on the trellis. "You dislike the subject that much? How unfortunate. It is one of the only things on my mind of late."

Perhaps she ought to have bitten her tongue rather than admit to such a thing. Yet he made it so easy to speak her mind. Something about the way he looked at her made her realize her words were safe with him. He wouldn't use them against her, wouldn't censure or judge. He listened, and always as though what she said had interest to him. That it mattered.

This particular admission caught him off guard, if the sharp rise of his brows was any indication. "Is it?" He studied her a moment. "Why would that be, I wonder?"

There. He'd phrased the question in such a way that she could answer if she wished or keep her thoughts to herself.

She surprised herself by offering up more on the subject. But...whom else could she talk to about it? "Because I am faced with the daunting prospect of finding myself a husband by year's end or my brother choosing one for me." She didn't look at the baron. She kept her gaze on the rose now bobbing in the light breeze. "Apparently, an unwed sister of five-and-twenty is a burden he can no longer bear."

Teague's mouth dropped open. She readied herself, but again, he surprised her with his tone as he said, "Ridiculous."

Her attention snapped to his at the unexpected heat behind that word. "Is it?"

"Yes. I'd not have let Isleen go if I thought her unhappy, and I would never force her or Fiona to go from our home unless 'tis what they wanted." The light, teasing tone he'd used earlier had completely dropped away. Now she heard impatience. "I apologize for so easily dismissing the subject when it is one that must haunt your waking hours. As I said, my sisters have well informed me on the unfairness of the female plight."

She stared at him with what she hoped was an open, curious expression. "It does seem unfair, doesn't it? Once I'm wed, by my choice or my brother's, I lose all independence. My will must necessarily bend to my hypothetical husband's."

"Hypothetical?" he repeated with a crooked smile. "Hm. Well. It needn't be that way always." He nodded again to where his sister greeted guests on the hill. "Isleen seems more willful than ever since her marriage."

Ivy glanced that way. "Indeed? She must be a happy woman, then, and in a happy marriage." She shook her head, then made a dismissive gesture with her hand. Looking beyond herself, she couldn't help but feel selfish for sullying the day with her worries. Best to put them aside for the time being. "The day is too lovely to talk of my worries. I am certain I ought to speak of the weather, religion, and fashion."

He obliged her with ease, moving into discussing the castle's grounds. Yet the more polite and appropriate line of conversation didn't seem to dull the mood between them. If anything, he seemed more than willing to speak on any topic she brought up. It was quite flattering, really. And different. When was the last time someone had listened to her with such unwavering interest?

Finally, several gentlemen came trotting across the lawn looking for others to challenge in a game of cricket. She released Lord Dunmore to their enthusiastic company with a laugh. She found her sisters speaking with Lady Farleigh—Isleen. They all stood about the refreshments, nibbling at biscuits and laughing.

"Here you are, Ivy." Isleen grinned brightly at her. "Goodness, isn't this a beautiful day? Perfect for the picnic. We're gathering some sustenance before watching the cricket match."

"It is. Yes." She set about making herself a plate of treats.

"We saw you walking with Lord Dunmore earlier," Betony said with a sly smile. "You seemed to enjoy his company."

This pricked Isleen's attention. "Oh, dear. I hope my brother is behaving himself."

"Of course. Lord Dunmore is a complete gentleman." Ivy sent a warning glance to her sisters, neither of whom seemed to care as they continued to grin at her. "I enjoy our conversations."

She had to remind herself that was all they were—conversations between two people who happened to be guests at the same party. Pleasant distractions from her worries and nothing more. She made her way toward the open stretch of lawn where others lined up beneath parasols to watch the match.

Lady Isabelle appeared, her enthusiasm making her bounce. "Betony, Rosalind and I want you to watch the match with us. Do hurry!"

Betony gave her sister one last playful smirk before hurrying off with the duke's daughter. Ivy tried to relax, keeping close to Isleen.

CRICKET WASN'T A DIFFICULT GAME. ONE MIGHT PLAY IT casually or with competitive vigor. Given the mix of individuals playing that afternoon, both in age and sex, Teague doubted he would see any of the gentlemen playing roughly. Although one of the girls, likely no older than fifteen, had a look about her as though she planned to use the cricket bat as a cudgel.

After the gentleman and boys had removed their jackets to play more easily in shirtsleeves, they formed teams. The girls playing rid themselves of bonnets and gloves. Only one married lady had asked to join the games, on the team opposing Teague's.

Teague jogged behind the bowler, long-off on the chance

the first batsman—an eager boy with a broad grin—struck the ball hard enough that it went by the other fielders.

Given the nature of a casual game, he was relatively safe to do no more than cup his hands around his mouth and cheer others on. The ball didn't come near him for long stretches of time, which meant that his mind freely wandered to his conversation with Lady Ivy.

That she used words like *hypothetical* and *serendipity*, that she shared deeper thoughts on subjects from books to gardens, had amused and intrigued him from the first. Yet he couldn't muster anything other than concerned dismay for her on the subject of matrimony.

In his usual talks with her, he often felt there was so much she wasn't saying, holding back an intelligence he wanted to explore. Now he understood a new layer of her reticence beyond the simple tenets of polite behavior.

The woman carried the burden of her future on her shoulders. The uncertainty of it doubtless made her less interested in idle conversation. He had let the subjects drift to the weather, the castle, and the gardens, even as his mind turned over her troubles, wishing for a way to help her.

With a thud that seemed to echo against the walls of Castle Clairvoir, the hard leather ball struck Teague squarely in the stomach. The force of the impact doubled him over, the breath whooshing out of his lungs in a single, violent exhalation. The pain was immediate and intense, a fiery brand that seared through his abdomen, demanding his full attention with ruthless efficiency.

There was a collective gasp from the onlookers, and Teague looked up to see the young lady with the wicked look of a conquering tyrant on her face as she ran to the opposite wicket. He scooped up the ball that had tumbled to the ground, but was really too late to do anything other than get it back to the bowler, who happened to be Simon for their loosely organized team.

Simon caught the ball and gave Teague a look of such disappointment that the Irishman felt his ears turn hot. "Distracted, Dunmore?" he shouted.

Teague rubbed at his stomach. The bruise would likely be impressive. "Not anymore," he called back. "Get me another like that and I shall prove I learn from my mistakes."

Lady Ivy's eyes were on him, her eyebrows raised, and her hand covering her mouth. She lowered it to wave and give him a sympathetic smile, but then Isleen said something that made Lady Ivy laugh. Of course she had seen him miss what would have been an impressive catch, had he been paying attention.

He certainly wouldn't let *that* happen again.

"I'd really hoped for better from you," Simon shouted.

Sir Andrew, on the opposite side of the makeshift playing field from Teague, shouted, "The English sport is obviously too much for our Irish friend!"

More friendly insults followed and Isleen's voice was heard booing the statement. Teague chuckled and made a show of rolling up his sleeves. "I'll not let you sully my countrymen. We're as good with bats and balls as the next man."

The harsh lesson delivered by the cricket ball served as a jarring reminder of the present, pulling him from the mists of distraction with a clarity both brutal and absolute. Yet even as he promised himself he would pay better attention, his eyes darted to where his sister stood with Lady Ivy and her younger sisters. His sister was, predictably, smirking at him. She'd not let him forget his mistake.

"Next one is easy," Sir Andrew shouted. "The Sicilian!"

A cheer erupted from the watchers as the Conte di Atella stepped in front of the wicket, his expression somewhat rueful. "Are you implying I lack talent or understanding of your game, Sir Andrew?"

"Both," the baronet shouted, moving closer. "Even if you hit the ball, it won't go far."

Simon bowled almost perfectly, the ball skimming the ground at quick velocity, heading straight for the wicket. Lord Atella swung but missed—and the ball narrowly missed the stumps, too. Teague, along with the other fielders, shifted and called out good-naturedly to Simon, who smirked and waved them off.

This time, as the ball was bowled, Lord Atella's expression turned fierce. He stepped forward, swinging the bat in a powerful arc. The ball made contact with a crack, the sound sending everyone scurrying to catch it. Including Teague.

He ran, backward, arms stretched out—and the ball struck his hands with enough force to make him grunt. It was a clean catch, and the duke—overseeing the game to ensure it was fairly played—shouted "caught!" The Sicilian ambassador was out.

"Excellent for your redemption, Dunmore," Simon shouted.

Teague held the ball aloft. "Was there ever any doubt that I'd do such a thing? Better luck next time, Atella."

The count executed a formal bow toward Teague. "I am certain there will be."

With that, it was time to change out. As Teague joined the queue of batsmen, ready to take his turn at the wicket, the other members of the team jested and advised one another with easy camaraderie.

Sir Andrew clapped him on the back, his grin friendly. "Let us see if you can hit as well as you catch, Frost," he teased, the twinkle in his eye betraying his genuine respect for Teague's earlier display of skill. Then he turned to face the crowd and waved toward his wife, Lady Josephine, who stood beside the duchess. His wife waved back and winked.

It was obvious the baronet enjoyed his wife's eyes on him. Simon seemed equally distracted in that moment, grinning toward his own wife. Indeed, most of the men who were married or engaged in the courtship seemed to spend at least a moment during the change of players posturing for their lady-loves.

Teague merely smiled, a nonchalant facade that belied the nervous energy simmering beneath. His gaze inadvertently swept across the spectators, landing once again on Ivy. Their eyes met and for a fleeting moment, the world seemed to pause —the chatter, the laughter, and the gentle breeze all fading into a hushed silence. Ivy's smile drew him in like a beacon, a silent encouragement stirring a tumult of emotions within him.

"Ready to lead us, Lord Dunmore?" one of the young ladies on their team asked with a bounce in her step. "Are you any good with the bat?"

"Am I any good?" Teague asked, hand going over his heart as he shook off the momentary distraction seeing Lady Ivy had caused. "Watch carefully, ladies and gentlemen," he announced with a playful arrogance that drew a round of laughter from his friends. "Allow me to show you how it's done."

Simon, standing next in line, apparently couldn't resist adding to the banter. "Just make sure you keep your eyes on the ball, not on the lady spectators," he quipped, sending a knowing glance towards Lady Ivy.

The man was far too observant. A good thing in a future duke, an annoyance in a friend. Teague waved off the comment.

The first ball came at him with a challenging speed, and Teague, mindful of Simon's jibe, focused entirely on the task at hand. With a swift, calculated swing, he connected, sending the ball rolling neatly between the fielders. Not a boundary hit, but a solid single that let him off the mark.

As he jogged to the safety of the opposite wicket, the mild success was met with cheers and a few exaggerated sighs of relief from his team. "Seems you've finally decided to join us in the game, Dunmore!" one of the players called out, his voice laced with humor.

Yet, even as the playful exchange continued, Teague's mind wandered, unbidden, back to Lady Ivy. Her presence, a constant on the periphery of his focus, was quite the distraction. He knew the balance between the joy of the game and the complexity of his thoughts about her was a delicate one.

As the match progressed, Teague found himself stealing glances towards Ivy, each look a silent conversation. There was an ease to her, and that intelligent curiosity that seemed to pull him in time and time again. Each time their eyes met, he felt a driving need to help her solve her matrimonial problem.

WATCHING THE CRICKET BALL DRIVE INTO LORD Dunmore's stomach had made Ivy gasp and even take a step forward, as though she ought to do something to ensure his well-being. A ridiculous, instinctive reaction that made her blush rather fiercely.

His sister, standing beside her, hadn't seemed to feel any sympathy at all given the way she shouted, "Keep your pretty head in the game, Teague Frost!" She shook her head and gave Ivy an exasperated look. "What in heaven's name would distract a man when he has a ball of leather flying at him?"

Ivy swiftly shook her head in confusion. "I haven't the slightest idea. The last time I played cricket, I was so worried the ball would take off my head I never took my eyes off it once." She winced in sympathy again, looking at Teague. He had turned a shade of red that made her wonder if he felt more embarrassment than pain. "Do you think he's all right?"

"It would take more than that to fell him," Isleen said with a toss of her head. "The man is stubborn as an ox and thrice as wily. How else could he have convinced the English lords to elect him to Parliament?"

"I had wondered," Ivy murmured, her eyes going back to the game. "Most of the Irish representatives chosen were quite old, with stronger ties to English peers through education or marriage."

Isleen hummed in agreement. "He campaigned rather hard. I think he leaned on the fact that he was young. They won't have to replace him any time soon." She smirked. "Of course, the moment he took his seat, he became quite an annoyance to the opposition."

Though Ivy found herself wanting to know more, it was difficult to concentrate on political discussion while trying to follow the game. Cricket wasn't her favorite sport as a spectator, but she quite enjoyed the moment when Lord Atella took up the bat. He was a touch older than her cousin, Simon, but had practically married into the family when he wed Emma Arlen, ward of the duke and former companion to Lady Josephine.

"Is everyone here related to the family?" she muttered aloud.

The Irishwoman chuckled. "In some form or another, it would seem." Then she cupped her hands around her mouth and shouted, "Don't let him hit it, Simon!"

Her husband sent a wink at his countess before bowling exceptionally well—but Atella hit the ball anyway, and it sailed through the air directly toward Lord Dunmore. Who was, Ivy saw with a confusing amount of elation, completely prepared to leap up and catch the ball, keeping Lord Atella from obtaining the opposite wicket.

She clapped and cheered as loudly as Isleen, bouncing on her toes with far too much enthusiasm. "There now, he's redeemed himself," she said aloud.

"That he has," Isleen agreed. Then she shouted, "For Ireland!"

That gave Ivy leave to laugh and shake her head. "You are

fiercely proud of your homeland. Your brother, too, seems to mention it every chance he gets. Is England really so different?"

"Fundamentally, yes. The history between our nations is one I think will forever divide us, even if we're ever fully accepted as equals." Isleen didn't speak with bitterness, but with a calm acceptance that made Ivy feel woefully ill-informed.

The time had come for the teams to switch places, which meant Simon and Lord Dunmore were jogging toward the lineup for batting. Isleen waved enthusiastically at her husband, and Ivy found herself making eye contact with the Irishman. The intensity of his stare momentarily took her by surprise, yet she found herself smiling her encouragement at him. He made a fine sight, running across the green with his white shirtsleeves bright in the sunlight. She half expected him to wink at her and was somewhat disappointed when he didn't.

Quite silly of her, really.

It seemed he would be the first to bat.

"I know things have been bad in the past for your countrymen," Ivy said quietly to her cousin's wife. "Is there really such enmity now? Things are changing for the better, are they not?"

Isleen gave Ivy a measured look, as though trying to determine if Ivy's interests were sincere or merely idle conversation. "We still live under the shadow of the Rebellion of 1798. The Penal laws keep Catholics from many rights, including representation in Parliament. A Parliament that dissolved Ireland's own government and will elect Irishmen to seats only as they see fit. Then there are the taxes imposed on Irish tenants, and the ways the poor are taken advantage of by the English who have estates in Ireland." She shook her head slightly. "If a man beats his horse with a stick instead of a whip, are things really better, or merely different?"

There was much to digest in Isleen's words, and Ivy nearly missed the moment that Lord Dunmore's bat connected satisfactorily with the ball, earning him a run to the opposite wicket.

When he'd obtained safety there, he looked directly at her again and her heart skipped a beat.

She clapped along with Isleen, though she didn't cheer aloud.

"I am sorry I am so ignorant of these things," Ivy said at last to her friend, for she did feel she and Isleen had at least become that much. "I ought to be more aware, given my brother's position."

"Often we are unaware or uninterested in the things that do not directly impact us," Isleen said without sounding offended. "It is a human failing, I think. There is much in the world I am ignorant of, as well. I think what is important is that when we learn of such things, we show compassion, interest, and understanding. If we can do something to make the circumstances better, then we act."

The gentle wisdom of those words made Ivy nod in agreement, her eyes still on Lord Dunmore. He glanced at her again and she wondered what she'd done to earn his interest. And whether she could manage to hold on to it a little longer.

CHAPTER 11

After dinner, Teague walked with Simon along the stone terrace that served as the castle's forecourt. They'd been abandoned by Sir Andrew the moment the man's lady-wife, Simon's sister Josephine, had batted her eyelashes at him. The man was incredibly besotted.

In truth, Simon was equally enamored with his wife, Isleen. But she had waved them out the door and settled in to play a game of cards with the Lady Ivy and her sisters, an event for which Teague felt immense gratitude. He needed to talk to someone, and Simon fit the purpose exactly.

"Marriage agrees with you," Teague said, looking into the darkness of the gardens. The only light came from the moon and the windows of the castle behind them. "And with my sister. You both seem happier now than you were when you met."

"I hope that holds true for many years to come." Simon chuckled and looked over his shoulder at the castle, his home, his inheritance. "Isleen has been good for all of us, in truth. She's a breath of fresh air. Whenever I talk to her, I feel as though I have learned a new secret to life or found a new way to look at things. Your sister is a wonder."

Teague nodded thoughtfully. "Sir Andrew and Lady Josephine seem equally happy."

"I couldn't wish for better for either of them, though I do still point out as often as I can that Andrew was my friend long before he was Josephine's husband. That must count for some sort of loyalty in our debates. Never seems to, though." Simon tucked his hands behind his back and cast Teague a curious glance. "You sound somewhat envious of we poor besotted fools. Thinking of trying marriage for yourself? I can highly recommend it, thus far."

Teague stared down at the stones beneath their feet as they walked. "I have given it considerable thought of late. My life has grown stagnant. Stale. My frustration with everything seeming to remain the same, no matter how hard I work at reform, has seeped into every part of my life. I need change. I need something to look forward to at the end of every insufferable day in Lords."

"Finding a lady for yourself might help, though I doubt it will solve all your problems." Simon, to his credit, sounded sympathetic rather than amused.

"Not all of them," Teague agreed, because he hadn't lost all his senses. Simon's reaction to what he said next would determine how many, exactly, he lacked. Perhaps he should have practiced the speech in front of a mirror. Then at least he'd know if he looked as mad as his friend might think him. "I've been considering asking Lady Ivy to marry me."

Simon stopped in his tracks, turning to face Teague with a mix of surprise and skepticism shadowing his features. "Marry Ivy? That's rather sudden, isn't it? You barely know each other."

The weight of his friend's gaze settled on Teague's shoulders, a reminder of the gravity of his somewhat impulsive thought. He had thought of nothing else since her revelation at the picnic three days previous. However, the restlessness that had been his constant companion seemed to quiet at the idea of a future with Ivy.

"I know it sounds mad, but something about her...it's as if she is the answer to a question I have been asking myself for months."

Simon sighed, the corners of his mouth twitching in a reluctant smile. "From what I know of you, you have always been one to follow your instincts, even when it leads you off the beaten path. But marriage is a lifetime commitment, not a solution to ennui."

"I am aware," Teague replied, well knowing the seriousness of his own proposal. "Only, I've seen the way you and my sister are together. How you've grown. I want that for myself, Simon. Not the stagnant pool my life has become."

Simon studied him for a long moment before speaking in a cautionary manner. "Then you must ascertain if she is a good match for you, or at least open to the possibility of a future with you. Love doesn't always start with fireworks, but there must be a spark, Teague. I've seen too many of my friends enter marriages the way a martyr goes to the gallows. I don't want to see you regret your choice nor see my cousin do so. You must consider your happiness. Promise me that."

Teague nodded, feeling a blend of appreciation and determination. Simon hadn't dismissed the idea as an impulsive mistake. Teague hadn't completely lost his senses, then. "I promise," he said. "I believe there's something between Lady Ivy and me. Something worth exploring."

Simon clapped him on the shoulder, a gesture of solidarity. "I'll stand by you, as always. Just be sure before you take that final step, my friend. Be *very* sure."

The exchange left Teague with much to ponder, the seriousness of his intentions now laid bare. Within his heart, the spark

Simon spoke of had already flickered to life, illuminating the path forward with greater clarity.

Perhaps it wasn't enough of a connection yet, but marriages had been built on less and thrived. The curiosity, the possibility of what could be with her, was irresistible in his thoughts. And *if* the chance existed for something genuine to grow, it was a gamble worth taking. Wasn't it?

There was an attraction, on his side at least. He found her beautiful, her eyes captivating. He had wondered if those lips of hers, with their slow and gentle smiles, would feel as soft as he suspected when he kissed her.

"You know her brother is pushing for her to wed." Simon stated the fact as though it was general knowledge.

"Indeed, I have come to understand that." Teague was a bit surprised Simon knew of it. "Do you think he would object to an Irishman paying court to his sister?"

"Half-sister. I'm not certain." Simon gave a shrug. "You're a baron. Respected in Lords, even if some find your ideas radical. An associate to my family, linked by marriage. On paper, you're an excellent choice for any English woman to wed."

"I am." Teague allowed himself a grin. "And I'm a hand-some fellow, too."

Simon choked on a laugh. "I doubt that comes under Lord Haverford's list of requirements for marital candidates, but it might have an impact on Ivy's thoughts on the matter."

Teague chuckled to himself. "Since her opinion matters more, I'll see what she thinks of the scheme first. There isn't any point in bothering her brother—*half*-brother—until I know her thoughts."

"How do you intend to approach her?" Simon stopped their walk and looked his brother-in-law up and down. "As though it's a business negotiation, or with some semblance of romantic interest?"

"I wonder if there's a guidebook for this sort of thing.

'Impromptu Proposals for the Impetuous Gentleman'—now there's a title."

Though he laughed, Simon said, "Be serious a moment, won't you?"

"Ah. Now I've given that matter a lot of thought. I think simplicity is best. Tell me what you think of this...."

CHAPTER 12

F inally, Ivy found her way out to the statuary gardens. She had a book tucked under her arm and a wide-brimmed bonnet on her head to protect against the freckling Fanny seemed intent on eradicating. Not that Ivy had many; only a few across her nose.

She took her time to observe the statues, created to bring to mind Greek gods and goddesses. One intriguing toga-clad gentleman looked remarkably like the duke. She stared up at him for a long moment, wondering if it had been commissioned that way or had been the sculpture's decision. Either way, it made her smile.

She found a stone bench tucked beneath the shade of an oak and went to it, determined to lose herself in a book, forgetting her problems for at least half an hour.

It was not to be, though. No sooner had she opened the book's pages than she caught movement from the corner of her eye. She looked up, watching as Teague Frost wound his way through the statues. He looked at none of them. Instead, he was focused on the tree—on her beneath it.

He raised his hand in greeting when he was close enough he

needn't shout to say, "Good afternoon, Lady Ivy. I hope you don't mind, but I have been looking for you."

"Have you?" She closed her book and rested it in her lap, then glanced behind him. "Sterling followed me out here. I think he's keeping watch at the top of the terrace. He could have told you where I had gone."

"But then he might've followed me down here," the baron pointed out with a grin, "and I'd like a word in private with you. If you and your present company don't mind." He gestured to the statues surrounding them. "Lively group, aren't they?"

Raising her eyebrows, she peered at the nearest statue, a maiden pouring a vase of flowers into the flowerbed below. "I like them well enough. They keep their opinions to themselves and haven't tried to interrupt my reading."

"I apologize for that unfortunate circumstance." He gestured to the other side of the bench. "May I?"

She shifted a little more to the side, giving him ample room to sit and still keep appropriate space between them. "You said you needed a private word?"

"A curious statement, isn't it?" He took off his hat and turned it about in his hands, looking at the brim of it and not at her. "First, I think it is important that you know that I respect you, Lady Ivy. I also find you quite intriguing. Every conversation I have had with you, I have come away feeling enlivened."

As each word fell from his lips, Ivy felt a growing sense of anticipation, though to what it built, she didn't dare imagine. She had heard enough tales of gentlemen speaking to ladies in this way, but she had not expected words like these ever coming from him. Or leading to the conclusion such words usually came to.

"I have been giving some thought to your situation," he continued. "I know it isn't truly my business, and what I say next will perhaps strike you as a bit forward. Please, hear what I have to say and consider it. What if I solved your problem?" He winced. "I mean, what if the two of us married. Each other." His cheeks darkened slightly. "It sounded better when I practiced this speech in front of my mirror."

Her mouth had turned dry, and her breathing stopped. She stared at him, unmoving and uncertain, for a long moment before four words slipped out. "I beg your pardon?"

This couldn't be real. Women didn't receive marriage proposals in gardens from men they barely knew. Men they wanted to know better. A man *she* wanted to know better yet hadn't dared hope for such a thing. He couldn't truly mean to ask for her hand.

He stopped twisting his hat and gave her a wry smile. "I know. I found the idea surprising when it first came to me, too. I have given it a lot of thought, though, and I am certain it's a good plan. Think of it. You know me; you have met my family. Do I strike you as the sort of man to demand my lady wife give up her interests or act a way contrary to her nature? Of course not. My sisters and mother would disown me and take up arms on my lady's behalf." His lilting words almost made his words sound teasing, yet the earnestness in his eyes kept Ivy from believing that possible. "You would have the freedom to be yourself, unbound by the constraints you have lived under as your brother's ward. I am proposing a partnership, too, where both of us will benefit."

He went silent, looking at her with obvious anticipation. She needed to say something, but her mind still wasn't quite latching on to what he was saying. "A marriage of convenience? Is that what you are suggesting?" A worse thought came to her. "In name only?"

It was not exactly what she had hoped for.

The sudden way his eyes narrowed and his lips turned up made it feel like her stomach had sprouted wings and swooped down, low, catching her expectations like an owl took hold of a mouse.

"Not at all, darling. It would be a marriage in truth, in every way. Every vow dutifully and most pleasantly kept. I want children. A family. A wife to come home to and solve the world's problems with over dinner as easily as resting on our pillows." He gave her a crooked smile. "I think we would get along well."

Her cheeks flamed and she had to look away, the playful glint in his eyes making her feel far too many things as his words conjured images of husbands and wives she had no business thinking of until she was wed herself.

"Lord Dunmore—"

"My name is Teague. I would like you to use it, especially given the intimacy of this particular conversation."

She frowned at him. "Lord. Dunmore. You barely know me. We've had a mere handful of conversations. I never expected this is what would come from confiding in you—which I realize now was a mistake. My sister-in-law has warned me that speaking my mind never leads to a good end." She turned away from him to massage her temples. "I am sorry if you thought this is what I was hoping for—"

"Not at all." He still grinned at her, though his gaze had softened somewhat. "I knew you told me a hard truth about your life. I'd no intention of making your problems my own until I couldn't stop thinking about them. There is much to consider, of course, in an arrangement such as the one I am proposing. I truly believe that together, we could not only appease your brother, but perhaps find something rewarding for ourselves in the process."

As Ivy's initial shock began to fade, her thoughts shifted from disbelief to something far more disturbing. Consideration.

Observing the Irishman carefully, she took a moment to reflect on the laughter she had witnessed within his family, a stark contrast to the cold pragmatism of her own situation. As Ivy looked at Teague, a realization softened the edges of her astonishment.

Here was an offer not merely of escape, but of belonging—to be part of a family with genuine affection, lively conversation, a chance at the kind of life she had only observed from the margins of their company.

It wasn't unthinkable. As it wove itself into the realm of possibility, tempting her with visions of a future filled with good humor, companionship, and the freedom to simply *be*, she found herself leaning toward him. Ready to hear more.

However, there was one important detail. "I cannot consider myself alone," she said with a firmness that made his head tilt to the side. "I have spoken with my brother about my sisters. I intend to keep them as part of my household when I wed. I want to provide them with a loving, comfortable home until they are ready to wed or set up households of their own. I want my husband to take over guardianship of them, leaving my brother to worry over his own children and nothing more. Juniper is nearing one-and-twenty, Betony is nineteen. They still need guidance."

His grin appeared again, with an ease that made her heart skip. She knew, before even he spoke, the gist of what he'd say. "That's fair enough, and presents no difficulty to my proposal, such as it is. I haven't done much planning, since I needed your answer before I dared build any imaginary castles." He put his hat down on the bench and leaned closer, taking one of her hands in his. "Marry me, Ivy dear. I think we shall both benefit. What's more, I think we can be happy together."

He did?

"You are in earnest about all of this?" She looked down where his bare hand held hers, admiring his strong grasp, secure in the knowledge she could withdraw with ease. "Lord—Teague." She met his gaze squarely, her heart tripping and flipping in fear and no small measure of excitement. "It could be a supremely bad idea. What if we do not get along?"

"What if we do? As we have so far, I'll remind you." He

gently pressed her fingers, his sincere smile making his handsome features all the more attractive to her. "I have every intention of giving you a happy home, Ivy. And your sisters. I feel you're not the sort who would do things by halves, either. Once you agree—if you agree— to marry me, we will both make a go of it with everything we have. I promise I will." His eyes shone with a determination that inspired her own.

"Then...yes. I agree."

It was the single most impulsive thing she had ever said. Fanny would certainly think so, anyway. But in that moment, Ivy searched her mind and her heart and found it the only answer she wanted to give.

Heaven help her. She had agreed to marry Teague Frost, Lord Dunmore. An Irish baron. All she felt in that moment was a sense of relief.

A burst of joy filled his expression, but he tempered it with a laugh, a light, somewhat giddy laugh. "Well, that's the best 'yes' I've ever heard. I promise, you won't regret it. We shall make a grand partnership, you and I."

He grinned and lifted her hand to his lips, where he brushed her knuckles with a soft kiss. No unrelated man had ever laid a kiss anywhere on her skin before. The sensation sent tingles up and down her arm, and they were most pleasant.

"Thank you, Ivy," he murmured softly. "We will make each other very happy. I'm certain of it."

That made one of them, at least. Ivy gently withdrew her hand. "You still need to speak to William. Though I am of age to choose whom I wed, William will need to be informed. There are still the contracts to arrange, and you will need to discuss the matter of my sisters with him."

Teague nodded along as she spoke, his grin never fading. "Of course. An easy enough matter. I will take my leave of His Grace and be on my way this afternoon."

That startled her into blurting, "So soon?"

"I don't intend to delay when I've set about a course of action, my dear." His smile, crooked and mischievous, charmed her. What would William make of her choice in husband?

What would Juniper and Betony think? "I need to tell my sisters."

Teague handed her the book she had forgotten and offered his arm. "Allow me to escort you inside, darling. Then we will part ways to spread the news of our betrothal."

Darling? Her stomach gave a happy little twist. She had never been anyone's darling before. She accepted his arm and his escort, though she said little else to him, trying to work out how best to share the news with her sisters.

THE DUKE OF MONTFORT SAT AT THE LARGE DESK IN WHAT was known as the Speak-a-Word room, off the pre-guard room, a long corridor most used to enter the castle from the portcullis. The room was a secondary office for him, set up for the sole purpose of allowing people from outside the castle to meet with him, for his tenants to "speak a word" with him regarding their farms, orchards, or families.

For a duke, the man was surprisingly available to the people who relied on him, a thing that made Teague respect the Englishman.

"Your Grace," he greeted the duke as he bowed on the other side of the desk. "Your steward said I might have a moment of your time."

Though in his early sixties, the duke had maintained a robust figure. His eldest son, Simon, looked much like him. Gray touched His Grace's temples, yet he remained an imposing man with his direct gaze and towering height. "Dunmore. You may have as much of my time as you like. You are family." He gestured to the chair opposite the desk from him. "Sit. Tell me how I can be of service to you."

Teague took the offered chair and found himself twisting his hat in his hands again. His father had died years before, and there hadn't been a man in his life whose approval he had sought since that time. Yet suddenly, before the duke, he became aware that had changed. The man before him had power, to be sure, but also possessed a degree of integrity and honor Teague aspired to attain himself.

"Your Grace, I have come to take my leave of you for a time, and to ask that my mother and sister remain until I return for them. I wish to leave them in your care, and to the enjoyment of your kind hospitality, while I see to an urgent personal matter."

The duke's expression darkened to one of concern. "I have only heard you speak that formally in Lords, son. Of course, your mother and Fiona are welcome here as long as they like. I must ask, though. Is something amiss? Do you need assistance?"

That he offered such a thing surprised Teague a moment, then he relaxed and smiled. He had come to expect Englishmen of power to peer down their noses at him, but he sometimes forgot the Duke was a man unlike most others. "Perhaps you could put in a good word for me with the fellow I plan to visit. Lord Haverford. Lady Ivy's half-brother. I intend to ask him for her hand."

At this, the duke sat back in his chair, his eyes widening slightly in the barest hint of surprise. "You want to marry Ivy? So soon after meeting her?"

It suddenly occurred to Teague that the duke's blessing might prove as important, and as necessary, as Lord Haverford's.

"Yes, Your Grace." Silence followed that simple answer, the duke only staring at him in his silent, questioning way. Teague cleared his throat, compelled to explain himself and choosing his words with care.

"In truth, Your Grace, my proposal to Lady Ivy is born not

from affection, though I hold her in the highest regard. It is a union conceived in mutual respect, in the recognition of shared ideals and aspirations. Lady Ivy possesses a strength of character and a clarity of vision I find most admirable. I believe, together, we can forge a partnership that will prove beneficial within the bounds of marriage."

He paused, his hands ceasing their restless movement as he placed his hat upon his knee, his posture embodying the sincerity of his intentions. "I have observed the manner in which she engages with the world around her—her compassion, her intelligence, and her unwavering integrity. These are qualities of the highest order. Qualities that promise not only a harmonious household, but a union capable of contributing positively to those around us."

The duke's expression softened, a reflective silence filling the room as he considered Teague's words. Finally, he leaned forward, resting his arms on the desk. "Teague, your approach to selecting a wife is not unusual, and I find no fault in your reasoning. Marriage, in its best form, is indeed a partnership—an alliance of strengths. If you perceive these qualities in Ivy, and she in you, who am I to question it?"

Teague swallowed some of his nervousness. "I hold you in the highest respect, Your Grace. If there is more you would say on the matter, I would hear it."

A smile, warm and encouraging, broke through the duke's reserved demeanor. "She is a cousin to my wife, yet my observations of Lady Ivy are quite limited. Her Grace speaks highly of her, though. She is spirited, intelligent, and kind. If she has agreed to this proposal, it speaks volumes of her regard for you. Your willingness to speak so candidly with me today reinforces my belief that you are a man of honor and intelligence. You two will likely do quite well together. Though I hope...I hope for more than a pleasant partnership for you, son."

Teague felt a weight lift from his shoulders, the duke's

words granting a sense of validation to his scheme he hadn't realized he sought. "Thank you, Your Grace. Your approval means a great deal to me. I assure you, my intentions toward Lady Ivy are honorable, and I am committed to ensuring our marriage is one of mutual respect, support, and affection." He relaxed a little. "I think I am, at least, already on the path to more than affection. She's enchanting. And lovely. I want her to be happy."

The duke steepled his fingers together and gave one deep nod. "Then you have my good wishes, Dunmore." He paused a moment before adding with a wry smile, "And my support, should you need it in your dealings with Lord Haverford."

"I am grateful, Your Grace. I do not take your support lightly. Truly, I may need it. Haverford hasn't been overly fond of me, at least politically."

"I am aware." The duke's smile inched upward. "You have made a name for yourself, and the more conservative members of the opposition tend to squirm in their seats every time you stand to speak. I enjoy the spectacle." The duke chuckled, then tapped the desk thoughtfully. "Now that I understand the situation, you ought to know that there is no need for you to leave Clairvoir. Lord Haverford is on his way here. He arrives in two days' time."

The shock of that went through Teague like a cold deluge. "He is coming here?"

"With his wife and children, yes. We could hardly host his half-sisters without extending the invitation for at least a brief stay for him as well." A gleam of amusement appeared in the duke's eyes. "In my study upstairs, I have a letter from him requesting the addition of another guest, a friend he wanted to introduce. We have rooms enough in the castle, and it matters little to me, so I agreed to extend the invitation to one Lord Martin Southersby. Have you met him?"

The name seemed vaguely familiar, but Teague shook his head.

The duke's amusement grew enough for him to chuckle. "Lord Martin is the second son of the Earl of Crighton. Their seat is in the west." He gestured vaguely in that direction. "Lord Martin has political ambitions but lacks an important connection to more influential members of Parliament. My suspicion is that Haverford wishes to introduce Lord Martin to my family for our support and connection, but I also wondered if he had another motive. Especially given that Lord Martin is a bachelor."

Teague leaned back in his chair, his posture dropping from stiff to casual as he took in His Grace's implication. "You think Haverford wants to try his hand at matchmaking his sisters?"

"Sister. Haverford is conservative to an extreme. He will want to marry off the eldest before giving attention to the other two." The duke chuckled. "I've no doubt Haverford will see an advantage to your proposal, but he may use his own candidate for Lady Ivy's hand as a way to bargain in the marriage contract."

"Lady Ivy already agreed to my proposal," Teague said, then winced at his own tone. He'd sounded somewhat possessive. Where had that come from? He pushed his hand through his hair. "This is a fascinating turn of events. Has Lady Ivy been informed of her brother's visit?"

"I believe Her Grace intended to tell the sisters this afternoon. We only received the letter settling the matter this morning." The duke's amusement hadn't faded, though Teague struggled to find the humor in the situation at the moment. "Never fear, Dunmore. As I said, you have my support. I am certain things will work out as they should. They nearly always do."

"To be sure, Your Grace." Teague's mind turned over the possibilities and possible difficulties ahead. "To be sure they do."

CHAPTER 13

The portrait gallery within the castle, situated directly above the long gallery where the family spent most of their time during the day, wasn't precisely where Ivy expected to find her sisters. Of course, once she realized they weren't looking at the artwork but rather creating their own, it made a great deal more sense.

The object of their watercolor paintings managed to surprise her. The sight that greeted her was one of serene domesticity contrasted with a hint of the comical.

Sterling, the footman and bodyguard, stood in the center of the gallery wearing his customary livery, sans the formal wig, but held a shield in one hand and a saber in the other, pointed downward. Both props seemed more suited to a stage than the portrait gallery of a duke's castle. Of course, he also wore a scowl that amused her. Poor man. How had her sisters managed to persuade him to model for them?

They had watercolor paper on easels before them. A white, thick canvas covered the floor beneath them like a carpet, protecting the room from stray water or paint.

"Ivy," Betony called when she saw Ivy standing in the doorway. "Come join us. We're turning Sterling into a knight."

The footman winced and sighed, adjusting his stance slightly.

Ivy came fully into the room, meeting Sterling's put-upon gaze and giving him an apologetic smile. "How kind of you to allow such a transformation, Sterling."

His eyes narrowed. "It is a pleasure, my lady."

She bit her lip to keep from saying she doubted that. Poor man. The combination of his good looks and serious nature had made him a target for her sisters' amusement and admiration both. From what she understood of his duties, Ivy knew he had to be a trusted servant to the duke. Most of the footmen were former soldiers, many of them tasked with acting as guards to the family and castle itself, like a small army.

"I suppose if we cannot fend off invaders, we can dazzle them with your art," she said, coming to inspect their work. Both had practiced enough that their work showed talent, though it was unlikely to ever grace more than a friend's wall.

Betony laughed softly. "Indeed. One look at the fierceness of Sterling's gaze and the enemy will run the opposite direction."

"Though I fear, in frightening off the invaders, our knight may not soon forgive us for putting him through this particular exercise," Juniper added, smiling innocently at the guard.

Sterling limited his response to a slight tightening of his lips, a testament to either his patience or his dedication to his position as a servant in the duke's household.

Poor man.

"Perhaps he would like a moment to rest while I share some important news with you both." Ivy gave him a nod, granting him permission to relax his stance. He bowed, placed his weapon and shield on a nearby table, and went to stand in the doorway, a silent protector and witness to anything that went on in the room.

"Oh, *that*," Betony muttered with a scowl, putting her paintbrush down. "Her Grace already informed us. Miserable, isn't it?"

Ivy blinked in surprise. The duchess couldn't know of her engagement. She doubted Betony would speak harshly, even if she disapproved, of anything that hinted at romance. "Oh dear. I think you have a piece of news I haven't yet heard."

Betony and Juniper exchanged a glance.

"You mean you haven't come to speak about William and Fanny coming to Clairvoir?"

"No." Her insides felt suddenly pinched and an unpleasant shudder went through her. Perhaps her half-brother and his wife didn't deserve that sort of reaction, as they weren't truly all that horrid. Yet she wanted nothing more than to recoil at the mention of them appearing just as she had grown comfortable in her situation. "When did you find out? When will they be here?"

"Day after tomorrow," Juniper said, adjusting her brushes and paints unnecessarily. "Her Grace told us before we started painting."

"Which completely destroyed all my former inspiration," Betony added with a huff.

"That is why we compelled Sterling to pose for us." Juniper glanced at the footman from the corner of her eye. "I think he pitied us enough in the moment to agree. I doubt he will make that mistake again."

This complicated things. Being beneath Fanny's critical eye meant tightening up her behavior and learning William's opinion on her decision to accept Teague Frost's proposal sooner than she had expected. She pressed her fingers to her eyes, already feeling tension building behind them.

"Ivy?" Betony placed her hand on her eldest sister's shoulder. "Ivy, dear, it won't be so terrible. They are only staying a short time. When they leave, we can return to enjoying Clairvoir as we had planned."

"I know." Ivy dropped her hand to her side and gave her sisters a wan smile. "You still haven't heard my news, though. William and Fanny coming complicates things, or at least gives me reason for anxiety."

Her sisters exchanged a glance, then Juniper asked, "What news, Ivy?"

Betony and Juniper both looked at her expectantly, trusting and interested, the best of sisters. She couldn't anticipate their reactions, try as she might. Best to get on with it, she supposed.

"Lord Dunmore has asked me to marry him, and I said yes."

A stunned silence greeted her announcement, finally broken by Betony's soft gasp. "Marry? You've known him less than a handful of weeks."

Juniper's reaction was softer, a smile blooming amidst the surprise. "If you have decided this, Ivy, then there is likely a good reason. Tell us, what made you say yes?"

Ivy took a deep breath, trying to organize her thoughts into something coherent, something that would make sense to her sisters who looked at her with curiosity.

"It's not what you might be thinking," she started, her voice steady despite the fluttering in her stomach. "This is not a love match in the way stories and poems describe it. Teague—Lord Dunmore—and I have agreed on a partnership, a marriage of convenience, if you will."

Juniper frowned, tilting her head slightly, running her fingers over the paintbrushes. "A partnership? So, this is about practicality?"

"Yes, exactly." Ivy smiled at her sister, grateful for Juniper's quick grasp of the situation. "He's offering me a chance for a life beyond the confines of William's guardianship. A life where I can be myself, and in return, I... We can offer each other companionship, stability. Of course, he agrees that you may both live with us until you decide otherwise."

Betony's eyes widened, her earlier dismay shifting to something more contemplative. "That's rather broad-minded of him, isn't it? And generous. Will you find happiness in such an arrangement?"

"I believe I will," Ivy replied, warming to the subject now that the initial shock had waned from her sisters' faces. "I believe we can find contentment, perhaps even happiness. He is kind and respectful, and we share many views on life and what we wish from it. And he has a lovely sense of humor. Our interactions have never been dull."

Sterling shifted slightly in the doorway, an unobtrusive witness to their discussion. His presence was oddly reassuring.

"Now, with William and Fanny coming," Juniper mused, setting her brush aside and giving Ivy her full attention, "it seems your decision is all the timelier."

Ivy nodded, a sense of resolve firming within her. "Exactly. Their arrival might complicate matters, but it also reinforces my decision. I won't be swayed by whatever opinions or objections they might have. This is about my future, our future," she said, gesturing to include her sisters in the declaration.

Betony, ever the most demonstrative of the three, wrapped Ivy in a tight embrace. "Then we are sincerely happy for you. Who knows? Lord Dunmore may be the sort of husband you have always wanted."

Juniper joined the embrace, adding, "If not, he'll have us to contend with."

"He is incredibly handsome," Betony said with a sly raise of her eyebrows. "Having a handsome husband won't be so bad, will it?"

This commentary made Ivy blush. "There is more to life than being attractive, Betony."

"Mm, but it does make life so much easier when one has a pretty husband to look at," Juniper said in a low voice. "I imagine it makes a great many things easier."

"Juniper!" Ivy gasped at her sister.

"And Ivy is beautiful." Betony tapped her lips thoughtfully. "They will make a lovely couple. Perhaps we ought to paint their portraits next."

Though usually the quieter one, it seemed Ivy's situation had brought out some mischief in Juniper more in keeping with someone of twelve than a lady of almost one and twenty. "Has he kissed you yet?"

"What?" Ivy felt a flush spread through her at the very idea. "Of course not!"

"That is terribly disappointing," Betony said with a deep, almost comical, frown. "One should always kiss after a proposal, at the very least. When it's accepted, of course. He rather looks as though he knows how to kiss."

Juniper nodded sagely. "Something about the way he smiles makes me believe that to be true."

"You are both rather horrid." Ivy laughed, despite her growing blush, and the other two joined her.

Their laughter filled the gallery, easing some of the tension that had coiled within Ivy at the thought of her impending confrontation with William and Fanny. Yes, their visit would be a trial, but she would see it through with her sisters.

As they broke apart, Sterling cleared his throat, a subtle reminder of his presence.

"Will you two release that poor man?" Ivy asked, her gaze briefly meeting the servant's. "He must have other duties to see to."

Betony pouted, but Juniper nodded. "Thank you, Sterling. We will continue another time, perhaps."

As Sterling bowed and departed, Ivy turned back to her sisters, their painting forgotten for the moment. The challenges ahead loomed large, but so did her gratitude for the two of them. Together, they would navigate the unexpectedness of Ivy's engagement and the arrival of their brother and his wife. Whatever the outcome, Ivy would manage so long as her sisters supported her.

CHAPTER 14

As the guests of Clairvoir gathered in the room adjacent the dining room, Teague kept his eye on the doorway, waiting for Lady Ivy. They had been engaged for a matter of hours, and he hadn't seen her since she agreed to marry him. Though he knew he hadn't imagined asking, and that she had really said yes, it still felt somewhat unreal.

"You look as jumpy as a fieldmouse," Simon said, appearing at Teague's elbow. "I thought you would have gone through with your scheme by now, but it seems you are still anticipating a conversation with Ivy."

Teague cast his friend an amused glance. "As a matter of fact, I *have* had that conversation. It went well, too."

Simon's eyes widened. "She accepted?"

Teague gave a succinct nod. "She did indeed."

"Congratulations are in order, then." Simon's warm grin appeared briefly, then vanished as he said, "Her brother is coming in day after tomorrow. I found out only hours ago. Will you speak to him then?"

"I will. It's a sight more convenient than having to go back to London for an audience with him."

"I suppose that is one way to look at it." Simon adjusted his waistcoat, then looked at the clock again. "Why do you appear nervous? It seems like the difficult part is over."

Teague raised his eyebrows and turned his full attention to his brother-in-law. "Was the most difficult part of your courtship with my sister asking her to wed you? Or was it perhaps the before and after that made things more complicated?"

The other man grimaced. "I see your point."

Isleen appeared on Simon's other side. "What point would that be, husband? Best not encourage my brother too much by agreeing with his side of anything. It's bound to set a dangerous precedent."

Simon immediately took his wife's hand and threaded it through his arm, as though the only acceptable way to stand beside her was to hold her as near as politely possible. "He does make the occasional good argument though, Isleen."

"Does he?" Isleen grinned up at her brother. "What are we arguing about this evening?"

"Which point is the most difficult in a courtship," Simon answered.

Teague shot him a warning look. "That was not precisely it."

"Oh, but I have the answer to that very question." Isleen affected a superior look. "Teague won't like it, though he'll have to concede it is true. The most difficult point is that right before marriage, when both parties are quite tired of all the well-wishes and parties, but especially all the nights of having to bid one another farewell until the next day. Nothing is so sweet as the moment you realize you need never part of a night again."

Indeed, Teague didn't fancy that explanation, as it came from his own sister. "I truly did not need to know that particular thought on the matter."

She grinned cheekily at him. "I am allowed to say things like that, now I'm a married woman."

"Not to your brother, you're not."

Simon chuckled at the both of them. "You will know the truth of things soon enough, brother-in-law."

Isleen's smile disappeared at that. "He will?" She looked from her husband to her brother, a look of shrewdness making her eyes gleam. "Teague. What does my husband mean? The implication sounds as though you will be entering a courtship."

He gave Simon a sharp glare. "It does sound like that, doesn't it."

"You may as well tell her," Simon said, completely at ease with revealing what Teague had intended to keep to himself until he spoke to Lord Haverford. "It is impossible to keep a secret in this castle."

Isleen leaned forward and raised herself up on her toes to better meet Teague's gaze. "What is he talking about, Teague? I'm nigh on bubbling over with the curiosity."

He rubbed at his eyes. Best to get on with it. "I asked Lady Ivy to marry me. She said yes."

She gasped so loud that others in the room quieted and looked in their direction. Teague winced. At least she kept her voice to a whisper for her next outpouring of sisterly questions.

"You're marrying her? Oh, Teague. That's wonderful! I knew there was something about the way she watched you during the cricket match. Did you fall in love so quickly?"

Slowly, he shook his head, keeping his gaze on his sister. "We're not in love, Issie. It's a practical match. Good for both of us. That is all." He had to smirk a little though as he said, "What's this about the cricket match?"

Her reaction surprised him as he watched her expression change from excitement to shock, the color draining from her face. "Oh. Teague, no. You cannot do that to yourself."

"Isleen, it is not as dire as you imagine," Teague attempted to reassure her, his voice holding a blend of humor and patience. "There are many forms of companionship, and respect and understanding can serve as a solid foundation for a marriage."

Isleen's features softened, but her concern remained evident. "Marriage is more than a partnership, Teague. It is sharing your life with someone, in every sense. Can you really be content knowing there is no love between you?"

Simon, observing the exchange, interjected as though seeking to mediate. "Affection can grow in many ways. It doesn't always start with romance. Your brother and Ivy are both sensible people. They are likely to find happiness in their arrangement."

"Indeed," Teague added, eager to shift the focus from his personal feelings—or lack thereof. "There's much to be said for a marriage that begins without the complications of a tumultuous courtship. We respect each other, and that counts for something."

Isleen looked from Teague to Simon and back again, the wheels of thought turning behind her eyes. Finally, she sighed, a gesture of reluctant acceptance. "I suppose you are both right. Who am I to judge the path you've chosen? If Ivy makes you happy, in whatever form that happiness takes, I'll support you and welcome her to the family."

The warmth in her voice was reassuring, and Teague felt a wave of gratitude for his sister's understanding. "Thank you, Issie. That means the world to me." He paused a moment, then said, "What was that about the cricket match?"

His sister raised her eyebrows at him. "Stuck on that, are you?"

"You said there was something about the way she watched me." He really wanted to know what his sister meant.

"Something about the way you watched her, too," Simon muttered, shaking his head. "The two of you will make an interesting pair."

Ignoring Teague, quite purposefully, Isleen nodded thoughtfully and addressed her husband. "He missed that catch because of her, did he not? You should have seen the look on her face. I thought she would run out on the field to ask after his wellbeing."

"That would have been amusing." Simon grinned and Teague folded his arms.

"The pair of you think you are quite amusing, don't you?"

"Ah, here comes your future bride and sisters-in-law now," Simon interjected, cutting through the remaining tension the conversation had stirred up.

Teague turned to face the doorway and found Ivy entering the room, her younger sisters on either side of her, all three of them looking directly at him.

"It seems Ivy told *her* sisters, given how they are studying you," Isleen whispered, her smile teasing.

Indeed. Lady Juniper and Lady Betony both had a knowing look about them, and they exchanged a glance behind their elder sister's back he thought communicated trouble of some kind. He swallowed.

With two younger sisters himself, he knew what sort of mischief they could make if they didn't like the idea of him courting and wedding their sister. Ivy seemed unaware of what was passing behind her as she focused on Teague, approaching him with a hesitant smile as though she was uncertain of her welcome.

He certainly could not have that.

"My lady," he greeted her, bowing with a flourish. "Good evening. I hope you find yourself as eager for the night's festivities as I am. Perhaps, after dinner, you may even grant my wish to partner me in whist?"

Ivy's tentative smile blossomed into something brighter, more assured, at Teague's greeting. The undercurrent of formality in his words did little to mask the genuine warmth in his voice, and her response carried a light, teasing tone. "Lord Dunmore, I would be honored to partner you in cards."

The tension momentarily clouding the air lifted as Ivy took

a step closer. Isleen watched the exchange with narrowed eyes, and Teague gave her a warning glance.

Lady Juniper and Lady Betony took on expressions which displayed more decorum, yet the spark of sisterly conspiracy lingered in their eyes. Teague recognized their shared glance for what it was—a protective scrutiny reserved for any challenge to their eldest sister's happiness.

Isleen immediately engaged Ivy in conversation about the gown she wore.

Simon, ever the observer, leaned in towards Teague, his voice low enough for only him to hear. "Remember, the approval of sisters is a prize worth winning. They can be your staunchest allies or your most creative challengers."

Teague nodded, well recognizing the truth in Simon's words. He had an opportunity to lay the foundation for familial bonds that would support or challenge their union. To make his home life, if the sisters came with Ivy to join his household, a misery or a joy.

THE DUCHESS TOOK CARE TO CHANGE THE SEATING arrangement each night at dinner, the better to entertain her long-term guests. Ivy straightaway had reason to suspect her dinner partner was chosen deliberately that evening, given that Teague sat immediately to her right. She had only to glance up the table at the duchess to see Her Grace offer a knowing smile.

"Seems news of our engagement is spreading," Teague murmured as he filled her cup of wine.

Ivy gave a nod of understanding. "Whom have you told? I have only spoken to my sisters."

"The duke. Simon. Isleen." He gave her a crooked smile, and

she couldn't help returning it. "Everyone will know by the end of the evening, I fear. My dearest hope at the moment is that I am able to tell my mother before another reveals it to her. She would never forgive learning of it from any source but my own two lips."

Her gaze dropped briefly to those very lips, then she blushed and picked up her cup, a response likely due to her sisters' teasing. "Do you think she will be happy with the news?" Ivy hadn't stopped to consider reactions beyond her own family. Juniper and Betony were her primary concern, of course, but what if William didn't approve?

"That's a thinking frown," Teague murmured at her side, bringing her attention back to him. "You get a little line between your eyebrows, just above the bridge of your nose." He tapped the matching location on his own face. "I've never seen someone think quite that hard before."

Ivy raised her eyebrows at him. "That's worrying, given that you spend so much time in Parliament. One would hope there is a lot of thinking going on in those chambers."

Apparently, he hadn't expected that response. His eyes widened slightly and he laughed, though he quickly covered the sound with a fist to his mouth and a light cough. "One would hope, but one would often be disappointed."

The amusement dancing in his dark eyes brought a smile to her face, too. She didn't often make people laugh, yet Teague seemed delighted by her every time they spoke. He had already secured her hand in their engagement, so he needn't try overmuch to woo her. His genuine reaction to her gave her the smallest, fleeting feeling of pleasure.

His next comment returned her thoughts to her concerns, however. "I have heard your brother and family are arriving overmorrow."

"Overmorrow?" she repeated.

"An odd word, isn't it? Means 'the day after tomorrow' but is much more efficient. So long as you don't have to explain it every time."

"It is efficient. And rather unique." She smiled despite the change in subject. "Yes. William and Fanny, their four children, and apparently a guest. I suppose I should be grateful, as having William here will make things easier to work out when it comes to legal matters."

"The true romance of a marriage," he said, tipping his head to the side. "Contracts. Legal terms. Negotiations. I wonder why those are never discussed in novels?"

She bit her lip to keep in her laugh. "Can you imagine? A beautiful proposal scene followed immediately by men in an office somewhere, writing out terms?"

"I suppose the point of novels is not always to relate the world as it is, but rather as we would have it be." He considered his own words a moment, then nodded. "That sounds particularly wise. Perhaps I should write it down."

"Why? To remind yourself of your own cleverness?" she asked, then immediately pressed her lips together. The comment wasn't one her brother would ever appreciate.

Teague seemed utterly pleased, though. "Indeed, and to quote myself, liberally, at every opportunity."

She ducked her head and pressed a napkin to her lips, trying to stifle the urge to giggle. Giggles were not appropriate at a dinner table, especially a duke's dinner table.

He lowered his voice and leaned a bit toward her, so no one else would hear as he said, "You've a lovely look when you're trying to strangle a laugh, my darling."

His teasing bordered on flirtation, and she found she didn't mind it much, even if she felt the tell-tale heat of a blush in her cheeks. Being called "darling" added to the charm, the unexpected enjoyment, of their conversation.

"You are going to cause me to be impolite if you keep trying to make me laugh," she countered. "Where are your manners, Lord Dunmore?"

"Oh, they are about somewhere, I would think." He gave attention to his plate for a short time, letting Ivy compose herself.

"I have wondered something," she ventured after several bites of the meal. "Your accent. I was given to believe that Irish nobility tended to be without such a strong indication of their origins, at least in speech. You could never be mistaken for an Englishman."

"Does it bother you?" he asked, eyebrows raised as his eyes flashed to hers, reacting in sharp surprise as though she'd pricked him with a needle.

She shook her head, startled by his reaction. It was easy enough to tell the truth. "Not in the least."

His crooked grin reappeared, and she detected the slightest touch of relief in his eyes. "Good. I don't try to hide it, the way some of my Irish peers do. I want people to know who I am, where I'm from. I'm not ashamed of it. When I open my mouth in Lords, they know at once where I stand from the sound of my words, if not the words themselves."

The confidence with which he spoke gave her more reason to admire him. How often had she been told the secret to success in society was to blend in? Fanny and William had driven that point into her again and again. Yet Teague made a conscious decision to stand apart.

"Could you speak like an Englishman?" she asked, still somewhat curious. "If you wanted?"

He smiled down at his plate. "I could if I'd a mind to. I finished my education at Cambridge, and mimicry became a talent of mine. Would you like to hear it?"

After a moment of consideration, Ivy shook her head. "I think it would shock me if you sounded like anything other than yourself."

That answer seemed to please him, given the way his eyes widened. "You like the Irish brogue, do you?"

Her cheeks warmed and she reached for her glass of wine again, sipping at it delicately. His fixed stare meant he wouldn't let the question drop, however.

"Perhaps," she said at last, lowering her glass to the table. Then she cleared her throat and gave her attention to the person on her other side, the local vicar invited for dinner, determined not to say another flirtatious word to her betrothed.

Not at the table, anyway.

TEAGUE HAD ASKED TO SPEAK HIS MOTHER BEFORE SHE turned in, but her response to his news of betrothal made him almost wish he had waited for morning.

"What do you mean, you are engaged? And to an English girl! Teague, when did this happen?" Lady Dunmore had her shawl wrapped tightly around her shoulders, sitting before the fire in the room adjacent to her bedchamber.

He hadn't expected his mother to look as shocked as she did. "I thought you would be pleasantly surprised."

"Surprised, to be sure, but 'pleasant' remains to be seen." She frowned at him and he had to resist the urge to pace while she stared. "Lady Ivy Amberton. She's a stranger, Teague. You don't even know her."

"People wed strangers all the time," he said, somewhat flippantly.

"Do not give me that, Teague Frost. You are not 'people.' This is a monumental decision. A life-altering choice. Are you sure you are not rushing into things?"

He tapped his fingers along his thigh, then went to kneel in front of his mother's chair to bring them to the same eye level.

"Máthair." He switched to the Irish tongue as he explained. "She is not a stranger. Every time we speak, I am delighted. Every time I see her, I am intrigued. We haven't known one another long, but I know enough to predict we will be content. It is a good match."

Looking into her eyes, he saw the woman who had loved him and raised him. Her gentleness, her understanding, were what he needed right then.

Lady Dunmore's expression softened, the initial shock giving way to a more contemplative look as she listened to her son. She placed a hand over Teague's where it rested on the arm of her chair, her touch warm and comforting as ever.

"I see," she said slowly, her tone more resigned than understanding. "Contentment, you say. Perhaps, in time, more than that?"

Teague could hear the unspoken hope in her voice, the maternal desire for her son's happiness not merely in practical terms, but in the depth of companionship and love.

"Perhaps," he conceded, a small smile tugging at the corners of his mouth. "Ivy is...different. In a world of pretense, she is refreshingly genuine. She values family, Máthair, much like we do."

Lady Dunmore's eyes glistened with a mixture of emotions as she absorbed his words. "If she has caught your eye and your interest in such a manner, then she must be quite special." She paused, then added with a playful huff, "Here I was, thinking you'd never settle down. An English girl, no less. You are full of surprises, Teague Frost."

He laughed softly, the tension easing between them. "Life is full of surprises, isn't it? And Ivy—Lady Ivy—she's one I had not anticipated, but am quite grateful for."

"If she has agreed to be your bride, I can at least appreciate her good taste," Lady Dunmore declared, the words somewhat teasing. "Teague, promise me this: do not let contentment be the ceiling of your aspirations for this marriage. Aim for happiness, for joy, for love. You deserve no less." She gave a firm nod. "Lady Ivy does, too."

Teague felt a lump form in his throat at her words. Rising to his feet, he leaned down and kissed his mother on the forehead. "I promise, Máthair. I will aim for the very heavens."

As he straightened, Lady Dunmore gave him a nod, her face alight with a mixture of pride and cautious optimism. "Now, go on. I need to rest, and you do too. You've a future baroness to woo. Remember, she is not only becoming a part of your life, but our family's life as well. Treat her with kindness, respect, and perhaps a touch of the Frost charm."

Teague chuckled and grinned at his mother with affection. He had no doubt she would do all she could to welcome Ivy— and her sisters—into the family. "I will. Thank you, Máthair. Good night."

"Good night, my son. Congratulations," she called softly after him as he exited the room, her words carrying the weight of her blessings and the hopes of a mother for her child's happiness.

Stepping into the corridor, Teague heaved a sigh of relief. His mother's concerns were valid, but her willingness to trust his judgment reinforced his confidence in his decision. As he made his way to his own quarters, his thoughts were filled with Ivy. Not for the first time, he allowed himself to consider that their marriage of convenience could blossom into something far richer and more fulfilling than he dared to hope.

CHAPTER 15

I vy had spent the better part of the night and the early morning in a restless state, her thoughts wandering to Teague with a frequency that surprised her. With her family's arrival looming over the horizon, she wished for a moment of levity, a brief escape from the anticipation and anxiety.

Still, she had a feeling of dread creeping up her spine too. How well did Teague know William? Chances were excellent that her half-brother would not show enthusiasm for their match, initially, though she doubted he would forbid it or outright condemn a union. Still. He would likely make things uncomfortable. She needed to speak to Teague.

If she were honest with herself, she wanted Teague's company as well, eager for the unexpected comfort his presence had come to represent.

Deciding to take matters into her own hands, Ivy ventured out of her room after a quick *toilette*, her steps taking her through Clairvoir's vast corridors. The castle, with its suits of armor, tapestries, and elegant artwork, was a pretty maze, but a maze nonetheless.

The carpets muffled most sounds, too, which made the

moment she turned the same corner as her quarry from opposite ends a true surprise.

The suddenness of the encounter sent Ivy stumbling, and Teague's quick hands steadied her as his shoulder hit the wall. He released an "oomph" as she crashed into him, forcing the air from his lungs. Ivy's hands pressed against Teague's chest and his arms went around her waist to steady them both.

Ivy looked up at him in shock, jaw dropped open, and he looked down at her with raised eyebrows, trying to draw in a breath.

Laughter bubbled up between them, the absurdity of their collision dispelling her initial desire to stammer out an apology.

"I seem to have found what I was looking for," Teague quipped, his eyes twinkling as he gazed down at her.

"You were looking for me?" Ivy replied, her laughter softening into a smile. "I doubt you expected finding me would prove hazardous to your wellbeing."

He grinned and carefully, gently, set her fully on her own two feet. His hands slipped slowly from her waist. "I find I don't mind the constant threat of danger if it means ending up with a lovely lady in my arms."

Goodness. Nothing about that could have been polite to say. Or...well. Ivy supposed things were different now. An engaged woman was practically a married woman. New rules applied.

Somewhat reluctantly, she stepped back, though the space between them thrummed with a tension she found oddly pleasant.

"I was looking for you, too," Ivy confessed, her cheeks warm with what she hoped was a pretty blush. "I thought we could use a moment together before the castle fills with my family and all the formality that will bring. We should probably talk about all of that. What to expect in terms of their reactions to our engagement. How best to respond. Not to give offense. Things of that nature." She winced as her thoughts clattered together and bit her tongue rather than babble.

Fanny did so dislike babbling.

Teague's expression softened, his initial amusement giving way to a gentle understanding. "I think that is an excellent idea. In fact, I know a place where we can escape for a bit, a walled section of the gardens. It's quiet, secluded, and perfect for a private conversation."

The invitation hung between them, an offer and a promise of a moment together. Ivy's heart skipped a beat at the thought, both at the prospect of discovering a new part of Clairvoir and of spending more time with Teague. Alone.

Something that would have been a scandal days ago was suddenly perfectly acceptable. Society was quite strange with some of its rules.

"Lead the way, Lord Dunmore," she said, her voice steady despite the fluttering in her chest.

As they walked side by side, their steps synchronized, they talked of mundane things. He asked after her health, she asked after his mother. They were strictly polite, cordial, as though needing to make up for their less than mannerly encounter in the corridor.

When they arrived at an ivy-covered wall, Teague took her hand as though it was the most natural thing in the world. "There's a grotto entrance. Here." He gently led her along, unaware that she stared at their joined hands.

She had never had a man treat her so gently, not since the death of her father. When her father had taken her hand to show her some new trinket or discovery of his, it hadn't at all stirred the rather interesting sensations in her stomach that Teague's touch inspired.

How fortunate for her that she found her future husband attractive. She couldn't help smiling to herself until they stopped in the midst of the garden.

"Her Grace calls this her Japanese garden," Teague informed her, looking about them with undisguised admiration. "The trees, the flowers, and most of it has been imported from the East. Even the little statues." He pointed out a stone shaped like a bird. "No one can see inside, even from the castle towers."

"Oh? Have you tested that theory?" she asked, taking in the garden around them.

"Lady Josephine informed me, and I doubt she would have reason to mislead anyone." He gave her a wide smile. "What do you think? I admit, I am enchanted by the place."

The walled garden, with its blooming flowers and the soft murmur of a fountain, offered a pocket of privacy in the vastness of the estate. There, amidst the beauty and tranquility, Ivy found herself relaxing.

"It is beautiful," she agreed, looking about with true appreciation. "I understand the Dowager Duchess is responsible for most of the gardens. Everything here is perfect, though. Clairvoir is a marvel."

"It's obvious why the family rarely spends time at any of their other houses." He hadn't released her hand yet, and now he walked her to a bench beneath one of the trees, a tree with red leaves, despite the time of year. "Though I met Simon first while he was visiting their Irish estate."

"I didn't know they had any land in Ireland." She sat down next to him, and only then did he release her hand. Not as though he wished to, though, but merely to put his arm along the back of the bench, his hand behind her shoulder. She felt it there, though he didn't touch her. An odd sensation.

"That's the 'Farleigh' part of the title." He gave her a wide grin. "Isleen has convinced him to spend part of the year there, to be nearer us when we are at home."

The need to discuss her own family's arrival became less urgent as Ivy found herself asking, "What is your home like?"

"Ah, Dunmore's barony. I suppose you would have reason to

wonder about it now, wouldn't you?" The lilt to his words became teasing, and she felt herself blush. "I hope you will like it there, Ivy darling. It's not a castle like this. More a house, built two hundred years ago by a Catholic family who ran afoul of the English during King James's reign. The English crown took possession and eventually gave it to one of my ancestors. Created a barony on the condition that no one in the family could be Catholic." He heaved a sigh, his dramatics discouraging her from saying anything pitying about that situation. "It is very English. My ancestors did their best to please their kingly benefactors."

"Goodness." She gave him her full attention, watching him as he spoke. She rather liked his mannerisms. His eyes were quite expressive, his lips quirked upward on nearly every word. "That is a bit disappointing. I have been in English homes all my life. I'd wondered how an Irish baron's home would be different."

He chuckled at that, and she felt his thumb brush lightly against her shoulder. It nearly made her shiver, but she kept her response in check. "We have put our little touches here and there, mostly in the art. Irish art is a wild thing to behold."

"I imagine so." She angled her shoulders toward him, putting the one he had touched in closer proximity to the hand on the back of the bench. "Do you have any flower gardens?"

"Half a dozen of them, at last count." He grinned at her, then nodded to the display around them. "None so grand or expensive as this. Though my mother takes special pride in the roses."

"I will be certain to praise them liberally when I see them," she promised with a grin. "What is your favorite part of your home?"

"I have two. Within the house, it is the library. That should not surprise you, given our conversation about books. But I think, along with all the books, it is the landscape painting hanging above the fireplace that makes that place feel the most comfortable. It's a piece by Thomas Roberts, a true Irishman."

Sensing his warmth for his home, Ivy could not help but feel her own excitement build. "And the other place you favor?"

"A hill about a mile from the house. On a clear day, I can see the land for miles, and even on a foggy one, I can stand on that hill and breathe in the free air in a way I have never been able to anywhere else."

As he went on to describe his home, not just in terms of its architecture but through the art that adorned its walls and the landscapes that surrounded it, Ivy found herself imagining a life there beside him. It was a life painted in the broad, bold strokes of his affection and excitement to share it, so different from the careful, constrained existence she had always known.

The realization came to her, when his thumb began to draw a circle on her shoulder, that she wasn't merely learning about a place; she was discovering the man who called it home. She found herself anticipating exploring both—the place and the man beside her.

She blushed. Did people explore each other? An odd thought, but it immediately sank into her mind.

The thought of visiting Dunmore's Barony, of walking through its gardens and standing beside Teague on that hill, filled her with a sense of adventure she hadn't known she was seeking, as well as the hope that she would belong there, somehow.

He fell silent after a time, his gaze unfocused, his dark eyes thoughtful. Then he blinked and the moment shifted. His easy, teasing smile returned. "Listen to me, blathering on about a place you will see for yourself soon enough. Assuming your brother doesn't run me out of England for daring to ask for your hand."

The peace that had settled in her heart abruptly vanished, though she managed a smile for Teague. "I liked hearing about it. That topic of conversation is far more pleasant than thinking about William and Fanny." She winced. "That isn't fair of me to say. They have done their duty by me and my sisters. They have kept us safe, housed, fed, and seen to our education."

For a moment, Teague appeared troubled. The teasing light in his eyes dimmed. "A thing one would expect from a brother. Or any decent folk."

Something about the way he said it bothered her, like feeling a draft without knowing from whence it came. She ignored the feeling and continued. "Regardless, I think it's important we talk about their coming."

He hesitated, then nodded his agreement. "We should. I don't plan to wait long between their arrival and asking for an audience with your brother. Is there anything you think I ought to know going in to such an interview with him? Announcing my intention to wed you might be a bit of a surprise." He raised his eyebrows as his words took on their teasing quality again.

"I imagine it will be," she mused, trying to picture William's face when Teague spoke in his lovely accent to make such an announcement. It was difficult to say which of his many expressions of dismay he might wear.

"Added to the fact that he's bringing his own candidate for your husband with him, I cannot think he's even considered the possibility of you finding your own groom."

Her breath caught and she gave Teague a startled look. "What did you say? Who is William bringing with him?"

"You didn't know?" Teague's smile faltered, replaced by an expression she had not seen him wear before, though it was so briefly on his face she may have imagined it. Was it worry? "Lord Martin Crighton. A bachelor trying to get a seat in Commons because he's a younger son."

"Ah." She heaved an impatient sigh. "He did threaten to choose someone for me. Knowing William, his 'candidate,' as you say, will be the farthest thing from what I would choose for myself that I can imagine."

"Perhaps." Teague studied her quietly a moment. "Though I would not consider myself a gentleman without saying this: If you like him better than you like me, I'll release you from our agreement."

Had he plunked a bonnet on his head and announced himself the Queen of England, she could not have been as shocked. Her lips parted and she felt a surge of feelings that were as confusing as they were quick to come to the surface. He would set her aside, easy as that? He would be willing to release her? Did he even want her as his wife to begin with?

Suddenly, both his hands were on her shoulders and his eyes were wide. "Ivy. I can see what I said upset you. Take a moment, darling. I'd no wish to give offense. That is the furthest thing from my mind."

She stared at him, aghast. Colorful words she had heard the men in her life mutter from time to time all came to the tip of her tongue. Again, the strength of her reaction surprised her, but she squared her shoulders beneath his hold and tilted her chin up. "Then you had better explain what you meant in clear terms, Lord Dunmore."

He clicked his tongue against the roof of his mouth, and the humor returned to his eyes. Horrid man. "I'd no notion you liked the idea of being an Irish baroness so much."

How dare he imply that was the crux of the matter? She nearly said something about it, too, but he preempted her.

"Think, darling. I had this whole mad scheme to marry you when I found out you needed a husband, and I was under the impression that our company was mutually agreeable." He sounded like quite the politician in that moment. "You agreed for the same reasons, added to it you want to look after your sisters. Gain some independence. What sort of man would I be to hold you to something you had agreed to before you knew there were other options? It is not the mark of a gentleman, I'd say."

She pursed her lips. That was hard to argue. It would not mean much if a man who offered her freedom did not give her a choice in how she obtained it.

He nodded slowly, as though he felt her indignation cooling. "There you are. Better." Then his grin reappeared, quick as a wink. "I intend to make myself the more attractive of the two choices, you understand. It's in my nature. The Irish never give up when presented with a challenge. In fact, I think it is only fair you know precisely what I offer."

With that pronouncement, he leaned forward and kissed her.

TEAGUE HAD NOT PLANNED TO KISS HIS BETROTHED. NOT for a while, at least. The upper classes could be stuffy about that sort of thing on occasion, and downright dismissive of it at others. He had hoped, though, to do a lot more flirting before taking Ivy in his arms and sharing a first kiss.

Call him a romantic, but he had wanted to make the occasion memorable.

His impulsive nature, coupled with her adorable, indignant expression when he had suggested he would let her out of the engagement, took command of his actions. Mentally, he had hesitated for only a moment. His heart had already begun racing, though, and it dictated that he act in that moment.

As he cupped her face gently in his hands, the softness of her skin against his palms was a contrast that sent a shiver down his spine. The initial contact was tender, a hesitant query into whether she would permit him this sort of connection. But as Ivy responded—a silent assent woven into the press of her lips against his—the kiss deepened as Teague grew in certainty of her approval.

Teague was acutely aware of every detail: the warmth of Ivy's lips, the subtle sweetness that lingered upon them like the taste of a honey, and the faintest hint of her breath mingling with his. The world around them fell away, leaving nothing but their touch for him to take notice of.

As he pulled away to catch his breath, Teague was met with Ivy's wide-eyed surprise. They had entered uncharted territory for her.

He tried to find his reassuring grin from before, but it felt a bit shaky. "There now. Not a bad sampling, was it?"

The kiss, though brief, was imprinted upon Teague's senses, a vivid memory he knew would haunt him with its sweetness and the promise it held. It was a mere taste of what he offered her in a courtship and marriage.

At least, he hoped she took it that way. There hadn't been a response for several moments, the only sound the rustling of leaves overhead and the distant drip of water into a fountain. Until, finally, Ivy took hold of herself.

Ivy's cheeks turned a lovely shade of pink. "That was—how dare you?" She spoke without any true upset. More likely she said the words she thought she ought to say, which gave him leave to relax.

"There's nothing wrong with a kiss between a betrothed couple." When she continued to gape at him, Teague tucked a curl behind her ear. "Ah, I've stunned you into silence. Must have been a good kiss, then."

That jogged her back into thought and voice. "Lord Dunmore—"

"Teague."

"—you cannot simply kiss a person without any warning, then assume it was a *good* kiss."

That brought his eyebrows up and he leaned back,

squinting at her. "You didn't think it good? Shall I have another go?"

"No!" She swiftly came to her feet and glared down at him. "You will not 'have another go' at kissing me." She seemed to struggle for words. "It isn't polite."

"You've a fetching look about you when you blush," he said, unable to help teasing her.

"Not. Polite." She paced away from him, then back, seemingly to say something scathing, then thinking better of it.

He tucked his hands behind his head and watched her. "Ivy. It was a kiss. You needn't fuss so, darling."

"William and Fanny will be here tomorrow," she stated with the woebegone air of someone announcing a funeral. "You don't understand. They insist upon everything being appropriate. Polite. Above reproach."

He had always carried a certain disdain for the rigidity of English society, a disdain that had not ebbed despite his years navigating its peripheries. Lord Haverford was a fitting representation for all things Teague found wrong with the English. It made him wonder, yet again, how Ivy had turned out so differently from her brother.

English ladies had always seemed to him like delicate hothouse flowers—beautiful, perhaps, but far too sheltered from the harsher realities of life. Or they were cold, aloof, and uninterested in speaking with him the moment they heard the Irish in his voice.

Ivy was different. Her curiosity for the world, her resilience, and the intelligence he had seen in her eyes—these were qualities he was grateful she hadn't hidden. She challenged his notions of the English, her strength and sincerity carving through his usually justified prejudices.

"I have met your brother. I am well aware of what he's like." He chuckled. "I've debated him, too. And won. His expectations need not govern everything in life." Yet she seemed genuinely distressed. He took in the look of her again, the way her eyes had turned large and troubled, the stiff way she held her shoulders.

He rose from his seat and approached her, noting the way she wrapped her arms around herself. He lowered his voice, speaking gently. "Ivy, I understand the weight of what we're stepping into. It's not just about us—there are expectations, familial duties. Things will be done properly."

She looked up at him, her dark brown eyes searching his, weighing his words.

"Know this." He put his hands on her upper arms, holding her steady, his grip gentle. "I respect those duties and your feelings above all. If you need more time to think things through, or you wish to talk more about what this betrothal means for us, I am here. Fully and truly here for you."

A tentative smile curled her lips upward, and Ivy's expression softened. "Thank you. That is...you seem most sincere. I am afraid I am overwhelmed at present. The thought of stepping so fully into the unknown is daunting."

"I know," he agreed, his thumbs rubbing circles on her arms, soothing her as gently as he could. "I will not pretend otherwise. However, I believe that together, you and I have the intelligence and fortitude to face anything that comes our way. You have a strength to you, Ivy, that perhaps you've not been given enough credit for—not even by yourself."

She drew in a sharp breath, and the look she gave him was skeptical rather than accepting. "Even if that is true, there will be days when I falter. I am not used to being as bold, as forthright, as you seem to be."

"Ah, it takes practice to be as brash a fellow as I am." He allowed himself a wink at her, a playful lilt to his words. "On those days, darling, you have me to depend upon, whether you need me for my boldness or my expertise with debate. Whatever need arises, I will be there the moment you have need of me."

Something of her confidence returned, along with the slightest of smiles. "I shall hold you to that, Lord Dunmore."

"Teague," he corrected again, softly.

She hesitated a moment, then nodded. "Teague. I will hold you to your promises."

"As you should, Ivy." He grinned with pleasure, already feeling the tension leaving her shoulders beneath his hands. "I promise to guard you from any scandal, too."

"You are more likely to cause them than I am, I should think." She spoke with the slightest hint of teasing, which immediately heartened him. "Please. Do not antagonize William when you speak to him. He is less likely to take issue with our arrangement if you are the picture of propriety."

"Antagonize my future brother-in-law?" He affected a scandalized tone. "I am capable of avoiding that disaster, my dear."

She gave him a doubtful look that made him laugh and want to kiss her again. Instead, he slid his hands from her arms to her wrists, then to lace his fingers with hers. Touching her was, he realized with a grin, a pleasure he wanted to enjoy more often. And he could, at least in private.

The quiet apprehension in her gaze finally made him heave a sigh. She carried too many things on her shoulders, and she had done so alone for so long. She needed his reassurance more than his teasing. "Ivy, I know this will bring a new set of challenges. I need you to understand, despite my giving you leave to choose the course best for you, that I am here. I am committed to making things go as smoothly as possible. I've no wish to upset anyone, or to have you worry after me."

Ivy dropped her gaze to the ground, away from him. "I worry about the reception of my family. About what they will say. I am sorry if I seem silly."

"Not in the least, darling. I would never think you silly when you are trying so hard to make everything go well." He squeezed her hands gently. "I understand completely. When I speak with Lord Haverford, I will do so with the utmost respect for you and your family's position. It is important to me that he see the honor in my intentions."

Finally, a tentative smile reappeared on her lovely face. "That means a great deal to me. My family's relationships are rather complex. Sensitive, at times."

Encouraged by her response, Teague continued, "While I cannot change that we come from different backgrounds, I can promise that my regard for you will keep me trying my best to understand your position and your family. More than that, I hope to prove myself a man who will support you through whatever challenges and triumphs will come our way."

That reassurance brought a more confident smile to Ivy's lips, her trepidation disappearing from her eyes, for the time being. "Thank you." She took a deep breath. "Thank you for listening to me, most of all."

"Always," he promised easily, then offered her his arm. "Now. Shall we return inside and see if any breakfast remains?"

She accepted his escort. "That sounds like a good idea."

Ivy had made him reconsider a great deal of what he thought he knew about the English. For so long, he'd seen a pattern in their behavior. A stiffness, an arrogance, that had made him feel as though he worked to bring down a wall of English opposition. Maybe they weren't all as alike as he had thought. Perhaps there was more potential for his work in Parliament than he'd given himself leave to anticipate before.

CHAPTER 16

T he Guard Room of Castle Clairvoir, with its elegant beauty and silent sentinels of armor and weaponry, was the setting for a meeting that held the weight of Ivy's future. Standing to her right were Juniper and Betony. Somehow, Teague had managed to take the spot on her left.

He seemed quite pleased with himself, too.

The other principal guests of the household would have introductions later, but Their Graces stood waiting as well for the imminent arrival of William, Fanny, and Lord Martin.

Ivy kept twisting her fingers behind her back, hiding the fidgeting yet unable to stop it. She kept glancing at her sisters, making certain they behaved. She didn't want Fanny criticizing them first thing.

A warm hand covered hers, stilling the twists, and Ivy looked up in surprise at Teague. He raised his eyebrows at her, gave her hand a gentle squeeze, and murmured, "It'll be over in a trice, darling."

She wanted to say something especially clever back, but that was when the doors opened, revealing William, Fanny, their four children, and a man Ivy had never seen before.

Ivy's attention was momentarily torn between the newcomers and Teague. She could feel a sudden tension in his hands, a subtle stiffness belying his usually composed demeanor. It was a reaction she had not expected and told her a great deal—despite his reassurances, the man was nervous. He released her hand an instant later, then the introductions began.

Finally, William stood before her with Lord Martin at his side. William's voice filled the room, carrying with it a sense of self-satisfaction Ivy knew all too well. "Lady Ivy, my dear sister, allow me to introduce a friend. Lord Martin Alistair Crighton."

As their eyes met, Ivy was taken aback by the immediate and unwelcome sense of connection.

"Lady Ivy, it's a pleasure to meet you at last. Your brother has told me a great deal about you." Lord Martin was everything society deemed perfect. His striking looks and confident tone were underscored by an air of genuine warmth radiating from him.

She hadn't been prepared for him to be pleasant. Rather, she had expected William's choice for her to look, sound, and have the air of William himself.

Next to her, Teague shifted ever so slightly nearer, a movement most might miss, but to Ivy it was a declaration. It was a reassurance, a silent promise that he was there, truly there, with her.

"The pleasure is mine, Lord Martin," Ivy managed to reply, her voice betraying none of the turmoil that Lord Martin's presence had stirred within her.

Teague smoothly entered the conversation with his usual warmth and charm. "Lord Martin, your reputation precedes you. I've heard of your ventures in estate management. Fascinating work."

The compliment, Ivy sensed, was genuine, and Lord Martin's response a blend of appreciation and modesty. "Thank you, Lord Dunmore. I believe there's much we can all do to better the lives of those who depend on us. It is a shared goal, I presume?"

The two of them began speaking lightly on the responsibilities of landlords to tenants, a subject Ivy suspected both could go on about for hours, when Fanny finally came close enough to claim a sisterly kiss to the cheek from Ivy and Juniper and Betony.

"My dear sisters-in-law. It is good to see all of you looking so well. Her Grace has taken marvelous care of you," she said, voice meant to carry through the room. Then, more quietly, "Ivy, you haven't been wearing your bonnet in the sun, have you? There are more freckles on your nose."

She turned to Juniper next. "And you, dear. I didn't know you brought the yellow gown. It makes your skin seem a little sallow, doesn't it?"

Before she could turn a critical eye on Betony, Ivy stepped forward. "Oh, Fanny, it is lovely that you're here at last. I have so much I should like to show you. Her Grace has the most excellent saloon, and I think you will find yourself most comfortable spending an afternoon there."

Betony glowered the instant Fanny's attention returned to Ivy, but she smiled in the genteel way Fanny preferred.

"Yes, of course. I am thrilled at the prospect of touring the house at the earliest opportunity." Fanny fluttered a hand toward the children, whose governess and nursemaid had arrived to shepherd them to the nursery. "As soon as everyone is settled."

The duchess returned, graciously offering to show Fanny to her room. "You must be exhausted from travel, Lady Haverford. The journey from London always leaves me a little out of sorts until I have had a nap."

Fanny simpered and put a hand to her temple, quite delicately. "Oh, yes. That would be ever so helpful in restoring my constitution."

Ivy refrained from rolling her eyes, but barely. Then she realized Teague was speaking with her brother, William. The Irishman appeared quite relaxed, but William was frowning and his gaze darted toward her. He motioned with his hand, beckoning her.

Oh dear. Teague was not wasting any time, it would seem.

She approached them with a polite smile. "Have you need of me, William?"

"Lord Dunmore has asked for a private conversation with the two of us." William's brows furrowed. "Have you a moment?"

That he wouldn't immediately insist on knowing the subject of said conversation was surprising, but Ivy nodded. "Of course."

"His Grace said we are permitted to step into his office off the Pre-Guard room." Teague gestured back the way William and his family had entered. "If that is acceptable to you, Lord Haverford."

The three of them quietly moved away from the rest of the guests, going to the Speak-A-Word room Ivy had heard much about but hadn't entered herself. It was well furnished, masculine, with comfortable chairs and a simple décor. It was a room that would certainly inspire directness without being harsh about it.

William glanced about with vague interest before turning to face Ivy and Teague, who stood side by side. "What is this all about, Dunmore? Has my sister done something for which we must make restitution?"

Ivy's eyes widened. What on earth could William be thinking?

A chuckle escaped Teague. "Not at all. Lady Ivy is a delight." He looked at her with his usual cheery grin. "So much so that I've asked her to marry me."

The man certainly knew how to get straight to the point.

Ivy darted her gaze to William's, speaking swiftly as she saw shock widen her half-brother's eyes. "I said yes. I want to marry Lord Dunmore. As a baron with a place in the House of Lords, you must agree that he's an excellent match. He also has the means to support me, and he's agreed to take responsibility for Juniper and Betony, too, if you approve."

Teague chuckled the moment Ivy paused for breath. "That sums it up nicely." He tucked his hands behind his back and smiled at William. "I am having my man of business draw up papers and send documents here for you to look over, to prove I am capable of providing for your sister, as well as a draft of a potential marriage settlement."

William looked between them, brow furrowed. "I hadn't any notion of this. Ivy, you have not said a word in your letters."

"It all happened rather suddenly," she admitted with a little shrug.

He looked at Teague. "But you're an Irishman."

Teague's grin broadened. Of course it would. "Through and through, I'm afraid. But, as you know, my sister is the future Duchess of Mountfort. She's Irish, too."

With a heavy sigh, William clasped his hands behind his back and regarded Ivy with a stern gaze. "What of Lord Martin? He has come to see if you are a match for him."

"I did not know about Lord Martin until after I had agreed to an engagement with Lord Dunmore," Ivy pointed out. "He will have to manage his disappointment."

"Or—" Teague raised a finger to speak "—as I suggested to Lady Ivy yesterday, we can continue this engagement informally, with the knowledge that it isn't set in stone until the paperwork if complete. If she finds Lord Martin a better candidate, I wouldn't dream of preventing her from making a more desirable match."

Ivy had to bite the insides of her cheeks to keep from scowling at him again. "Do you want out of your agreement?"

she asked, voice sharper than it ought to have been. Especially in front of William, who gave her a startled glance. "You have brought it up twice now."

He chuckled, eyes on her. "Trying to be a gentleman, darling."

"It sounds as though we ought to proceed with negotiations, if both of you have already agreed," William said with ill-concealed confusion. "Though I appreciate the acknowledgement that there is still time and opportunity to make changes. Still. I believe my sister ought to be a woman of her word." His chest puffed out. "There is no harm in Lord Martin coming to know her or the other girls."

After William's statement and the group's tentative agreement on how to proceed, the tension in Ivy's chest constricted. Her thoughts raced as she evaluated her brother's words, Teague's offer of an open-ended engagement, and the unwelcome yet undeniable intrigue Lord Martin presented. The conflict within her was as sharp as the swords displayed on the Guard Room's walls.

"Thank you, William," Ivy finally said, her voice steady despite the storm of emotions within. "I appreciate your thoughtful support." She stole a glance at Teague, seeking some sign of his true feelings behind his gentlemanly actions. His smile was supportive, yet there was a depth in his eyes she hadn't noticed before, an underlying seriousness.

Teague caught her look and his smile wavered for a moment. "Lady Ivy," he began, his tone shifting to something more solemn. "I meant what I said. Your happiness is paramount. If, in the end, Lord Martin or any other situation seems a better path for you..."

Ivy couldn't hide her surprise at the earnestness in his voice. "Lord Dunmore," she interrupted, her decision to defend their bond made on the spot. "I agreed to marry you, not because you were the most convenient option at the time, but because...because I believe we could be truly good for each other." She ignored the surprised look from William and the slight softening in Teague's expression.

William cleared his throat, his discomfort with the sudden intimacy of the conversation quite apparent. "Well, then. It seems we have much to discuss and prepare for." He glanced at Teague. "I shall await the details from your man of business."

When they exited the Speak-A-Word room, Ivy felt the weight of the moment settle on her shoulders. Teague offered her a small reassuring nod as they parted ways a moment later, a silent promise of conversations to come.

Ivy found herself blessedly alone, her steps leading her towards the castle's gardens, a place of solace amidst the turmoil.

The sunshine and clear air of the afternoon was a balm to her frayed nerves. Ivy wandered the pathways closest to the castle, her thoughts a tangled mess. The possibility of Lord Martin being a better match gnawed at her, a question of *what if* she hadn't wanted to consider. Teague seemed determined that she do so, with full sincerity in his voice, despite their conversation and the kiss from the day before.

"Why must this feel so complicated?" she whispered to the bobbing blossoms of a rosebush. She had agreed to marry Teague, moved by instinct and the stirrings of a deeper interest. The prospect of stepping back to evaluate other options, even with Teague's blessing, felt like a betrayal of her own good sense.

As she reached a marble bench tucked away beneath a blossoming tree, Ivy sat, allowing the quiet of the gardens to envelop her. She watched the flowers bob in the breeze, their soft pinks and yellows making her wonder what they'd look like in different hues. In blues and greens, through lenses of different colors. What lens ought she to look through to make the best choice for herself? For her life? The one her brother offered, or the one she already held?

The thought of exploring a connection with Lord Martin, or anyone else, stirred a sense of loyalty to a possible future with Teague Frost. A strange thing, given the brevity of their acquaintance, perhaps. But every time Ivy spoke to him, she felt more herself than she had in ages. He did not mind her voicing strange thoughts or strong opinions. In fact, he seemed delighted by everything she said. He valued her words. He liked her younger sisters.

He liked Ivy. And she rather liked him.

"Perhaps," Ivy mused, gazing at the stars peeking through the foliage, "the real question is not about the better match, but about where my heart will be happiest."

CHAPTER 17

Teague understood why the family's favorite room in the castle was the Long Gallery not long after entering it for the first time. The room was enormous, over one hundred and thirty feet in length, with windows stretching from floor to ceiling and comfortable groupings of furniture throughout. The setting made it possible for everyone to be in the same room, within sight of each other, and still able to pursue separate activities.

He sat in a chair near one of the windows, elbow on the arm of the chair, chin in hand, glaring at the sunny sky. Teague was seriously wondering what had come over him, to insist Ivy give the newly arrived Lord Martin even a moment's thought.

"I must be daft," he muttered aloud.

"I've never disagreed with that assessment," Isleen said from beside him, where she worked with an embroidery hoop and needle on a white expanse of cloth.

Why were women always embroidering things? Not every handkerchief needed roses along its edge, surely.

"Your brother seems to have a specific reason for believing his statement, Isleen." Simon turned another page in his book, not entirely focused on the conversation, but sitting near enough his wife that his arm stretched along the back of the couch, allowing him to brush her shoulder with his thumb.

They were remarkably happy together. Teague admired how they made something so simple as sitting side by side look like the best thing a person could do. Relaxed as they were, content as they were, it made his own feelings of discontent sharper.

Isleen sighed and looked up at Teague long enough to ask, "Why do you think yourself daft, brother?"

He considered them, his sister and brother-in-law, both focused on their own activities, neither aware of the colossal fool he'd made of himself. He would have to tell them if he wanted any help or advice. He badly needed both.

"I told Ivy she ought to consider Lord Martin's suit for her hand."

Simon snapped his book closed and Isleen hissed and shook out her finger, apparently having pricked herself with the needle. She immediately held her finger to her husband, who studied it, gave it a kiss, then held her hand.

"You *are* daft, Teague." Isleen shook her head at him. "Unless...you do not want to go through with the engagement?"

"I want to marry her," he stated firmly. He had made his mind up about that already, or he never would have asked.

"Then why would you tell her to even so much as glance at another prospect?" Simon asked, brow furrowed. "That seems counter to your wants."

At this moment, Isleen made a sound somewhere between a scoff and a laugh. "Teague is ever and always his own worst enemy. He is more worried about Lady Ivy's perception of the matter than what he wants."

"How do you mean?" Simon asked.

Isleen gestured to Teague. "Look at him. He wants her to

like him. He wants her to *choose* him. What he does not realize is how Lady Ivy will feel unwanted—"

"Oh, she made her feelings known on that matter," Teague interrupted, a little of his confidence returning. "I think I cleared things up on that front."

"I do not like the look in your eye when you say that." Isleen looked him over with disapproval. "Fine. If you made your intentions and reasons clear, why are you sitting here fretting about things now? What's done is done. Set about courting the lady and kindly stop sulking."

"Courting the lady. There is where we enter the trouble-some spot." Teague leaned closer to his sister. "As an engaged couple—because that is what we are—we haven't a need for chaperones. As I've provided her a way out, should she want it, do you think she will insist on them?"

"Given that we are at a house party, surrounded by both your family and hers, I doubt there will be any great need for one. Chaperones are for stilling the tongues of gossips and those that would delight in scandal. You are among people who trust you and want what is best." Isleen gave a little shrug. "I would not worry over it, but I know you are a gentleman. You won't do anything scandalous."

Simon gave his wife a look of surprise. "Of course you'd think that. You're his sister."

Isleen sent her husband a narrow look. "Have you reason to believe otherwise about my brother?"

"None," he admitted. "I think you make a fair point. I only meant to say there are things sisters wouldn't imagine about their brothers."

She shook her head at him. "Keep to the matter at hand, Simon. What do you think? Does Ivy require a chaperone to be going about with my brother around your home and lands?"

"I agree with what you said. Most of us are related in one way or another. This is a family event. No one will say a word—

especially if Ivy weds someone at the end of summer. Preferably Teague, I suppose." He gave his brother-in-law a wide grin. "Should I tell Sir Andrew it's to be a competition? He will want to place bets."

"I will remind you that a wager is what brought our courtship about," Isleen said softly. "I would not tease on that end too much."

Simon chuckled and nodded to Teague. "There, now there must be a wager. It's practically good luck for your relationship to be involved in one."

"Irish don't need luck. We make our own," Teague responded, folding his arms over his chest. At ease over the chaperone question, he let his eyes travel to the end of the room where Lady Ivy and her sisters were sitting beneath the critical eye of their sister-in-law and the kindly eye of the duchess. "They all look as though they are ready to be eaten by a dragon."

"I thought only my grandmother had that effect on people," Simon muttered.

"Damsels love being saved from dragons," Isleen pointed out, returning to the ridiculously large white square of embroidery. "Perhaps she needs a knight in shining armor, brother."

"Perhaps you're right." He rose and moved in the direction of the ladies. He had crossed half the space required to join them when Ivy met his gaze and, ever so subtly, he saw her head shift. It was the tiniest of motions, a little back and forth, a silent plea in the negative.

No. Don't come any closer.

He paused, raised his eyebrows. *Whyever not, darling?*

If only it were possible to speak to a person without saying a word. The way her eyes darted from him to her youngest sister made him follow her gaze.

Lady Betony had struck him as the cheeriest of the three sisters, smiling and carrying about her beadwork, never holding back from sharing a charming observation. He had found himself hoping little Fiona would get to know Lady Betony, as the two seemed rather similar in temperament, but Betony had a decade of experience learning how to fit into a world that had not been made easy for ladies with spunk.

At the moment, however, he saw none of her usual lightness of spirit. Lady Betony appeared pale, and there was a tightness in her brow that made him wonder if she had a headache.

Ah. Ivy didn't wish for rescue if it came at the expense of leaving her sister behind. He understood that.

Very well.

He affixed his charming smile in place and kept coming. For a moment, Ivy's eyes widened in alarm, but she turned her full attention to her sister-in-law as though she hadn't even marked Teague's approaching form.

He interrupted without a moment's pause. "I beg your pardon, your grace. Ladies. I've a need to kidnap one of these fair maids a moment." He turned his smile from the duchess and the countess to the sisters, only briefly meeting Ivy's frown before settling his gaze on the one most in need of rescue.

"Lady Betony, if you would join me a moment? My sister is thinking of adding beadwork to the bit of cloth she's at work upon, and we would like to know your thoughts on the subject. We've agreed you are the one with the best eye for such details."

The young woman's mouth popped open for an instant in surprise, but she quickly looked to her sister-in-law.

It was the duchess who waved them away. "Of course, Lord Dunmore. We wouldn't dream of keeping her from you. Your work is really quite fine, Betony."

"Thank you, your grace." Betony rose, made her curtsy, then accepted Teague's hand as he led her away. He looked over his shoulder once before he reached the safety of Simon and Isleen's couch, intercepting a look from Ivy that sent his heart into a lively dance.

It was a short glimpse, yet he read several things in it at once. Approval. Appreciation. And, quite possibly, attraction.

He winked and turned before seeing if he had made her blush.

Betony settled happily in the chair he had occupied before, and Isleen—bless her—played along in asking about adding beadwork to the embroidery of the gown.

"Gown?" Teague looked down at the white swath of fabric again. "There's not enough cloth there for half a gown. Who do you plan to wear such a small scrap of a thing?"

Simon's ears went pink, but his sister gave him a measured look. "You really ought not to worry so about my sewing."

Betony coughed softly into her fist, though it sounded more like she was trying to hide a laugh at his expense.

"I thought it was an overly large handkerchief." His eyebrows went high, but Isleen put a finger to her lips. He scowled at her. "You've a secret you're not telling me?"

Her lips turned upward. "A little one. I shall tell later."

He huffed and looked at Simon, but the man had grown tight-lipped and appeared to be trying to melt into the pages of the book in his hand. Fine. He had enough to worry himself about without diving into whatever secrets his sister and her husband wanted to keep.

In conversation with Isleen, Lady Betony relaxed and was soon herself again, though perhaps speaking at a lower volume than he thought necessary. Perhaps she didn't like being her full self in front of her sister-in-law. Pity she had to temper herself at all.

He went to one of the tall windows, folded his hands behind his back, and looked out over the stretch of land sloping downward from Clairvoir's hill. He had saved a damsel from a dragon. Hopefully, that would win him another fair maiden's hand.

Ivy and Juniper both relaxed the moment the Irishman swept away their little sister. Fanny had not been cruel, and likely as not thought herself helpful, but she had done nothing except correct every gesture Betony made from the moment they sat down in the Long Gallery. She had admonished Betony to temper her smile, to sit straighter, to put her knees closer together, to keep her ankles apart, tilt her chin up, keep her shoulders back, and on the list went.

Perhaps Fanny meant to make up for lost time, given the fortnight the sisters had been away from her care. Betony had drowned beneath the shower of criticism like a flower in a pot overflowing with rainwater. That Teague had understood in the few seconds he'd had to assess the situation, then done something about it, struck her as deeply sweet.

She had every intention of telling him so, too, the moment she freed herself from Fanny's conversation. Unfortunately, Teague left the room with Lord Farleigh some time before Fanny had finished regaling all of them, even the patient duchess, with stories of her last two weeks in London.

Juniper looked as though she were ready to wilt from the overabundance of information by the time Fanny allowed the duchess to steer the conversation, and Fanny herself, elsewhere.

"Do come look at the nursery with me, Lady Haverton. Now that James is ready to move on, I would appreciate another mother's perspective on how to keep the rooms for younger children pleasant when we have guests."

Fanny preened, obviously overjoyed at the idea of a duchess wanting her opinion on anything.

The moment the doors closed behind the pair, Juniper slumped over against the arm of the furniture and released a soft moan. "The duchess is a saint, and Lord Dunmore ought to be knighted for his rescue of Betony."

"I think a knighthood is a step down from being a baron," Ivy said with a soft smile. "It was not so bad. She has obviously stored up a great deal of things. Stories to tell. Gossip to share. Critiques to distribute."

Betony appeared standing before them. "Ivy, if you do not marry Lord Dunmore, I might have to." She spoke as though earnest, her hand over one heart. "I truly expected he had come to steal you away, but I was the chosen one." She fluttered her eyelashes. "A most valiant man. Kind. Thoughtful. Witty."

Ivy's cheeks warmed and she folded her hands tight in her lap. "It was kind of him to whisk you away."

"You will marry him, won't you?" Betony asked, her usual cheerful grin returning. "No more of this Lord Martin—oh." Her face turned red and she leaned closer to whisper, "He just came in with Sir Andrew."

Indeed, the handsome gentleman accompanied the baronet into the room, both immediately coming to where Ivy and her sisters were.

"Lady Ivy, Lady Juniper, Lady Betony," Sir Andrew said, bobbing a brief bow to all three. "We are in search of more gentlemen. Or nobles, I suppose, since everyone here seems to have a title, and they're all higher than mine." His broad grin made it seem more a joke than an actual observation. He sighed heavily and looked to Lord Martin. "We are swimming in lords and ladies."

"Lord Farleigh and Lord Dunmore left perhaps ten minutes ago," Ivy answered, gesturing to Isleen, who was still working at her embroidery. "Perhaps they told Lady Farleigh where they meant to go next. Otherwise, I am afraid I cannot help."

"I shall ask Isleen," Sir Andrew said, turning at once to speak to the countess.

Lord Martin shook his head as the baronet strode away. "I

have never met a man so happy to poke fun at people with higher ranks. It is remarkably refreshing to be in his company."

"I think one must lose their awe of such things as rank when one's best friend is a future duke." Ivy had stood to speak to him while her sisters both sat on the couch, watching Lord Martin with a critical eye. "I understand you won your seat in the House of Commons recently, Lord Martin. Does that mean you have not socialized much with the men here who are in Lords?"

"Very little politically, though quite often when it comes to parties and gentlemen's clubs. I went to the same schools as Farleigh and Sir Andrew, though I was behind them in age." His carriage was correct. His tone polite. His smile quite friendly. Nothing negative could be said or even thought of his presence.

That did not stop Juniper from trying to poke him. "Strange that we haven't met you before, Lord Martin, and yet you're well acquainted enough with our elder brother for William to invite you here."

Betony's smile curled up eagerly, too. "Truly. I had not heard him mention you before, either."

Ivy could blithely throttle them both. As it was, she cast them a warning look, the look of an older sister reminding the younger to play nicely with others. They ignored her, keeping their innocent smiles on Lord Martin.

If that was not enough, she caught the guard, Sterling, out the corner of her eye, smirking, as though he was enjoying the show her sisters were putting on to disconcert Lord Martin.

The man appeared unflappable, perhaps even amused. "Alas, your brother and I have known each other these six months and I have barely won his approval, it seems. I am afraid some of our political views are at odds. I am more closely aligned with His Grace's party than Lord Haverford's. We recently came to an agreement about better practices for tenancies. I think knowing that I have it in me to compromise is what finally gained his attention."

Betony immediately raised her eyebrows and Juniper wrinkled her nose. Neither were fond of discussing politics, as they did not take much of an interest. Not like Ivy did. He had provided them an answer to their somewhat rude queries and bored them.

Ivy had to resist laughing at her sisters as she turned to Lord Martin. "I am glad he finally brought you to meet us. Most of my brother's friends have little interest in discussing politics with the earl's younger sisters."

"Perhaps I am brighter than they are," he responded with a charming smile. "I have a question I must ask, though it is likely all three of you are tired of hearing it. Your names are quite unique—plants. Ivy, Juniper, Betony. It is somewhat unusual in the nobility to find nary a Mary or Elizabeth in a family. Did your mother have a special love for horticulture?"

Betony's wicked grin came an instant before her answer. "Oh, no. It was our father. *All* of us have plant names." She batted her eyelashes. "Even our brother."

Lord Martin's eyebrows drew together. "Your brother's Christian name is William, is it not?"

"It is," Juniper said with a tamer version of their youngest sister's expression.

"Father named him after one of his favorite flowers. *Sweet William*," Ivy said at last, wincing somewhat. It was not her half-brother's favorite piece of family history, that he had been named for a flower, even though the name itself was quite respectable and common for a man of his station. The fact that his name came from a plant rather than a conquering king wasn't one he liked.

Lord Martin, to his credit, immediately covered his laugh with his fist, then cleared his throat. "That seems like dangerous information for me to possess if I want to stay on his good side."

Easy as that, he had pleased her sisters enough for the two of them to laugh and stop glowering at him. Indeed, Ivy relaxed somewhat, too. He was not a bad sort at all.

When Sir Andrew came back to fetch him, he said, "They have gone to the boat house. There's talk of a rowing race if we can gather more interested parties. Do you row?"

"I did well enough at university," Lord Martin answered, some eagerness in his tone. He bowed to the ladies. "It sounds as though I am needed in the boathouse. Good afternoon, ladies."

After the two men left, Juniper tilted her head to the side and gave Ivy a speculative look. "There isn't anything wrong with him. At least, not that I can spot easily."

Betony sniffed. "I still like Teague better."

Ivy absently corrected, "Lord Dunmore. You should not use his Christian name."

"He gave me leave to after rescuing me." Betony grinned happily. "As I hope to call him brother before long, I intend to accept that invitation, at least in private conversation. Besides, you have already said yes to him."

"I know." Ivy gave an impatient roll of her eyes. "Betony. I am quite aware of that. He is the one who has said I ought to consider Lord Martin as an option."

"Does Lord Martin know about the engagement yet?" Juniper asked, hands folded properly in her lap. With an expectant tilt of her head, she added, "It's unsporting if he does not know he's in a competition. Can you imagine being in a race without knowing about it? Just leisurely walking while the other person darts ahead?"

"It is not a competition. And I do not know what he knows." Ivy slumped into the chair where Fanny had perched not a half hour before. "He strikes me as the sort of man who would not give attention to a woman already engaged. I will assume he does not know."

"Not fair, Ivy." Juniper shakes her head.

"Who exactly does know?" Betony asked. "I have not spoken of it outside the three of us."

"Nor I," Juniper added. "I thought it best to wait until you or Tea—Lord Dunmore announced it." She blushed when Ivy sent her a glare for nearly using Teague's given name.

"I have spoken only to our family about it. William, the two of you, and Teague himself." Ivy winced. "I believe Tea—Lord Dunmore told His Grace, Lord Farleigh, and possibly his sister."

"A tight-knit group, then." Juniper glanced toward Sterling, whose face was a mask of indifference. "And whatever servants have been about to hear, I suppose. There must be gossip."

"It is not really a secret," Ivy protested softly, with a sinking feeling in her stomach. "Perhaps I should speak to William about it. You're right. Lord Martin should know the circumstances under which he was brought here have changed, if he truly was only brought to meet me."

Juniper tapped her chin thoughtfully. "A younger son of a nobleman is a fine catch, so long as he has his own means of support. Perhaps he will turn his attention to one of the other ladies present."

"Whom do you think he would turn to next?" Betony bounced a little in her seat. "You, Juniper dear?"

Juniper's cheeks flushed and she shook her head. "No. I am not at all looking for a husband. Yet."

"You aren't any fun." Betony tossed her curls and turned her gaze back on Ivy. "Why would Teague want you to consider another man? Is he trying to get out of marrying you? He did not have to rescue me unless he really liked you."

"Or he is kind and would have done it no matter what," Ivy put in, somewhat defensively. "He says he is trying to be a gentleman by considering my feelings first. He says if Lord Martin is the better prospect, I deserve that if I think I would be happier with him."

"That is ridiculous. I am certain if we made a list of their attributes, of all the good reasons and bad, they would come out quite equal. The worst thing about Lord Dunmore," Juniper said with an even tone, "is that he lives in Ireland. That is far away. But if we go with you, it is not too terrible. You did say we could go with you if William approves."

"Precisely." Betony gave her hands a clap. "If they are similar in terms of positive reasons for marriage, I still choose Teague."

Ivy gave her sister an exasperated look. "It is not your choice, Betony."

Betony childishly stuck her tongue out and all three of them giggled. Fanny certainly would not have liked that behavior.

"Really, though," Juniper said at last, voice softer. "This is not a fair situation for Lord Martin. Nor for you." She stood and went to sit on the footstool directly in front of Ivy's chair, solemn.

"What do you mean, for me?"

Juniper leaned closer to Ivy, her voice soft but firm, carrying the weight of her convictions. "Ivy, while I understand Lord Dunmore's intentions might be noble, suggesting you consider Lord Martin places you in an unfair position. It is not just about choosing someone as if they are books on a shelf. It is about where your heart truly lies. Lord Martin... he deserves to know the full picture, too. It is only fair to him and to you."

She paused, her gaze thoughtful as she considered her next words carefully. "Marriage isn't a competition or a list of attributes to compare. It is about finding someone who complements you, who brings out the best in you and stands by you through every challenge. Whether that person is Lord Dunmore or not, it is a decision that should be made with clarity and honesty, not under the shadow of doubt or obligation."

Ivy stared at Juniper in silent admiration for several long moments. Though the oldest, she had often suspected that her middle sister had more clarity of thought, if not outright wisdom, than Ivy possessed. Juniper's strengths were lovely and unique to her, and they were part of the reason Ivy wished to wed and get both her sisters away from Fanny's censuring and William's indifference.

"Thank you," she said quietly. "It feels like so much to consider. It would be easier if...if there was love involved."

With a sigh, Juniper reached out, taking Ivy's hand in hers. "Whatever you decide, know that Betony and I are here for you. We want your happiness above all else. So, let's ensure everyone involved has all the information before any more steps are taken. It is the only way to navigate this with integrity and respect for everyone's feelings."

Betony grumbled from her place on the couch. "Does Juniper always have to be right?"

The other two laughed, but Ivy nodded. "This time, I think so."

She needed to have a rather important conversation with Teague.

CHAPTER 18

Waiting outside a woman's quarters like a rogue of the worst sort had Teague on edge. It did not help that Sterling, positioned at the end of the corridor, wore a somewhat disapproving frown instead of his usual mask of indifference. Teague kept glancing at the guard, nearly speaking several times, but wound up saying nothing.

What would he say? *Stop looking at me like I should not be here?* Ridiculous. He had every right to stand in an empty corridor, waiting to speak with his betrothed before dinner and the subsequent musical evening.

Still uncomfortable, he leaned against the wall opposite to the quarters shared by the three sisters. His shoulders had barely brushed the wallpaper when her door opened, and he practically leapt forward to intercept her.

"Lady Ivy." Her loveliness immediately set his heart pounding. This evening she wore a gown of soft pink, which complemented her dark eyes and the soft flush in her cheeks. "You are stunning."

The pink cheeks turned red. "Thank you, Teague." She smoothed the skirts of the gown along her hips, a self-conscious

SALLY BRITTON

movement he found as endearing as it was enticing. "Are you waiting for me?"

"I am. I thought we could have a chat, if you are amiable to that." He held out his hand, bending at the waist in a near courtly bow. "Please?"

After watching her, speaking with her, slowly coming to know her, Teague fancied himself able to read some of the emotions in her expression. The subtle lightening of her eyes, the tiny forward tilt of her head, told him he had done something that merited her approval. He intended to do more.

She placed her hand in his and he guided it to the crook of his arm, walking down the corridor toward the ballroom staircase. She spoke first. "Did the men reach an agreement about a possible boat race?"

He chuckled. "Indeed, we did. We should have enough to man four boats, if everyone Farleigh invites accepts his invitation. There's talk of going to the river rather than doing the thing in the lake, as they've done in the past. Have you an interest in boat racing?"

"None at all," she admitted with a slight upturn to her lips. "But the men in this castle seem quite obsessed with it."

"Including our newest addition, Lord Martin." Better to bring up the subject they needed to address than continue to dance around it, he supposed. "He's quite the sportsman."

"I am not the least surprised," she said, giving him a rueful glance. "He is charming, well-spoken, athletic, and was a delight to partner in cards last evening. Truly, nothing like the kind of man I expected my brother to offer for my consideration."

Teague agreed with her assessment and wanted nothing more than to lock Lord Martin in a closet for all his good qualities. "He's logical when it comes to his politics, too. Thinking ahead."

"Should you not speak more disparagingly of him?" she asked, amusement in the tilt of her head. "Or are you trying to push me toward him? I confess, I know not what to think from one moment to the next."

He gave her his best innocent expression, all wide-eyed and narrow-lipped. "I wouldn't wish to insult your intelligence or judgement by suggesting he is anything other than a good match for a lady. Though perhaps I am a bit too self-assured in thinking you will still find me the better choice."

"Oh?" She raised her eyebrows at him. "What advantages do you have that I ought to know about?"

Teague couldn't resist the opportune moment, and there was a wonderfully situated little alcove for him to tuck her into —so he did. He backed into it, bringing her with him with one hand on her wrist and the other going gently around her waist, drawing her against his chest.

"I have plenty of advantages, darling." He released her waist to tilt her chin up, barely grazing her skin. He did not need to direct her much, as she seemed quite eager to lean forward.

She wanted a kiss, did she?

He smiled to himself, then touched his lips chastely to her forehead. "There now. Wasn't that grand?" he teased, looking down into her eyes as they glowed first with surprise, then indignation.

For a moment, she opened and closed her mouth soundlessly, looking as though she wished to lecture him, but with enough confusion on the matter that she couldn't settle upon what to say.

"You can either be upset I did not give you the kiss you wanted, or you can be upset you wanted it in the first place," he informed her with a smug little smile as his hand went back around her waist. "I don't think you can say a word against *me* in this case."

"You are rather infuriating." When she spoke at last, it was in a hushed voice. "I can say that much against you."

"I think you like it," he protested with a grin. "I'll not kiss you again until you ask me to, Ivy."

"You are a beast." Then the slightest pause before she said, "What makes you think I will ask?"

"Nothing but a great deal of hope." He tilted his head to study the flush of her cheeks, the way she pursed her lips, and that little wrinkle at the top of her nose. "You wished to speak with me, did you not?"

"You were the one waiting for me in the corridor. Like a tiger preparing to pounce."

He chuckled softly. She hadn't stepped away from him, which told him enough about how much she enjoyed his nearness. "Let us say I sensed you needed a word with me, so I made myself available." He had caught her glancing at him every time they had been in close proximity that day. It had not been difficult to surmise she had something on her mind.

Given how willingly she stood with him, tucked out of sight, he didn't think she meant to break off their engagement. Lord Martin had been present for three days. He could not have won her over yet, not when it was Teague who had worked for weeks to coax her into expressing herself more openly.

It simply wouldn't be fair. Not that he expected much fairness out of life. But he hoped for it from her.

"Astute of you to notice," she muttered, hardly impressed with him. "It is about Lord Martin. I have decided it is not fair for him to be here, expecting to get to know me and court me, when I am already engaged. Even in your spirit of fair play, or whatever you wish to call it, he ought to know."

"If he knew, he wouldn't be any sort of gentleman to continue pursuing you, as you've already given your consent to marry another," Teague pointed out. "I have no objection to telling him, of course. I merely think you will deprive yourself of the choice."

"I would rather be honest," she returned, and his heart

warmed with approval. He had yet another thing to admire about Ivy: her integrity. Before he could give her a compliment on that hand, she added, "And honorable. I already gave you my word, Teague. We ought to announce our engagement properly and stop playing games."

"But I do so enjoy games," he protested, already wishing to gather her close in his arms again. She did not want to consider her other option, despite the attractions he held. It was a boon to his pride, for certain, and an immense relief. "You truly do not want to consider him? Even though your brother agreed?"

"Truly. Unless you wish to end our engagement for your own reasons, I would rather proceed. Openly. No games."

The way his heart stuttered and skipped ahead to make up for the stumble almost hurt, and he had to step back a little. Had to breathe. Didn't quite know what to do with the gift she'd handed him.

The way her eyes watched him, raptly, not missing a thing, made him smile. She looked as though she was holding her breath, waiting for his response.

"That is music to my ears, darling. And here I was planning a variety of schemes to win you to my side."

"A gesture or two to show your enthusiastic approval of my decision would not go amiss," she said, her eyes narrowing. "A lady likes to feel appreciated. Especially when she is giving her entire future into the hands of the man who asked for it." The softest note of vulnerability entered her voice, a thing he felt more than heard.

He gentled his hold on her, tilting his head down and speaking with all the sincerity in his heart. "Ah, and that's a grand gift indeed. I'm honored you trust me with it. I swear on my life to be a worthy keeper of that future."

She rested her forehead against his, a shaky breath escaping her lips.

Teague squeezed her hand. "Now then, my darling. Let us find His Grace and see about making an announcement."

WILLIAM AGREED TO TAKE LORD MARTIN ASIDE AND TELL him of Ivy's betrothal between dinner and the evening's entertainment, insisting that he'd been the one to set the man's expectations, thus he would be the one to inform him of the mistake.

His Grace suggested they make the announcement after the entertainment ended, making it the final, happy note on which to end the evening. All the castle guests, consisting of family and extended family, would be present, and most of their neighbors from the gentry class upward.

"Who does not want to leave a night of enchanting music with a notion as romantic as a betrothal?" the duke had asked with a somewhat wistful smile, and Teague had immediately agreed to the idea.

The one problem with such a thing waiting that long would be that it added to Ivy's nerves. She had been practicing her piece for the evening since the ladies had originally discussed it. Choosing music that had spoken to her heart, feeling free to do so, not realizing Fanny would then be sitting on the second row of chairs in the music room, listening and watching for any sign of inappropriate playing.

Betony and Juniper had chosen a duet, and Ivy would perform before them. As Lady Farleigh had taken the reins of the hostess from the duchess that evening, she carefully ushered each woman up at their turn and informed the guests of what they would play.

Ivy sat with William and Fanny on one side, her sisters on the other, and gripped the music in her hands tightly. She did not think she would need it, as she loved *Nocturne*. It had been

composed by John Field, an Irishman, who had spent his lifetime composing and selling his music in England and
throughout Europe.

After the duchess named her and her somewhat unconventional piece, she didn't dare look at Fanny. Her sister-in-
law had always insisted the sisters never play or perform a
piece not well established as socially acceptable. Polite. Well-
known.

Ivy sat at the piano, hesitating before placing her fingers on
the keys. This song reminded her of evenings long ago, her
father humming while she drifted off to sleep. Everything about
it was gentle. Soft. Loving.

And that would be how she played the piece.

Under the tender glow of candlelight, Ivy's fingers glided
across the ivory keys, each note of John Field's *Nocturne*
unfurling into the hushed room with all the warmth in her
heart. She closed her eyes, allowing the music to flow gently.
Peacefully. It was as though the piano itself sighed under her
touch, its melodies not just played but felt—each phrase a
memory, each arpeggio a whisper of happier days.

She thought of her father, showing her illustrations of
faraway lands. His hand taking hers to walk through the garden
with a magnifying glass to look at insects. His proud smile when
she grew heated in her conversation about a book.

Her approach to the composition was less a matter of tech-
nique than of heart. Ivy did not merely interpret Field's work;
she infused it with her soul, her body swaying with the swell of
the music, eyes closed to better inhabit the world it conjured.
The world where she'd been safe to be herself with her father. It
was a performance that blurred the boundaries between musi-
cian and melody, where each note was a testament to the joy
and gentleness of her past.

The last notes trembled in the air as her fingers trembled on
the keys and a tear slipped through her lashes, along her cheek.

She missed her father. What would he have thought of her current situation? Her betrothal?

She dearly hoped he wouldn't be disappointed, that he would understand her choice. She opened her eyes with a serene smile.

When she turned her head to acknowledge the genteel applause, her gaze went first to Teague. She had not meant to look to where he sat, across the room from her family, but her eyes were drawn to him in a brief, hesitant glance.

His expression made her breath catch.

There, in the depths of his eyes, she found not the veiled concern or polite detachment she had braced herself to encounter, but a glowing approval, a warmth reaching across the room like the gentle touch of moonlight through a window. His gaze held a mixture of pride and tenderness. As though he had found the music, and perhaps its player, beautiful.

He was not ashamed. Was not worried. She dared put on a smile as she curtsied, her turn over, her nerves settled. Relief touched her heart...yet quickly faded the moment she turned her gaze toward her family and met Fanny's disapproving frown and reddened cheeks.

She had upset Fanny.

William did not seem concerned, politely clapping, gaze not truly focused. Betony and Juniper were beaming. But Fanny would have words for her the moment she sat down.

Somehow, she made it to her chair without stumbling. The *contessa* took her turn at the keys, playing an Italian ballad to compliment her ambassador husband. Ivy sat, gripping her music, as the first notes began. Everyone's attention now on the new piece, the new player.

Everyone except Fanny.

"Ivy," her sister-in-law said, her voice saturated with reproach, "Your playing and crying at the keys is an inappropriate display. Such depth of feeling! It is improper. Music, my dear, should mirror grace and restraint as much as skill. What you did was shameful. What was that song? I did not give approval for it."

Still emotional from her heart's journey to the days she had been safe beneath her father's watchful eye, his smile, where laughter filled the air and Ivy and her sisters could simply be— she did not have words to respond to the harshness of the critique. To Fanny, there were two ways to play that had little to do with the music itself. There was appropriate and inappropriate.

"What will people say about a young lady who weeps at the piano?" Fanny hissed softly. "In the duke's home. What will they think of you?"

Another tear slipped down her cheek and she brushed it away with her ungloved hand.

"Excuse yourself at once at take hold of your emotions, child."

Ivy nodded and silently rose, slipping away, out of the room and into the quiet of the corridor, where she covered her mouth and leaned against the wall opposite the now closed door. She choked on a sob.

Would she forever be a disappointment to the people around her, merely by being true to herself?

A man cleared his throat, and she glanced up to find Sterling suddenly standing at her side, but facing the doors. He had one hand extended, holding a handkerchief. "My lady."

She accepted the unadorned linen square. "Thank you, Sterling," she said, almost gulping for air. Her lungs burned.

He tilted his head to the side. "No one is in that room, my lady, should you wish for quiet."

She looked at the closed door he indicated and nodded, then went straight in. Heart hurting. Tears escaping, unchecked.

CHAPTER 19

Teague gave his mother's hand a squeeze, noting her happy smile as she listened to each performance with pleasure. His mother adored music, and she had expressed her joy that so many pieces played that evening would be compositions by Irishmen. She seemed especially touched by Ivy's selection.

As had he.

He bent forward slightly, looking down the row of chairs, hoping to catch a glimpse of Ivy to offer her another congratulatory smile. Yet he realized at once her chair sat empty. His eyebrows furrowed. He sat back again.

Where had she gone? Why hadn't he seen her leave? He bent toward his mother. "Lady Ivy. She's left the room."

"Perhaps she needed to compose herself," she whispered back, eyes focused forward. "The music touched her heart. Not every lady wishes to sit still after expelling such emotion. Step into the corridor. You will likely find her there, her heart all aflutter." She gave him a warm smile. "She plays beautifully, son. One can tell she has a gentle soul. I think you chose well."

He took his mother's hand and gave it a gentle squeeze, thanking her in the Irish tongue. "*Go raibh maith agat,*

Máthair." He kissed her cheek, then rose and carefully wound his way through the chairs and out the room.

Stepping out of the music room, he immediately found Sterling at attention, another guard at the side of the door. Their gazes flicked to him, then away. Other than the two of them, the corridor was empty.

He raised his eyebrows at Sterling. "Lady Ivy?"

The guard posing as a footman tilted his head to the side, glancing at a door. "Through there, my lord."

He grinned his thanks and went to the door, ready to praise his betrothed for her skill. The moment he opened the door, however, he caught sight of her standing with her back to him, her shoulders hunched, head bowed, body shaking with sobs.

The moment he understood what he saw, he approached. "Ivy, my darling." He took her shoulders and turned her gently toward him. She lifted her face, her cheeks shining with tears and her eyes clouded with sorrow.

He guided her into his arms, her cheek against his chest, and held her as though he could offer shelter from the storm of her heart.

He should not hold her like this. Then again, he should not have kissed her. Should not have pulled her into the alcove to tease her. Their engagement had given him—had given both of them—more freedom. He justified being there through that reasoning. She needed him. He stood as her protector. Who else but he could hold her when she so clearly needed to be held?

She cried into his shoulder, a handkerchief pressed over half her face. He let her, running one hand gently up and down her back in what he hoped was a soothing motion. He murmured nonsense words to her, assurances that everything would be all right, that she could cry as much as she wished, half in English, half in Irish, until her shoulders ceased shaking, and her body shuddered with one last sobbed breath.

Then he finally dared ask, "What happened, *a stór?* How did you come to this after such a radiant, beautiful moment?"

Still leaning against him, she shook her head. "Does it matter?"

Carefully, he eased back from her, hands coming up to hold her forearms. He gazed down into her eyes, studying the sadness within them. "Everything about you, your life, your heart, matters. Especially to me."

He didn't know where the words had come from, though he knew they were true, spoken from the deepest recesses of his heart. They were not married. She was not his responsibility. But he wanted to be her protector, the one who soothed her. He did not want her to think, for even a moment, that she did not matter.

"Ivy. Tell me true. What has happened?"

She swallowed and lowered her gaze to the level of his cravat. "I disappointed my family. Fanny, and likely William. I didn't behave how I ought to behave. The way a *lady* ought to behave."

His fingers tightened slightly, and her head tipped up in response. "What do you mean, the way a lady ought to behave? Did I miss something? Did you turn a handspring after your performance? Or perhaps you tripped the next lady to go up? Or were you saying slanderous things about the duchess?"

She made a soft sound that could have been a laugh, but he suspected her throat remained closed from her tears. "Teague. Don't be ridiculous."

"Then you don't be ridiculous," he returned with a gentle smile. "I cannot imagine for a moment you did a single thing that one could call unladylike."

Her head shook in denial. "I was too emotional as I played. The piece wasn't the right choice."

"I have never been so moved as I was, watching you." He touched her cheek, inwardly upset it was a gloved finger that skimmed along her jaw. "You brought tears to my mother's eyes. We thought it beautiful."

Her cheeks regained some color, and uncertainty replaced her sorrow. "Fanny said it was shameful, the way I played."

"Fanny is a miserly woman and ought to be ashamed she hurt you," he said immediately, without a touch of respect. "If kindness were coin, she'd be a pauper. How dare she say a word against you?"

"She is my brother's wife—"

"Then how dare *he* allow it?" he countered, more heat in his voice, though he tried to temper himself for her sake. "The more I learn of this woman, the less patience I have for her. She has done her best to chip away at the most beautiful parts of your soul to shape you into some cold, helpless creature meant for display rather than the joys of life. Do *not* let her do it anymore, Ivy."

She stepped back from him, lowering her gaze. "William and Fanny have done so much for me. You do not understand all the sacrifices they have made. All the things put up with after my father died. They've done their duty by me and by my sisters. They have done so much for me."

"That may be true. But have they loved you enough, Ivy?"

HER EYES RAISED TO HIS IN SURPRISE AS HIS QUESTION seemed to hit her like a slap. No—like a revelation. A shocking one. She had never asked herself that question. It hadn't seemed relevant, given all the things she owed her brother and sister-in-law. Fanny was always going on about how important it was to show her gratitude.

"I suppose they have loved me—and Betony and Juniper—in their own way."

His gaze turned far too serious. "But was it enough? Was it what you needed?" He leaned closer, both his hands coming to take up one of hers. "Did you feel loved and cherished?"

It was a strange question for him to ask, perhaps, given he had offered for her without loving her himself. Ivy didn't let herself dwell on that. Instead, she focused on his words. On what he was really asking.

They had treated her with fondness, at times. Most often, though, she had felt tolerated until she did something out of step with William or Fanny's expectation. Then she had mostly felt like an annoyance.

Her eyes pricked with the threat of more tears. She looked up at Teague with shock. "No. I suppose I did not."

"I thought as much," he said as his expression softened, the usual teasing glint in his eyes nowhere to be seen. Instead, he seemed lit from within by a profound gentleness that made her heart twist. "You deserve so much more, Ivy. You deserve to be loved, to be valued and cherished for yourself, not for the way you behave in public. Not for whether you meet expectations set by someone else. For your own self."

For so long, she had equated William and Fanny's strict expectations and criticisms with love, believing that their guidance was for her benefit. She remembered countless moments of trying to mold herself into the image of perfection they demanded, each attempt leaving her feeling less like herself and more like a beautifully decorated porcelain doll, admired for its appearance but void of warmth.

She had questioned whether her father hadn't prepared her enough for adulthood. Wondered if he had somehow failed her, yet she had never dared to give voice to the thought. Her father had loved her, cherished her, and nourished her curiosity and passions. He had encouraged her.

Somehow, Ivy had let William and Fanny's disapproval hold more weight in her heart than her father's love. Yet in the last several weeks at Clairvoir, in a home where loved ones teased and talked, encouraged one another and laughed together, she had felt confused. Utterly and completely confused that she never heard anyone give censure. Never seen the duchess wince at a word or action undertaken by her children, by their spouses. Indeed, the duke and his wife were quick to laugh. Quick to praise.

For the first time since her father's death, Ivy had felt happier, more like herself. No one had turned away from her, either. Her cousins had sought out her company. People seemed to enjoy being around her. Juniper and Betony were acting with greater confidence.

She looked up at Teague, seeing the intensity of his stare as he waited, patiently, for her to speak. He never rushed her. Never discounted what she said. He teased and flirted and he listened. Intently. As though she mattered.

"Why do you like me?" she dared ask.

His brow wrinkled. "Now that's quite the question."

Where William and Fanny had often been quick to point out her flaws, Teague had celebrated her strengths. His laughter and shared moments of genuine joy felt like a balm to the wounds of her spirit, wounds she had not fully acknowledged until now. Teague's concern for her happiness, his easy acceptance of her emotions, and his encouragement for her to express herself freely made her feel seen and valued.

"Do you have an answer for it?" She needed one. Desperately.

His gloved hand brushed her cheek again as he studied her closely. Measuring words, perhaps. Fitting the right ones in the right place. "The first time I saw you in that theater box, watching the play as though you wished you were part of it, I thought you charming. The joy and excitement on your face, merely to be a part of a crowd watching the story unfold, stirred my interest. When you were here, I thought myself the most fortunate man in all of Britain." His lips curled upward in a smile. "There are whole lists of things I like about you, my darling. Every time I see you, every time you speak, there are more reasons for it. I think it will always be that way for me."

His answer had exceeded anything she hoped for. She covered his gloved hand on her cheek with her own. "You like me for my own self."

A slow nod confirmed her words. "I do." His eyes softened, crinkling at the corners as he regarded her with a fond smile. "I always have. I always will."

It was quite the promise.

"When we are wed, Ivy, our home will be a place where you are always free to say what you wish, play the piano how you wish, read what you wish. Your sisters, they will come with us and never know a moment's unkindness. Juniper can read her novels and spout her opinions unchecked. Betony can smile and laugh without anyone quieting her."

Her heart warmed as he spoke, and she leaned into the palm against her cheek. He meant every word he said. He would provide the sort of home she had grown up in, and he would give her the freedoms she longed to have.

A new realization settled in her heart. The place he wanted to give her would not be at all what he said, not unless he was there. It was Teague who would make wherever she was feel like home.

"It will be grand," he said, everything about him seeming perfect to her in that moment. He looked as though he would say more, his lips slightly parted, hesitation in his eyes—

The door opened slowly, giving them both plenty of time to lower their hands and step apart. Sterling entered, eyes on the ground as he bowed. "My lord, my lady. The entertainment is nearly at its close."

Teague's smile turned crooked. "Is it now? I suppose we had

better return, then, to make our announcement. If you still wish for that, Ivy?"

She relaxed and nodded. "Indeed. I think it is past time for it." She took his arm and he led her past Sterling, whose handkerchief she returned with a grateful smile.

CHAPTER 20

"I have never been so humiliated in my life." The calm, icy tone Fanny used made all three of the sisters wince. William stared at his wife with an incredulous frown. They were in the sitting room assigned to the ladies, the room that connected Ivy's bedchamber to Juniper and Betony's. "How could you agree to this, Ivy? Marrying an Irish baron? And announcing it like that, after your inappropriately emotional performance!"

The memory of Teague's arms about her, his look of pride when he announced their engagement, kept Ivy from apologizing. Her betrothed had praised her performance and found beauty in the way her emotions influenced the music. She much preferred his kindness to her sister-in-law's criticism.

Fanny's reaction was not at all what Ivy expected; she acted as though personally insulted by Ivy's decision. Ivy cut a look to William but found him staring at his wife with perplexity.

"His Grace thought it a good time to make our engagement known," she said slowly, clearly.

"But you said yes to him. Without consulting your brother or me first." Fanny clutched a handkerchief in one hand and the arm of her chair in the other. Her knuckles were white. "After we brought a suitable husband with us, practically delivering him into your hand, this is how you repay our generosity? Our thoughtfulness?" Perhaps that was the issue at hand, then. Fanny didn't like her own plans circumvented.

Ivy kept her spine straight as a steel rod. "I am of age. When Lord Dunmore proposed, I knew nothing of your coming, nor of Lord Martin. I made the decision that best suited me. I still think it best, too."

The scornful, sharp laugh Fanny emitted made Ivy wince. "A selfish, foolish decision. You cannot let her go through with this, William." When she turned to her husband, Ivy did as well.

William stared at his wife with a bemused expression and said, slowly, "We are already in negotiations. Lord Dunmore is a fine choice, and he offers much for Ivy in both stability and respectability. I have no objection to the match. She will be a baroness."

"An Irish baroness, which may as well be an Irish scullery maid," Fanny insisted, tone growing petulant. "Honestly, William. How can you condone this?"

Never before had Ivy seen her half-brother and his wife at odds with a decision. That he didn't fall in step with Fanny this time surprised her, and likely the others in the room, too. "I gave Ivy my preferences for her marriage prospects before she left London. Lord Dunmore fulfills all my expectations. What's more, he seems to genuinely like her. I think he will make my sister quite happy."

Fanny's eyebrows threatened to become one with her hairline. "Like her? Happy? They barely know one another. Think of the scandal."

"The Duke and Duchess of Montfort have overseen their interactions and have vouched for Lord Dunmore. I cannot think of anyone who could object under those circumstances."

William's tone crept toward impatience. "The Frost family is already connected, intimately, with the Dinards. Lord Dunmore's sister is the future Duchess of Montfort."

The red in Fanny's cheek marked her as someone who objected to *all* the circumstances. Strongly.

Daring a glance at Juniper, Ivy saw her sister as startled by the unfolding conversation as herself. Betony's hands gripped each other tightly. It seemed Fanny and William had not discussed the matter at all. Fanny had not even known of the engagement until they had announced it before everyone went home or turned in for the evening. William had not thought to tell his wife, and she had not thought a monumental decision regarding his sisters would be made without her.

"Be that as it may, it was wrong of her to keep us ill-informed of her intentions. If she meant to chase after an Irish baron, she ought to have told us."

Heat flared from Ivy's chest up her throat and into her cheeks. "I did not chase after anyone," she said, her words firm. "I behaved myself as a lady ought."

"I somehow doubt that."

Juniper opened her mouth, her brow furrowed, and Betony looked ready to jump to her feet, so Ivy moved first. She stood, chin up, arms at her side. "I have conducted myself in a manner that is appropriate for a lady and I have been respectful to my hosts. I have done nothing wrong. In fact, for the first time in ages, I have happily been myself. Lord Dunmore found that to his liking and proposed. I found him to *my* liking and agreed. After discussing several important points, I might add, including his acceptance of my sisters into his household."

Better to get it all out now, she knew.

Fanny gaped at her, then looked at William. "What does she mean, husband?"

"Lord Dunmore has agreed to take over guardianship of Juniper and Betony until they come of age or wed." William massaged his temples. His forehead was wrinkled and his mouth turned down in a frown. "As you have made it quite clear that looking after them is a drain on your energy and time, that you would rather focus on our own children, I thought it an excellent suggestion. I have already agreed."

"Without speaking to me first?" Fanny's voice went uncomfortably high for all of them, but William managed not to wince. "We cannot give your sisters into the control of a near-barbarian."

A spike of indignation prodded Ivy to speak before William formed a response to that unflattering opinion.

"Lord Dunmore sits in Lords," Ivy said, tone cool. "He is a respected Peer of the Realm. He is a guest of the duke and a gentleman. Do not call him anything less within my hearing again."

Betony's happy gasp was immediately drowned by Fanny's impatient huff.

"How dare you speak to me like this? After everything I have done, all the sacrifices I have made, the patience I have shown. What ingratitude and disrespect—"

"Fanny." William's low warning tone caught them all by surprise. "What is the meaning of this? Why are you acting as though Ivy's engagement is a personal affront to you? To us?"

"You cannot mean to say you approve of how she spoke to me—"

"She will be a married woman in three weeks. She has every right to defend her husband, as I would hope you would speak to defend me if someone called me a barbarian within your hearing." William no longer looked perplexed so much as weary. "It is done, Fanny. The negotiations are underway. Ivy will marry Lord Dunmore and become Lady Dunmore. So long as Juniper and Betony have no objections, they will go to live with her after they have returned to our home and supervised the packing of their things. Of course," he turned to his younger sisters, "if either of you are uncomfortable with the circumstances, we may discuss them. You will always have a home with us."

"Thank you," Juniper said. "I would like to go with Ivy, please."

"As would I," Betony added quickly, perched on the edge of her seat. "Ireland sounds lovely."

Fanny finally rose to her feet, hands clutched over her heart. "After everything we have done for you." Then she turned to William. "You would trust *Ivy* to look after the other two?"

"She will be married." William gave his wife an incredulous frown. "It is perfectly appropriate, and they all seem to have turned out well enough. Fanny, I thought you would be relieved."

So had Ivy. Fanny had only really ever made her feel like a burden. William had tolerated them all, with occasional moments of fondness, but really, he had mostly left Fanny to see to them.

"We are grateful, Fanny," Ivy said, having to keep her head still lest it shake and deny the words as she spoke them. "You took care of us after Father's passing. Now you are free to see to your own concerns."

For a moment, Fanny looked affronted, then she glowered. "An Irish baron. Well. You have made your bed, Ivy Amberton. I hope you enjoy your lie-in."

Ivy shocked herself and everyone else by laughing. "I truly think I will. I feel happier and more myself in this moment than I have felt in years."

Fanny gasped. "Well, I never!"

Ivy thought of Teague, of his wit, his quick tongue and charm, and said with a grin, "That is a shame, Fanny. Perhaps you will in future."

Fanny sniffed in offense and swept out of the door without waiting for William.

He stood, slowly, and looked at Ivy. "Perhaps she is merely shocked. It will be a significant change in our household."

Ivy voiced her thoughts on the matter with more gentleness. "She needs to feel important, I think. A new project may help."

William looked at his three sisters, appearing somewhat concerned for them, as though he did not know if he ought to leave them or if there was something more he should say. "Ivy. Congratulations. I am certain Fanny will come to see the good points of your match. Juniper. Betony. Good night."

She had never felt so thankful for Teague's place in her life. In the weeks since she had met him, he had told her to trust to her own happiness and judgement. Without his kindness, his gentle encouragement, she would have crumbled completely under Fanny's disapproval, if only to keep the peace.

After the door shut behind him, Ivy looked at her sisters. "I had not expected this evening to go in that direction. Not in the least."

Juniper's smile was soft and encouraging. "Well, it seems our evenings have become far more thrilling than any society ball. Who knew our sitting room could rival the theaters of London for drama?"

Betony, quick to find the humor in any situation, chimed in with a wistful sigh, "And here I thought our lives would be limited to choosing ribbons and attending teas. Now we're to be the heroines of our very own adventure, living among the barbarians of Ireland."

Ivy, despite the seriousness of their discussion, could not help but smile at her sisters' attempts to restore their good humor. "Indeed, we must ensure our decorum is impeccable, lest we scandalize the Irish with our English manners."

Their shared laughter was a gentle balm to the evening's tensions, a reminder of the joy and resilience that lay at the heart of their family.

"I daresay," Ivy added with a twinkle in her eye, "our experiences in Ireland shall make for the most captivating theatrical. *The Amberton Sisters: An English Adventure in the Wilds of Ireland.* How does that sound for a title?"

Betony nodded, her eyes alight with mischief, "Splendid! But let us not forget to dedicate a scene to navigating the perilous waters of family gatherings. Or it could be its own play entirely. *The Great Engagement Announcement: A Comedy of Manners.*"

As their laughter filled the room once more, Ivy's profound gratitude for her sisters kept her worries over Fanny's reaction at bay. She and Teague would marry, her sisters would be with her, and they would build a new family. A happier one. Imagining Teague sitting with her, laughing as Betony went on dramatically and gently teasing Juniper into sharing her own thoughts, came quite easily. That she could picture him as part of their conversation, seamlessly fitting the sisters into his life, made the last of her anxiety over Fanny's outburst fade away.

She had made the right choice. She knew it. Felt it in her heart. Teague was the right choice. He was everything she had hoped for, and quite a few things she had not even thought she needed.

Thinking of him made something inside her feel aglow, like a lamp in the window lighting her way home.

All would be well.

CHAPTER 21

The day after the musical performance and Teague's betrothal announcement, a large party of the house guests summoned carriages for a trip to Lambsthorpe, the local village. The Amberton sisters had all piled into the same carriage as Isleen, Lady Josephine, and Lady Atella. The men accompanying them, Teague included, elected to ride on horseback.

"A terrible idea, most likely," Lord Atella said cheerfully as they discussed the decision, riding ahead of the ladies' carriage. "We are giving them yet more time to discuss the men in their lives while we are not present to defend ourselves or refute their claims."

"Lady Ivy, as a newly engaged member of their set, will likely be treated to an extensive discourse on the management of a husband." Sir Andrew sounded far too cheerful, almost gleeful, about that prospect.

That the baronet relished the idea told Teague exactly how disastrous it might be, but Simon looked over his shoulder and gave Teague a broad grin. "Given that Dunmore's sister is one of the married ladies dispensing advice, he ought to be terrified."

Teague gave an easy shrug, his mood eased rather than irritated by the banter. "I am neither afraid nor intimidated. If you lot can survive matrimony, I am certain I shall find great success in the endeavor."

The good-natured teasing did not rile him in the least, though he noticed one of the gentlemen with them looked less amused than the majority. Lord Martin had applauded with the rest the evening before, not appearing surprised at the announcement thanks to Ivy's brother speaking to him ahead of time. He had known Ivy too short a time to have developed any feelings for her, yet Teague could well imagine the frustration of being thwarted at winning such a lady's favor.

Had Teague's offer to Ivy ended with her choosing Lord Martin—the thought itself caused a feeling rather like a knife through the ribs. He had been fortunate she had chosen him, all things considered. Incredibly so. While comforting her the evening before, holding her in his arms, he had found himself grateful he was the one to offer understanding, reassurance, and...other things. Things he hesitated to name just yet.

He'd lost himself in thought and came back to the present amid the men's laughter.

An unexpected warmth flooded him as he took in the ease of being in their company. Simon began to regale them with an anecdote from a London ball involving an overly enthusiastic member of Commons attempting to solicit the duke's support through delivering a speech to Isleen while dancing with her.

Lord Atella chimed in, his tone light but the joke sharp, "Imagine, Teague. This will be your bride soon, dodging the pitfalls of a politician's life with the agility of a seasoned dancer."

Laughing, Teague shook his head. "I expect I shall step on more toes than she ever would," he admitted, sincere yet unconcerned. "Lady Ivy has a better understanding of polite English conversation than I do."

"Likely true. Wise of you, to take an Englishwoman as your

bride," Sir Andrew said with a chuckle. "My lady-wife thinks your betrothed a good fit for the job."

"I think my *contessa* makes a far better ambassador than I ever will," Lord Atella quipped.

Lord Martin, who had seemed likely to continue the ride in silence, offered a remark. "I've found the key to navigating the world of English politics is knowing whom to trust and whom to steer clear of." Lord Martin's gaze briefly met Teague's. "It seems you are off to a solid start, given your choice of bride and aligning with this lot."

The remark, meant in jest, struck a chord with Teague. Glancing around at the group, he realized that amidst the laughter and shared stories, he had woven a thread of friendship he hadn't anticipated. Simon, Sir Andrew, and Lord Martin—the duke, too—were English to their core. Yet they were not the adversaries he had long expected to face on every front. Instead, they were allies. Even friends.

Lord Atella, the only true foreigner present, spoke with his usual thoughtfulness. "It is often the unexpected friendships that stand the tests of time and trials. It seems like you will be bound to us in more ways than you might have guessed, Lord Dunmore."

As they approached the village, the lighthearted conversation not only reassured Teague, but subtly softened his view of his future in Parliament. Perhaps, just perhaps, there was a place for an Irishman among the English—in politics, and certainly in these growing bonds of friendship.

After they arrived in Lambsthorpe, the gentlemen dismounted and Simon handed each of the ladies out of the carriage. The women looked no worse for their ride together, and indeed came out into the sun with laughter and bright expressions.

Teague had every intention of giving his escort to Ivy immediately, but before he could, her sisters darted forward and each took an arm.

"Oh, no you don't, Teague." Betony gave him a broad grin most would think unbecoming a lady of nineteen years.

Juniper's smile wasn't as wide, but it still had a teasing curve to it. "Quite right. Ivy may have agreed to wed you, and William might approve, but you have yet to secure our blessing."

He looked over their heads at Ivy and found her pressing her lips together, as though to keep herself from speaking, yet the way her eyes danced told him she found the whole situation entertaining.

Hm. He didn't mind entertaining her or her sisters in the slightest, not when it made her dark eyes dance like that. He played along, releasing a sigh and a shudder of dread. "I had thought to circumvent the two of you entirely. Alas, you're both too cunning."

Betony, despite being the youngest sister, seemed to possess the most confidence, at least when she was not under the eye of her sister-in-law. Given the way Ivy and Juniper had reacted that afternoon when he had rescued the younger woman from a simple conversation, Teague suspected the two of them had done much to protect Betony from the countess's sharp tongue and criticisms.

"Indeed, we are quite artful and wily," Juniper said with a dry tone and a little roll of her eyes. "How ever will you manage adding all three of us to your household? It will be constant chaos."

He couldn't help but chuckle. "I welcome such, I assure you. Though Fiona is likely to make anything the two of you get up to look relatively tame."

"Oh! I get to be a big sister of sorts," Betony said suddenly. "I hadn't stopped to consider it. Do you think you will mind if I set a very poor example for Fiona?"

"How could you? Isleen has already done that work for

you," he quipped, noting his married sister was within hearing distance.

In every family, there were often patterns and roles played out time and again, things that the members of the family accepted without knowing it. Adding a wife would necessarily put most of the burden of learning how to be part of the family on her. But bringing Betony and Juniper into his household, his life, meant learning about them. Their roles. The dynamics the sisters shared.

Isleen did not let his statement remain unchallenged, as she turned about while on the arm of her husband and raised her eyebrows at him. "I am the very best example of femininity and strength, Teague Frost. That you do not know how to cope with it is a mark against you, not me."

Betony snickered and Juniper ducked her head, smiling.

It struck him as an intriguing challenge to meld their families and discover how they would all fit together. Fiona, Máthair, and himself adding three entirely new people to their home would necessitate many changes. Most of them, he hoped, pleasant. Thankfully, Teague loved a good challenge.

Ivy sighed, hands lightly clasped before her. "If this is how every family conversation will be, I wonder that you have not yet lost your sanity, my dear."

It was the first time she had used an endearment for him, however mild, and it made his heart tick a touch faster. He sent a grin her way, hoping to show his full appreciation.

Lord Martin had approached, an appropriately friendly smile in place. "It seems your sisters have robbed you of your betrothed, Lady Ivy. Might I dare to offer my arm until such time as you can reclaim his?" There was nothing in the man's disposition that suggested jealousy.

He was a good man. He'd likely have been a fine fit for Ivy, too. Yet Teague was grateful he had asked for her hand first, and more so that she had chosen the Irishman over the Englishman rather insistently.

Ivy accepted Lord Martin's arm, and the large party broke into smaller pieces as they roamed the village. Teague allowed Betony and Juniper to direct him while he played escort. Lord Martin and Ivy following along behind, snatches of their casual conversation occasionally meeting his ears.

Devoting himself to the younger Amberton sisters felt important. Becoming a brother-in-law to Juniper and Betony would, apparently, mean being as much a target of their teasing as it meant being their guardian.

They entered the shop of books and stationary sundries, a tidy establishment with a lending library and shelves full of uncut paper, bottles of ink, and pens in cases on display. Betony explored the ink, releasing Teague's arm in her eagerness to ask questions of the shopkeeper. Juniper's eyes lingered on the shelves of books, though.

Teague drew her toward them after a quick glance at Lord Martin, who nodded and kept Ivy near the youngest sister.

"Have you as much interest in literature as Ivy?" he asked Juniper.

She lowered her head and her cheeks went pink. "I am not certain you could call my favorite things to read 'literature,' so much as 'written follies.' I prefer a Gothic novel over a centuries-old romance. Ivy reads Daniel Defoe and Jonathan Swift. I prefer Anne Radcliffe, Percy Shelley, Robert Huish. Francis Lathom."

He raised his eyebrows, finding it difficult to believe Lady Haverford approved of such sensational novels. "Your personal library is full of thrilling adventure and darkest towers, then, isn't it?"

"Oh. No." She shook her head a little. "I do not keep them. I borrow them from libraries or friends who share my interest. I haven't any place to put books of my own. My brother and his wife insist that all books in the household belong in one place, and Fanny wouldn't countenance *Italian Mysteries* being on the same shelf as something she deems more respectable. Displaying books of that sort would not give the right impression of the family."

"I had not really thought the purpose of bookshelves to give a good impression. Except, perhaps, when it comes to showing a care for reading. Perhaps a glimpse of the personality and values of the reader." He looked at the books on display in the shop, and his mind immediately went to a title he recognized by Stanhope. *The Crusaders*. He plucked it from the shelf and held it out to Juniper.

"Have you read this one?"

She took the book gingerly and her eyebrows raised. "Oh, no. I have read her other books. *The Nun of Santa Maria Di Tindaro* was a favorite." She opened the book and saw the slip of paper inside marking it as available to be lent or bought. "I will take it back with me this very day."

"Excellent. What else shall we add to your list today?" He took up another book. "*The Munster Cottage Boy?*"

"Oh. I have already read that one."

"Yes, but would you like to add it to your permanent collection?" He waited, hand extended to pluck the book from the shelf.

Juniper stared at him a moment, uncomprehending. "But...I already told you, I do not keep the books."

Teague tucked his hands behind his back and fixed her with the most serious stare he was capable of, the one that made the opposition in Lords brace themselves for a long argument. "Juniper, my soon-to-be-sister, from this moment forward, you will have a personal collection of books. A whole library, should you wish it. We will keep it at Dunmore House in Ireland, in any room you wish, private or public, until the day you make your home elsewhere. Then we will pack them up in as many crates as it takes and send them along with the rest of your personal effects."

One would think he had just handed her the crown jewels, the way she gasped. Then, throwing aside what he had come to think of as her usual stoicism, Lady Juniper Amberton embraced him. Right there in the shop.

Lady Haverton certainly would not have approved.

When he returned Juniper's hug with a gentle pat on her shoulder, he looked over her head to see Ivy watching them with wide eyes. She came across the shop, looking from her sister to Teague.

"Is something wrong? Juniper?"

Juniper stepped back, wiping at her eyes, and wrapped her arms around Ivy instead. "It is a good thing you are marrying him, Ivy, or I would kidnap him to Gretna Green at once. He is going to let me have novels!"

Ivy's look of confusion melted away and the warm smile she gave Teague was enough to make him willing to buy all the books in that shop, that very instant, if she would keep looking at him like that. "That is marvelous, Juniper."

"Quite a good thing we are to be family, then, as I do not care for the idea of being kidnapped and wed across an anvil." He smiled at them both and picked up another Gothic-sounding novel. "What of this one?"

Juniper turned to the serious matter of taking books from the shelves to add to her arms. They were all used, lent out by the shopkeeper, but he would see to it that she had prettier editions with custom binding soon enough.

Ivy gave him another look of soft gratitude, then drifted back to where Betony and Lord Martin were discussing the benefits of the new pens over using quills. Teague watched her go with a sense of anticipation stirring in his chest. Something about the way Ivy had looked at him made him think, perhaps anticipate, a different sort of thanks shown him in future. If being generous with her sisters made her that happy, he would buy up everything the village had on offer.

"What does Betony like?"

Juniper was distracted by her growing pile of books and spoke without turning. "Beads. Embroidery. She is very good at making things look pretty."

He grinned and looked over his shoulder, catching Ivy's eye when she glanced his way again. The way her cheeks pinked was apparent even from where he stood.

"Then we're off to the sewing and sundries shop next."

FOLLOWING HER SISTERS ABOUT AS TEAGUE SPOILED THEM with purchases and treats made Ivy feel rather light-headed. Her betrothed took in everything her sisters said with cheeriness and the occasional serious frown. He had not mocked them, teased them beyond what was entertaining, or belittled them and their conversation even once.

Not that she had expected him to. She had seen him with his own sisters, of course, and found his behavior endearing. Somehow, she had not expected his actions would move her so much as they had.

Lord Martin, to his credit, was friendly and seemingly amused by the situation as he escorted her from one shop to the next. "Your sisters are enamored by Lord Dunmore. Tell me, in future when I wish to court a lady, is the swiftest way to her heart through the people she cares for?"

She gave him a sideways glance, though she detected no bitterness in his words. His curiosity seemed genuine enough. "I imagine such things vary from lady to lady, Lord Martin. Though I would wager you are kind to everyone, as a rule, I cannot think it would be a hardship for you to behave that way."

He gave a little shrug as they entered the bakery and coffee house. "Perhaps not. Though seeing the man in action has made me wonder if I would be so quick to act as a brother to those I barely knew. He is a good man. It has been a pleasure to meet him, in all truth. And a pleasure to meet his future baroness."

While they waited at a small table for the others to join them, Ivy gave Lord Martin what she hoped he would see as a kind smile. "I am sorry things did not work out the way you wished."

"As am I. However, rather than be resentful, I think it better to declare myself pleased to have come here at all. I am now on more familiar terms with some of the most powerful men in Britain. I do not have the good fortune to leave Clairvoir with a wife; but I leave with a better position for my own political ambitions."

She laughed at that. "You have a gift for optimism, your lordship." She sipped at her coffee. Some said that tea would overtake coffee in terms of popularity, but Ivy doubted one drink would ever outdo the other in permanence. She liked both far too much to choose a favorite for herself.

"Indeed. Ah," he stood and bowed. "Lady Farleigh. Would you join us?"

"I would like that, very much. Though, Lord Martin, I seem to have lost my husband to a debate with Lord Atella. They are yet now in the street, trying to determine the fate of the world when it comes to a tax on imported coffees. Would you be so kind as to break their tie? Perhaps then they will join us." She settled with the grace befitting a future duchess, removing her gloves at the table.

"Of course, my lady." He bowed and a moment later the bell over the door merrily announced his leave-taking.

Isleen gave Ivy a commiserating smile. "I saw your sisters delaying Teague as well, to stare at hats through the milliner's window next door. I think they have wrapped him around their little fingers. Smart ladies. Teague will move mountains to make the people he cares for happy."

Ivy poured coffee for her future sister-in-law. "I am coming to understand that, yes. He has a generous heart." She took up her own cup once more. "It makes me wonder, though, who looks out for him in that way. He is forever showing kindness to everyone around him. Does he receive as much as he gives?"

"Doubtfully." Isleen winced somewhat. "The two of us used to look out for one another, but I felt at every turn he saw more of my needs than I did of his. That you have noticed this habit of his reassures me, though. If you have noticed his affection through his actions, then you know how devoted he already is to you."

Warmth spread from her heart through the rest of her. Yes, Ivy had noticed. He had shown kindness from the beginning, and his attraction through his touch, glance, and that stolen kiss. Yet it was not until he had spoken of his care and understanding aloud that she realized what all the little gestures had added up to—something stronger than mere affection.

"I wonder," she murmured aloud, not strictly expecting an answer, "if that is how best he would receive a declaration of devotion, through action rather than words. Though I confess, I often do not believe a thing until I hear it spoken. Words are powerful things."

"You speak as though the two are separate languages. Action and words." Isleen chuckled and wrinkled her nose. "I would have both."

"As would I," Ivy said with a laugh. "Yet I cannot deny they are not equal in my heart." Perhaps they were not equal in Teague's. Her words of reassurance, that she wished for their engagement to continue, had not seemed to penetrate his understanding. Not until she had fairly demanded that they make the announcement of their betrothal. He had seemed to float about the castle since that moment.

Perhaps he needed action more than he needed reassurances.

When he came into the bakery a moment later, Juniper and Betony chatting with excitement, she met his gaze for what seemed like the hundredth time during the outing. His eyes sparkled with amusement, his smile stretched wide across his handsome face, and he winked at her.

Despite a desire to duck her head as a modest lady ought, Ivy winked back. Somehow, his smile grew warmer, his posture more relaxed.

Ivy was determined to show him exactly how much she had come to adore him at the first available opportunity.

CHAPTER 22

"The thing about Catholic emancipation at this juncture is simply that other things take precedence," Lord Haverton spouted from his place standing near the hearth in the library. "I do not disagree that the practice of keeping men of faith from taking part in the government is archaic. However, there are still many concerned with the fact that orders could come from the Pope himself, giving Rome a say in matters where it ought not have any say."

The men of the house party were scattered about in the library, a few of them with pipes in hand, some sitting in chairs, others lounging on couches, and a few standing like Haverton. The windows were open to keep the scents from settling and letting in cooler air from the courtyard below.

Teague was near the doorway, arms folded, trying to keep his tongue in check. Haverton had not expressed his own view, only one that was generally held by his party. The Irishman cut a glance to Simon and then the duke. Simon was staring out the window, back to the room, listening more than speaking. His father, though, sat in a chair near the hearth with the look of a king sitting upon a throne.

He spoke with a measured tone. "The majority of our Parliament is made up of Anglicans, whose official head is the king himself. Yet we have a fair share of Protestants, Methodists, Agnostics, and the like. I believe the only time a man's religion ought to be considered is when he proclaims to loudly follow its tenets and then proves himself dishonorable by going against what he has sworn to uphold. Which is, I am afraid, most of our government's representatives."

Teague lowered his gaze to the carpet and allowed himself a smile. The duke's library hosted nearly two dozen men that day. Most were guests at the castle or at the Lambsthorpe inn, as they had a hunt planned for the next day, and everyone was enjoying His Grace's hospitality for the evening.

"I believe we will see a change in the way we regard Catholics before the end of the decade," another gentleman remarked, a representative from Commons. "It is something the people want. Something they deserve. Lord Atella could tell us, I am certain, that there are politicians throughout Europe who attend Catholic mass and are not told how to vote or rule by the Pope."

The Ambassador for the Kingdom of the Two Sicilies tipped his head forward in acknowledgement. "It is true enough. Only those angling for service to Rome would consider such a thing necessary. We are in a more modern era. While religion may play a part in a man's life, we see it less and less when it comes to governance. Science and philosophy hold higher esteem. Things that are provable, regardless of what one believes."

Sir Andrew, standing near Teague, leaned closer. "Not chiming in today?"

"I haven't the desire to argue at present," Teague answered with a shrug. "I am in too good a mood."

"Yes, I suppose love will do that to a man," the baronet said with a smirk. "One cannot be bitter while also being besotted."

The word *love* stirred Teague's mind and heart. Though he had yet to say it directly to Ivy, he had not been able to stop expressing it. Not when he had stolen a thousand glances at her over the past several days, not when he had held her in his arms after her musical performance, and possibly not since the beginning.

It was an odd thought to turn over in a library, surrounded by men and pipe smoke. Yet one could hardly help when or where an epiphany came into being. Teague stood still, letting the acceptance of his feelings sweep through him like flood waters, spreading widely, seeping into every inch of his heart and mind until he the tenderness he felt for Ivy saturated his being.

He loved her. Fully. Completely.

A soft hissing sound snapped him from his startling revelation, making his eyes dart down, then behind him. Standing between Teague and the wall, crouched as though to keep himself hidden, was Lord James.

The boy's eyes darted from Teague across the room to where his father, the duke, was speaking again about the state of prejudice that existed in Parliament. The lad obviously had no wish to be seen.

"Lord Dunmore," he whispered, his eyes comically wide. "Fiona needs you." He jerked his head toward the doorway, then hurriedly slinked along the wall to slip out of it.

Teague glanced at Sir Andrew, who raised his eyebrows. "Do not look at me. I have been involved in more misadventures with the children of this castle than can possibly be fair. Off you go. See what the little miscreants want."

As the conversation in the room had been informal, Teague did not take his leave of the crowd. He left the room without haste, however. In a true emergency, a servant would have come for him. Lord James and Fiona were obviously plotting something.

He came out into the corridor and raised his eyebrows at the two of them. Fiona stood in the middle of the long carpet, hands on her hips, and James had joined her with a wide grin on his face.

"We have been looking everywhere for you," his little sister proclaimed. "Now Ivy will think it is our fault that you are taking so long."

That brought him up short. "Ivy sent you?"

Both children nodded rapidly.

"We are supposed to give you a message," James said, puffing out his chest a bit. "Then you must find her."

"But it is not hide and seek," Fiona said with a little scowl. "She only gave us a clue. I think she doesn't want us coming after you both, which means it's something to do with the two of you getting married." She rolled her eyes with disgust. "Are we really going to have the ceremony here at the castle?"

"We are," Teague informed her, opting to be amused rather than impatient with the messengers. "Before we go home to Ireland in September." He looked at James. "What is the message?"

James shrugged. "I have no idea. She told Fiona. Fiona recruited me, but then she didn't want to go in the library with all the men present."

"It smells of tobacco pipes in there," Fiona said with a shake of her curls. "Do you know how awful a smell it is to get out of a lady's hair?"

"Fi," Teague said before she could begin an argument with the duke's youngest. "What is the message?"

"Oh. That. Ivy said she wanted to meet you in the place where you gave her an 'Irish sample.' Whatever in the world did she mean by that, Teague?" His sister tilted her head, curiosity in the gesture. "Did you let her try the toffees we brought from Belfast?"

He cleared his throat. "Something like that." He glanced

back the way he had come, but didn't hesitate a moment more. "Thank you for the message. Now, you had both best get back to the nursery or wherever it is the younger guests are milling about. I'll be off to see Ivy."

"The others are not all that fun." Lord James scrunched up his nose. "Everyone is so stuffy, especially Ivy's nieces and nephews. I'm surprised they haven't already tattled on us for slipping off."

Someone down the corridor cleared his throat. Fiona and James both winced and looked back to see one of the footmen there, his eyebrows raised. The boy huffed. "All right, Brockton. We are coming."

Fiona laughed and gave James a shove. "Told you they would send someone. We are lucky we escaped this long."

"Off with you both," Teague instructed, taking himself to the nearest staircase. "Mind your manners, Fi."

He didn't run through the castle. Even an Irish baron had more respect for proper decorum than that. But he did take the stairs to ground level two at a time and stretched his stride as long as he could to eat up the ground between himself and Ivy as quickly as possible.

The only sample he had given her of anything had been the kiss. If she had brought it up, even through an unlikely messenger like Fiona, he had every hope she had finally decided to ask for a bit more.

What sort of man would he prove to be if he denied her such a thing?

He took the walkway through the rose gardens, down another spot of the terraced gardens, then came along the stone wall to the grotto entrance. He did not pass another soul after the rose gardens.

Yet when the entrance to the Japanese Garden came into sight, his steps momentarily slowed. A sudden weight pressed upon his chest. The echoes of the day's discussions about acceptance and prejudice lingered in his mind, mingling with his worries for his countrymen. His responsibilities as an Irishman, as a peer, a member of Lords, had come first for so long. Yet now he found himself about to take an English bride. While he had found a sympathetic listener in Ivy, he hoped she would never have cause to question his stance on the things that mattered most to his people.

Even as she was now the person who mattered most in all the world to him.

Before stepping through to the Japanese Garden, Teague allowed himself a rare moment of quiet reflection. The garden's tranquility, a stark contrast to the lively debates inside, reflected the serenity he felt whenever he thought of his future with Ivy. Yet with this tranquility came an acute awareness of the profound changes his life was about to undergo.

Marriage was not merely a union but a transformation. Was he ready to be the husband Ivy deserved? She deserved all the love and admiration, all the support and the praise he could give her.

He took a deep breath, letting the fresh air and scent of green and growing things strengthen his resolve. Love meant more than acknowledging a feeling. It meant making a decision to embrace every challenge and the joy that came with it.

When he stepped through to the Japanese Garden, its tall stone walls sheltering the peace within, Teague caught his breath at the picture Ivy made sitting on a bench beneath the sprawling branches of the magnolia tree. The late afternoon light casting dappled shadows through its leaves. The deep green of her gown complemented the lush surroundings, making her appear as a part of the garden itself—an embodiment of the natural beauty around her.

"Ivy, darling. I hear tell you have a need to see me?"

Her dark hair framed her face in soft curls, catching the sunlight and teasing the shadows. The same dark eyes that had so often met his with intelligence and warmth watched him draw nearer, a subtle mischief playing within their depths.

What was she up to?

As Teague approached, she stood, the deep green of her gown highlighting the rosiness of her cheeks and the pink of her lips, which parted slightly in a welcoming smile that held not just affection, but a promise of something more. Something almost secretive.

"Indeed. I' a relieved my messengers found you, and more so that you came. I wished to speak with you in private."

This vision of her, poised and graceful, reinforced all the reasons why he had fallen so irrevocably in love. Ivy was not just his betrothed; she was a revelation, continually defying every expectation he had once held about English ladies. Her strength, her compassion, and her keen mind challenged him, comforted him, and inspired him.

She held her hand out to him and Teague closed the distance between them quickly, taking her hand when near enough and stepping still closer, bringing them nearly toe-to-toe.

"You have my full attention, darling." He loved looking into her eyes. Loved knowing he belonged to her. Knowing that he loved her. She had his whole heart.

"Good." She squared her shoulders, lifted her chin, looked him directly in the eye and said, "*Tá mé i ngrá leat*, Teague Frost." Before he could quite recover from the shock of being told, in the tongue he had learned first, that she was in love with him, Ivy rose up on her toes and kissed him.

What a kiss it was.

Teague stood, momentarily frozen, as the soft, lyrical words in Irish echoed through his heart. The language of his homeland, spoken so tenderly by Ivy, pierced through all worries he had ever held. The earnestness in her voice, the openness in her gaze, undid him.

She loved him, truly and deeply.

As her lips met his, every thought but one vanished: he was utterly and irrevocably hers. Her kiss, fervent and bold, was a seal on a vow he had not even realized he had been waiting to make. The world narrowed to the warmth of her mouth on his, her hands coming up to thread through his hair, pulling him closer, as though she couldn't abide even a small distance between them.

When they finally parted, a need for air pressing them apart, Teague's breaths came in heavy. He rested his forehead against hers, his voice low and full of longing.

"Ivy, my love," he murmured, the words slipping from him as naturally as prayer. "You have captured my heart completely. *Mo ghrá thú*—I love you. More than words in any language can convey."

Her smile was radiant, her cheeks flushed with the same overwhelming affection that filled his chest—a mixture of joy and awe.

"I hoped as much," she whispered, her fingers tracing the line of his jaw tenderly. "I can't imagine going another day without telling you, without showing you how I feel, Teague. Not a single one."

All his remaining uncertainties about their different backgrounds, the challenges they would face together, dissolved under the weight of this truth between them. They were more than a lord and his lady; they were partners, equals in the most important endeavor of their lives.

Proclaiming her love in Irish and kissing the man she loved was the most daring thing Ivy had ever done. Yet she had never felt more certain of anything in her life. All the yearning to be heard, the wishing to be told her thoughts and feelings had value, had quieted in her heart. The more time she had spent with Teague, the more she had felt like herself. His love gifted her that wonderful feeling of acceptance.

"I am so glad we were both at the theater that night," she said, standing in the circle of his arms. He hadn't stepped away after their kiss. He had continued to hold her close, head tipped forward to rest against hers, as though he needed that contact to remain. Needed her to remain by his side.

"Then here at the castle together," he added with a little grin. "Serendipity, indeed."

She laughed and tipped her head up enough to brush a kiss at the corner of his lips. He smiled and turned his head to steal another. She stepped back and looked up at him, her heart full to bursting with happiness. "We are fortunate to have found one another."

"I think it had to have happened, sooner or later, given the ridiculous way the two of us are connected through family." He let her escape his arms but retained a hold on her hand. "My lovely Ivy. My heart. My lady with the multi-hued lenses."

She felt her cheeks warm. "You are an incorrigible flirt."

"Only for you, Ivy."

"Is it flirting even after we marry?"

"Of course. We Irishmen, we always flirt with our wives. It's the best of sports." He gave her one of the crooked grins that made her stomach flutter and her chest grow warm. "Not a day will go by without me trying to make you blush or smile. I'll drive you to distraction at every possible chance."

"I look forward to that," she confessed, squeezing his hand. Her gaze swept over his face, memorizing each line, each curve that had become dear to her. "I will take each day to remind you of my love, in words, in deeds, in every glance shared across any room we enter."

Teague's eyes softened, the dark brown of them reflecting her love back with tenderness. "You've changed my world, Ivy.

Not just by loving me, but by being you. By being the one who sees past the surface, beyond what things are, to how they make you feel. To what they could be."

The sincerity in his voice, the earnestness of his words, stirred something profound within her. This was no simple affection; it was a promise of endless support and devotion.

"Teague," Ivy began, her voice barely above a whisper as she stepped closer again, reclaiming the warmth of his embrace. "I never imagined love could feel like this. Like home. Like the safest harbor after the longest storm."

He chuckled softly, his breath stirring her hair. "I didn't know it could be a grand adventure, one worth every risk." His fingers traced the curve of her waist gently, his touch sending shivers down her spine. "But here we are, about to embark on the greatest journey either of us has ever taken."

She knew there would be challenges ahead, moments of doubt and trials, but with Teague by her side, she felt equipped to face anything. To help *him* face anything.

"I promise you this," she said, leaning back to lock her eyes on his. "No matter what comes, I will support you. With all my heart and unwavering trust."

"Thank you, my love. I will do the very same for you, for the rest of my days." Teague sealed their vow with another kiss. As their lips parted, the world around them seemed to pause, acknowledging the beauty, the depth of their commitment.

Hand in hand, they walked the garden path, their steps light, their hearts full. No matter what the future held, they had already conquered the greatest challenge of all—they had found and chosen each other in a world that often seemed too vast and indifferent. That, she knew, was the truest victory of all.

EPILOGUE

I vy stood at the front of Clairvoir Castle's chapel in a gown of green, trimmed with Irish lace, and holding a bouquet of flowers made up for her by Juniper and Betony. Never in her life had she felt so beautiful, yet she was quite certain she would have felt the same in even the plainest wool gown, given the way Teague looked down into her eyes. It was his love, his adoration, that made her feel like a fairy queen.

The little chapel only held their families. All the duke's other guests had long since departed, and William and Fanny had returned for the ceremony the day before. Tomorrow, they would begin the journey to their home in Ireland, with Betony, Juniper, Fiona, and Máthair Frost, where they would stay until Parliament opened mid-winter.

Every day that had passed since Ivy's confession in the garden, Teague had found a way to tell her he loved her. He had begun to list the things he loved about her, too.

"I love your laugh. It makes me want to tease it out of you at every turn. I love your thoughtful little frowns when you are reading. I love the way you speak of the books you read. I love that you treat everyone around you with respect."

She never grew tired of hearing his declarations, as each one acted as a balm to her heart. When Fanny had criticized her wedding dress that morning, Ivy had laughed with true amusement, and found it a little sad that Fanny tried to spread misery rather than joy.

For Ivy's part, she had endeavored to show Teague how she felt. Every day. She learned more Irish words from his sisters to surprise him, even by asking for silly things in his tongue, like passing the salt at the table. She winked when she caught him staring. She made a point of brushing his hand or arm when she passed near him. And she had whisked him away to private nooks and corners to surprise him with a kiss or two.

Her feelings for him grew, branching out like a tree reaching for the sunlight. She loved him with everything she had, yet startled herself by continuing to grow in that love.

She listened to the words of the vicar and spoke her vows with full feeling, her heart thrumming along happily in cadence with her voice.

"I, Ivy Amberton, take you, Teague Frost, to have and to hold, from this day forward, for better, for worse, for richer, for poorer, in sickness and in health, to love and to cherish, till death do us part...."

The love that shone in his eyes assured her, every time she saw it, that she had come home.

THERE HAD NEVER BEEN A PRETTIER BRIDE THAN IVY, OF that Juniper felt quite certain. Her sister looked lovely in her Irish lace and the deep green her new mother-in-law said was the perfect shade for an Irish bride. Truly, as Juniper watched her sister at the wedding breakfast the duke and duchess had provided, she felt as though her sister's happiness was her own.

Yet after a time, with all the merriment and laughter, Juniper's mind grew far too crowded to sit still amid the sea of voices and clatter of celebration. When the celebratory meal came to a close, she gave Betony a look that her sister knew how to interpret.

Betony raised her eyebrows in a question she needn't voice aloud. *Do you need company?*

Juniper gave a subtle shake of her head, then slipped down a quiet circular stairwell. It led to the bottom of the ballroom stairs and out the doors to the stone terrace.

It was a great relief to know Fanny wouldn't upbraid her for her disappearance later. Earlier that summer, her sister-in-law had proclaimed she had washed her hands of the Amberton sisters and their abilities to behave themselves in public. Truly, having Teague and Ivy take responsibility as guardians until Juniper and Betony wed had been a gift, one Juniper intended to take advantage of.

No more balls. No more hours spent in crowded sitting rooms during visiting days. She would do what Ivy asked her to, of course, but she knew Ivy would give her plenty of room and time spent away from all the noise and bustle of Society.

Truly, Juniper dreaded nothing so much as she did the exhaustion that inevitably followed too much time spent among noisy strangers.

She leaned her elbows on the balustrades, looking down into the tiered gardens, her eyes taking in the landscape she had come to love with true appreciation. She would miss Clairvoir Castle. It represented so much to her now—her freedom, her peace of mind, her tranquility of spirit. Hopefully, Dunmore House would become as dear to her in time. The way Ivy's in-laws spoke of it, it was beautiful and serene.

They were so eager for her and Betony to love it. The sweetness of the Frosts would make up for any disappointments, were there any to be had, as would her already growing library of Gothic and adventure novels.

A small scrape of shoe on stone alerted her to the fact she was no longer alone. Juniper straightened her posture and looked over her shoulder, hoping it was not Fanny, nor anyone else who would demand an exuberant conversation.

It was one of the guardsmen. Sterling. The poor man was dressed in full livery for the wedding celebration, which included a rather stuffy looking white wig. She had to bite her lip to keep from smiling, though she certainly had sympathy for him. September, while cooler than August had been, was not pleasant weather for warm head coverings.

Sometimes, she wondered why the duke did not simply let his guards be guards and his footmen be footmen, but apparently the secret of men like Sterling and their true abilities did not extend outside the family. Therein lay the only benefit Juniper could think of. If one wanted to attack the duke, one would not expect a footman—no matter how strapping and capable in appearance—to whip out a pistol or blade and counter the attack.

It was rather romantic, come to think of it. Certainly something a hero in a Gothic novel would do. Though the heroes usually dealt with brigands and villains themselves, the heroes were not usually dukes of three-score years.

She smiled at Sterling, but he only gave a slight bow and remained a dozen steps away from her.

"I wonder," she said aloud, not certain if he would answer a direct question, "why a guard feels the need to follow me around when I am only distantly related to His Grace. Yet one of you has always been nearby when my sisters or I step out of doors."

His expression remained stoic as ever, but he was looking at her rather than staring vacantly beyond her position. That was something.

"It is rather nice, of course, to know someone is near in case I should have some terrible emergency. Perhaps I will be attacked by a shrubbery." She shivered in pretended horror.

He did not react at all.

A shame, really. He was quite handsome. When he had spoken a time or two, his words spare, he'd had a delightful voice. Low and even. Nothing about it could possibly agitate her, even after a long day of chatter.

"You are excellent company, Sterling," she said, smiling a little. "Certainly my favorite among the guards. It will be strange to leave and not have a protective shadow hovering behind me when I take walks in gardens. Though I imagine you will be most relieved to have only His Grace's immediate family to watch over."

She turned away again and released a little sigh of contentment. "I will miss this place, though I hope to visit it again many times in future. Perhaps I will see you again. But on the chance that will not be the case, thank you for making me feel safe."

For a long moment, she felt certain he would not answer. That was fine. Probably for the best, to be truthful. He was a guard. She was sister to an earl.

Then that low, comforting voice spoke softly. "You are most welcome, Lady Juniper."

She smiled to herself, not turning around. Oh yes. She would look forward to future visits.

If only to hear that voice again.

THANK YOU FOR READING IVY AND TEAGUE'S STORY. I HOPE you've enjoyed it and that you are as excited as I am to return to Castle Clairvoir.

Juniper and Sterling are likely a surprise couple for a few

readers. However will such a pair work out? Make certain you keep up with me so you don't miss their romance. It's going to be a lot of fun.

Sign-up for my newsletter to find out all about what's coming next. (You can do that here: https://geni.us/AuthorSally Britton)

AUTHOR'S NOTES

This is one of my favorite parts of writing a book, because it's on these pages that I get to speak directly to my wonderful reader. Hello, you incredible person! Thank you so much for taking this book in your hands and giving it a chance. Ivy and Teague have been in my head for a very long time, and it's such a great thing to finally share them with others.

Their story is light-hearted, fun, but not without its hiccups. It's also quite personal to me. Throughout our lives, there are people who try to minimize our personalities. A lot of the time, these people are well-meaning. Other times, they are not. "Be small, don't take up space, smile even if you don't feel like it, act your age, etc...."

I believe we should always be kind. But I don't believe that means we should pretend that things are fine when they are not, or that we ought to diminish who we are to please the people around us. We are precious souls with unique views and experiences of the world. We ought to celebrate those things rather than attempt to hide them through conformity. Yes, I realize this is a strange thing for an author of Regency romance to say - because that society was governed by so many rules based entirely on keeping up appearances. But you know who stands out in history from that time period? The people who disregarded those rules.

In case you missed the dedication of this book, this is what it said:

To each woman who's felt pressured to silence her inner voice, may you find the courage to be authentically yourself.

Be you. Skip through the grocery store. Dye your hair blue, pink, green, or black. Wear the earrings that you aren't sure you can pull off—because you can. Sing as loud as you want. Roll your eyes at the people who give you odd looks. (Really, they're just jealous they're not as awesome as you are.) Be authentic, wonderful, fearless, and adamant about being yourself. The people who matter will love you no matter what. And maybe you'll inspire someone who has been silenced and small too long to do the same.

Ivy is my heroine who has been shushed and belittled too long. Teague is my hero who reminds her how wonderful it is for her to be herself.

Go for it, just like Ivy did.

As for my usual notes about historical accuracy, here's my disclaimer: I did my best, I altered a couple of little things to make them fit the story, and I had such fun doing it. Claude Glasses were an especially fun insert. I'd never heard about them before listening to the awesome podcast "The Thing About Austen." I highly recommend it.

Now, my favorite, *favorite* part: Thanking everyone who helped me with this story!

Thank you first and foremost to my critique group - they are incredible authors and you should read all of their books. They are: Laura Beers, Heidi Kimball, Laura Rollins, Mindy

Burbidge Strunk, and Anneka Walker. They really helped, especially toward the end when I was starting to lose my mind.

All my gratitude for my marvelous assistant Marilee Merrell. She is my second brain. My handle on sanity. Truly, she makes it possible for me to focus on the writing while she handles a lot of other complicated stuff. She's amazing.

Many thanks also to my incredible alpha reader, Shaela Kay, who also creates my fabulous covers for this series. She's amazing. Love you, Shaela!

A special thank you to Amanda M., who beta read this novel for me in a pinch! She helped iron out a few things and generally made me feel a lot more comfortable with publishing.

Appreciation also goes to my editors! Emily Poole for her early story support and Karie Crawford for helping me pull it all together at the end.

This one is a little unique, but I must express my appreciation for Camilla Evergreen. She writes contemporary romcom and contemporary fantasy. Her books have recently made my brain happy. If you're neurodivergent and want to read positive, joyful, uplifting depictions of people who struggle with ALL the things, pick up her books. They're lovely.

Last but not least, my undying gratitude for my incredible family must be expressed. Thank you to my husband, who is the best partner in life and my best friend. Also to my children, all four of the delightful little gremlins, for celebrating my successes and hugging me through the difficulties.

I hope you've enjoyed the time you spent in this book and the low-stress world of Clairvoir Castle. I can't wait to have you back for another visit!

Most Happily,
Sally Britton

ALSO BY SALLY BRITTON

CASTLE CLAIRVOIR ROMANCES:

*A Duchess for the Duke | Mr. Gardiner and the Governess | A
Companion for the Count | Sir Andrew and the Authoress | Lord
Farleigh and Miss Frost | Lady Ivy and the Irishman*

THE INGLEWOOD SERIES:

*Rescuing Lord Inglewood | Discovering Grace | Saving Miss Everly |
Engaging Sir Isaac | Reforming Lord Neil*

RETURN TO INGLEWOOD:

Romancing the Artist

DEVOTED HEARTS:

*Martha's Patience | The Social Tutor | The Gentleman Physician | His
Bluestocking Bride | The Earl and His Lady | Miss Devon's Choice |
Courting Miss Ames | Penny's Yuletide Wish*

STAND ALONE ROMANCES:

*The Captain and Miss Winter | A Haunting at Havenwood | Her
Unsuitable Match | An Unsuitable Suitor | Mistletoe for Felicity*

LOVE UNAWARES

His Unexpected Heiress | Her Unsuitable Match

HEARTS OF ARIZONA SERIES:

Silver Dollar Duke | Copper for the Countess | A Lady's Heart of Gold

ABOUT THE AUTHOR

Since Jane Austen isn't releasing any new titles, Sally decided to try her hand at writing a few. Those attempts led to a happy career doing what she loves most: telling love stories.

Sally Britton, her husband, their four incredible children, their dogs, the cat Willow who tolerates them, and a snake named Basil live in Oklahoma.

Sally started writing on her mother's electric typewriter when she was fourteen years old. Reading her way through Jane Austen, Louisa May Alcott, and L.M. Montgomery, Sally fell love with the elegant, complex world of centuries past.

In 2007, Sally earned a bachelor's in English Literature. She met and married her husband not long after, and they're quite busy living happily ever after.

All of Sally's published works are available on multiple retailers and you can connect with Sally and sign up for her newsletter on her website, AuthorSallyBritton.com.